The Carpathians

Also by Janet Frame

NOVELS

Owls Do Cry
Faces in the Water
The Edge of the Alphabet
Scented Gardens for the Blind
The Adaptable Man
A State of Siege
The Rainbirds
Intensive Care
Daughter Buffalo
Living in the Maniototo

STORIES AND SKETCHES

The Lagoon
The Reservoir
Snowman Snowman

JUVENILE

Mona Minim and the Smell of the Sun

POETRY

The Pocket Mirror

AUTOBIOGRAPHY

To the Is-Land
An Angel at my Table
The Envoy from Mirror City

The Carpathians

JANET FRAME

GEORGE BRAZILLER   NEW YORK

Published in the United States in 1988
by George Braziller, Inc.

Published simultaneously in Great Britain by Bloomsbury, Ltd.
and in New Zealand by Century Hutchinson.

Copyright © 1988 Janet Frame

For more information address the publisher:

George Braziller, Inc.
60 Madison Avenue
New York, New York 10010

Library of Congress Cataloging-in-Publication Data

Frame, Janet.
   The Carpathians.

   I. Title.
PR9639.3.F7C3   1988   823   88-16754
ISBN 0-8076-1205-7

Printed in the United States
First printing

Grateful thanks to the members of the Frank Sargeson Trust, the cities of Takapuna and Auckland, and the many people who made possible the building and furnishing of the Frank Sargeson Centre. As the first Frank Sargeson Fellow I found the conditions for writing were almost ideal. I dedicate this book to the writers who will work in future in the Frank Sargeson Centre.

I also thank my friends J., S., and J.

Note:

The characters and happenings in this book are all invented and bear no relation to actual persons living or dead.

Writing this, my second novel, I became absorbed not in my power of choice but in the urgency with which each character equated survival with maintaining point of view, indeed with *being* as a point of view. The coincidence of the rediscovery of the legend of the Memory Flower, and the discovery of what I have called the Gravity Star, tended to make both memory and point of view (removed, overturned by the Gravity Star) the characters and the scene now of celebration, now of battle.

I quote from a Press Association Report:

'A survey of distances to galaxies has revealed something that at first seemed implausible: a galaxy that appears to be both relatively close and seven billion light years away . . . the paradox is interpreted as being caused by the focussing of light from a distant quasar (starlike object) by the gravity of an intervening galaxy.'

I have been greatly influenced by my mother (recently dead) and by my father. My mother's short visit to New Zealand and my father's life-long marriage with words have inspired this book.

J. H. B.

Part One

The Gravity Star

1

There is a legend of Maharawhenua or Memory Land with its town of Puamahara or Memory Flower. A young woman, chosen by the gods as collector of the memory of her land, journeys to a region between the mountains and the sea to search for the memory; and as in all legends, the helpers, human, animal, insect or vegetable who are themselves guardians of the inner world of searches, make or find time to stand at convenient places — corners, crossroads, shores, boundaries — to offer advice, to warn, to encourage and inform; and many times to demand a sacrifice with no promise of reward. The journey is one of choices, judgments, of logic — if . . . then . . . and also . . . if not . . . therefore; the small words that have little use alone become instruments of power.

The legend describes how the young woman released the memory of the land when she picked and tasted the ripe fruit from a tree growing in the bush: where Eve tasted her and Adam's tomorrow, the woman of Maharawhenua tasted the yesterday within the tomorrow, and realising that her search was over, she called together the people of the land. For many years with no human function but that of a story-teller, she recounted the memory, and one day when the listeners returned, they found the memory-collector had vanished and in her place a tree grew with one blossom named, then, the Memory Flower from which, it is said, fruit invisible to most eyes from time to time may grow.

The town of Puamahara grew where the memory tree first blossomed. It is said that the orchards on the outskirts of Puamahara bear some relation to the seed of the first fruit thrown in the bracken by the first keeper of the memory of the land.

2

Poets who live in unimaginable reality have always known of the Gravity Star; now all have been given the fact as an everyday physical truth. Ordinary perceptions are denied, overturned, the mind is thrust into a channel of the formerly unknowable because then unimaginable. New seasons are born, new weathers, climates; the old well-loved legends rise to the surface; the Gravity Star may shine in every street of every town.

Was that how it was in Kowhai Street, Puamahara? At the time of the strange happenings, the town of the Memory Flower had no wood-cutters' cottages, no forests of northern spruce; no foxes or wolves that may have been long-buried in the minds of many of the inhabitants. The journeys and the searches elsewhere in the land were for coal, gemstones, earthquakes, volcanic eruptions, shifts of landscape, the appearance and disappearance of rivers, lakes and seas reflecting their inner spiritual equivalent, the growth and decay of myths and legends, seasons of rebirth, explosions as real as those enforced by geological events. There is havoc enough on familiar earth beneath familiar skies, but in a time of discoveries that overturn unquestioned beliefs, then, in small pockets of the everyday world, an inexplicable chaos may reign.

In Puamahara the legend of the Memory Flower, rediscovered and reinforced by the Tourist Centre, became the town's treasure. Cities, many knew, have thrived more on their legends than on their gold, oil, gemstones. At the entrance to a city's harbour, a statue depicting a loved story will entice more tourists than a street of wealthy merchants. The legend of Puamahara and Maharawhenua was seized, retold, enhanced, illustrated. A plaster sculpture of a tree with one large blossom suspended from the topmost branch was hastily erected at the entrance to the orchards on the edge of town. Puamahara, the Memory Flower.

And almost as reinforcement of the legend, Maharawhenua and Puamahara are natural horticultural areas where the fertility of the soil is fed by the crushed bones of vanished rivers and the blood of former generations, and where even the town gardens blossom amazingly with varieties of native and exotic plants. Puamahara itself has gradually con-cealed its earth beneath concrete. It is known as a town for travellers to pass through or rest in; it is most of the year without visitors. The main street, Tyne Street, part of the main north-south highway, carries massive trucks of sheep and cattle, petrol and milk tankers, huge vans proclaiming, We Move You Anywhere in the World; and travellers going north to the sun, noise, wealth, south to the mountains, shadows, space, and neighbouring continents of ice. The houses are arranged neatly east, west of the main highway, in streets named by the English settlers after rivers and towns they would never see again, or, by those with a sense of belonging to the land, after the native trees — manuka, rata, kowhai, kauri, the trees being the first heroes of the settlers, the conquered heroes that in time became the enemy.

Who lives in Puamahara? Even a small town of thirteen thousand citizens has its streets of the wealthy and the poor, the wealth observed in the elaborately built homes with their tall fences, spacious driveways, swimming-pools; the poverty in those sections where limbless cars lie abandoned in the overgrown grass of front lawns, and fence posts prop one another, severed from their original root in earth. Puamahara has three morticians, three veterinarians, the usual kindergartens, schools, churches; a medical centre; a library; a cultural centre within an old Victorian house staging exhibits of paintings, sculpture, craftwork, pottery; a marae out of town where the Maori families gather; an art shop offering the framing of paintings and the sale of prints of flowers, trees, wide-eyed children and kittens. Puamahara has its political parties and their headquarters, its real estate agents; a race course, a football field, parks, a show ground for the seasonal agricultural and pastoral show, the travelling circus and fun fairs; and, a few miles out of town, towards the mountains, a picnic ground near the river.

Puamahara, known as a 'good' place to retire in, has more than the usual number of homes and hospitals for the aged where the flower gardens, the mountains, are there to gaze at, the distant sea to dream about, while the convenient north-south road brings visiting relatives and friends. Everyone remarks that Puamahara is 'so convenient' for the placing of institutions, for living, for dying. Also, out of town, there's the Manuka Home for the Intellectually Handicapped of all ages; and, near the sea, the Home for Wayward Children.

Like any small town, Puamahara has its factions, frictions, fictions and fractions. Stratford with its mountain, Christchurch and Wanganui and Hamilton and Dunedin with their rivers, Napier with its foreshore and its memory of the great earthquake, Wellington with its harbour — none outshines Puamahara and its legend. It stands alone without the publicity of rivalries for visitors, amenities, harbour facilities, not even a Harbour Board courting perennial scandal.

Puamahara returns always to the consolation and pride of the legend; and of the sky. Puamahara has unrivalled sky.

And now, the Gravity Star.

Do not mistake me. This is not to be a sociological survey of a thriving New Zealand town of English, Scottish, Welsh, Central European, Chinese, Pacific Island immigrants; and of the original dwellers, the Maoris, who here are mostly poor in the material possessions that the country values highly, who live in the streets of the orphaned cars, who are often out of work, staying home to repair or rebuild their cars and to cultivate their flower and vegetable gardens. Their envied wealth is in their possession of time and in their being the only inhabitants for whom the legend has been a growth of love and not the sudden possession of a tale arranged to entice tourists and to make more money for Puamahara.

This is not, however, to be a discussion of the first and the last, an exhortation to perfection within an always imperfect society of human beings. Yet it may contain the longing for the 'unchangeable certainty of truth'.

It's another story of the town of the Memory Flower, of the Gravity Star, the prospect of the sudden annihilation of the usual perception of distance and closeness, the bursting of the iron bands that once made rigid the container of knowledge, the trickling away of the perception of time and space, although at first the shape persists as if still bound, yet if you examine it you see the widening crevices in what was believed always to be the foundation of perception. Near and far, then and now, here and there, the homely words of the language of space and time appear useless, heaps of rubble.

The smallest words have lifted the weight of centuries of knowing and carried it out of our reach.

How far away you have been, and now your death is near; I hold in my hand the most distant star; the dead of yesterday dine with me at my table.

14

3

At the time of the discovery of the Gravity Star, Kowhai Street, Puamahara, had its usual variety of residents. The street itself, the architecture
of the houses, the arrangement of the lawns, the fences and garden sheds
and garages were 'suburban comfortable', with the houses at each end of
the street bordering the two busy highways, Gillespie Street and Royal
Street, descending to 'suburban struggling' or 'poor'. An ordinary street
in an ordinary cluttered town made extraordinary, perhaps, only by the
Memory Flower and the Gravity Star.

The Memory Flower grows always from the dead. Where are they,
the long dead, the recently dead, the poets, the painters, the toilers, the
housekeepers, the murderers, the imposters: all who have held the
memory blossom? If you walk in mid-afternoon through the streets of
Puamahara you might suppose you walk through a neatly kept cemetery
where the graves are more spacious than usual, with flowers and vegetable gardens, fences, concrete paths leading to the door of the family
mausoleum. The silence, cavelike, may be entered. No sound of cars,
trains, planes, radios, people, dogs; and just as you become certain that
you walk in a cemetery, the sounds of the living intrude, the dream van-
ishes, and those whom you thought to be dead appear in the doorways
with brooms and brushes and motormowers and hedge-clippers to perform
the daily sweep and cut and snip, while others wheeling shopping trundlers,
riding bicycles, driving cars, set out in search of substance to feed on, to
sleep on, make love on, die on; to clean with, to look at, to spit on, to
sigh over, to read, to admire, to wear: all to make certain of one more
day of life, that is, to protect the habits of being human: housekeeping
their lives.

Kowhai Street is little different from other streets in Puamahara. You
may shiver with a sudden inkling of eternity as you sense or imagine that
perhaps your street is unique in the world, with the last two houses at
each end facing not a noisy frontier of State Highways but a verge of
darkness on the furthermost boundaries of the earth, that you and your
street may be suspended as a capsule in space and if you dig the thin skins
of your garden you may stare down at the spinning earth and the stars
or upward at the stars. Such feelings are common, too, in the largest
cities of the world where, walking to the end of your block, you gaze and
gaze at the seemingly endless street of similar houses, on and on to the
ends of the earth, and the further you gaze the easier it is to lose your

sense of being somewhere, of having your familiar place, with the warmth of being in your street changed to the desolation of realising that distance may transform your feeling and knowing into nothingness, that you yourself may destroy and declare not to exist what you do not now know and have ceased to become a part of. Then, desperately, you must forge links or deny whatever lives in time and space, your denial meaning the constant possibility that you may fall into the the darkness at the edge of the earth and may never be known again.

And so, whether or not the people of Kowhai Street are aware of their boundaries and beyond, they cherish their street, they cling to their place of being, their point of view to and from within, to and from the mountains, the sea and the sky. Even those not yet resident, like Mattina Brecon, nurture their feelings toward Kowhai Street, while the others too depend for their being on their certainty of place. Just as on the first of 'real' summer days, in December, the early morning spiders weave their webs on every object in the street (if you are absent for two days the mouth of your letterbox is webbed shut), so the people of Kowhai Street leave, in all months, their invisible mark of being, of recognition, people-mark their street, as even the cats and dogs do, touching the surfaces of plant and wall with their essence, linking themselves to the street and to each other. You who are nomads or homeless will say with truth that such links are not vital, that we may walk on earth without marking it and die leaving no trace, like the 'flower of the field': but the flower itself is a trace, a link, as is the 'wind that passeth over it and is gone'. Those who have no home may not ally their being to a house or gate or an item of furniture or adornment but they are possessed by and possess those other forces or presences that also are homeless — the sky, the wind, the elements, so simply listed and trusted in the days before the splitting of the atom and, now, the arrival of the Gravity Star. Those elemental links of loving and hating and knowing are as passionate and the architecture of their passions as noble or lowly as that of cathedrals, huts, three-bedroomed houses with ranchsliders, rumpus rooms, ensuites, and bar-becues in the back garden; and as varied in nobility, lowliness, artistic endeavour, success or failure, as, again, cathedrals, sheep-pens, prisons, castles, three-bedroomed bungalows with clinker-brick exteriors.

Have I now placed a burden on the residents of Kowhai Street, Puama-hara? Let me use the old-fashioned words in their old-fashioned meanings — my then, my here, my now, my up, down, far, near, my old, my new, as valued as the painter's blue, green, yellow, red, to tell the story and let these small words remain faithful to me in the brief time that may be left for all the old written and spoken languages.

4

Mattina Brecon took her wealth for granted as an instrument to satisfy desires that, for her, did not include the acquisition of goods, thought often to be the one certain use for money. In the past she had used her wealth first to enable her husband, Jake, to continue writing his second novel, and to give their son, John Henry, education at a private school in New York; then, to share with friends, mostly artists, who had little; finally, to buy services for herself, her family, and friends — the use of a private plane, priority on airline flights, gourmet meals from the ground floor restaurant on their 74th Street condominium. Like her dead father, a wealthy philanthropist, Mattina was happy to give away money, usually to penniless authors discovered at the publishing house where she worked as a reader of miscellaneous manuscripts. Now and then, should a fault be found in a household appliance, rather than have it repaired, Mattina would give it to someone whom she thought to be 'deserving', while she bought a new appliance. For her, money also bought or tried to buy perfection in others, total efficiency. Her endowment of intelligence and sensitivity was such that she seldom brought money within the boundaries of love and close friendship, although she never concealed the fact that she could always pay, and the hope that everyone knew of her wealth, with the result that, at times, in her presence, others were inclined to smooth the sharp edge of their honesty. Mattina, who was proud of her own honesty, never showed the brutality that some self-styled 'honest' people bring into their direct speech.

And as a rich woman she did not collect a wardrobe of fine clothes: she simply chose and wore the 'best' of sandals, jeans, sweaters, shoes, with one or two gowns for special occasions. Also, her sympathy with feminism had developed enough to make her willing to buy jewellery for herself and not keep to the rule she had learned long ago, she could not remember where, that it was unseemly for a woman to buy jewels for herself. Not having had to spend time worrying about acquiring money and (the common anxiety of the rich) about losing, spending or saving it, she knew the philosophical luxury of having time to think, to observe, to reason, and to dream, a luxury more likely in a lifelong absence of worry over money than after a sudden release from worry: unexpected riches may infuse the luxury with torment.

Yet Mattina was not a happy woman. She enjoyed her life, her marriage, her husband, her child, and, for a brief period, a lover. Her strong sense of humour, seldom spontaneous within herself, was awakened chiefly by the humorous perceptions of others: as excellent fuel for laughter she needed less a struck match than one of those slow-burning blocks of chemicals that are deadly if ignited incorrectly but if all is well can spark a long-burning fire.

An urgency within her demanded that she 'know' how the rest of the world lived, how they felt, and behaved, what they said to one another, what they rejoiced in, despaired of, and dreamed about; and so whenever she travelled, she sought the company of the 'natives', listened to their stories, and often, recklessly, felt the satisfaction of giving cheques towards needs that could not recognise or be fed by money.

As a New Yorker, Mattina was not one of the many who believed that in spite of the love they gave to their city, the city had failed them. Many of her friends were leaving to live elsewhere — in Vermont, New Hampshire, Long Island, Connecticut, and further afield, and as soon as they had gone, they appeared, to Mattina, to have lost the knowledge of being in New York City, as if elsewhere had given them the taste of the seed of their forgetting. 'They just don't seem to remember how it is, in Manhattan,' Mattina would complain to Jake or John Henry. This evidence of the power of distance began to obsess Mattina, and allied with her urgent need to know the lives of those distant from her, increased her restlessness. How might distance affect her and her family, she wondered. And her bond with her city and her country? She became absorbed in the power of the distance of time as well as of space, and when by chance she read in a New Zealand tourist brochure that apart from the main tourist centres there was one town, Puamahara, 'an attractive horticultural centre in the south-west of the North Island' known to be 'the source and setting of the legend of the Memory Flower', her curiosity was aroused. She read eagerly the précis of the legend. Perhaps, she thought, she might buy real estate in Maharawhenua or Memory Land, just as, over a number of years in a series of urgent journeys, she had bought land in Nova Scotia, the Bahamas, Hawaii, Portugal, Spain, each time living among the inhabitants as 'one of them', and each time on departure, with greater or lesser self-deception, scattering cheques that, falling, melted like snow.

Although Jake felt her journey to New Zealand was a hurtful exercise in altruism, for she understood too well his problems in writing his second novel and his need for solitude, he gave his blessing to yet another of her desperate searches, and when she had made her travel plans ('Rent a house while the owner is absent. Spend time in a friendly New Zealand town. Get to know the place and the people'), he went with her to the heliport and repeated the jokes their friends were making about 'little ole Noo Zealand', and Mattina's home for the next two months, 'Twenty-four Kowhai Street, Puamahara.'

'Kowhai! Is it a bird, a plant, a dragon, a person? You'll have kowhais flying everywhere and nesting in your garden.'

'Work well,' Mattina whispered as they said goodbye. 'You know you have it in you.'

'You can do better than that,' Jake said angrily. 'After all these years!'

'I know, I know. In two months we'll both be rejoicing, I'm sure.'

Was it only two days later, after her flight to Los Angeles, Auckland, Palmerston North, and the taxi to Puamahara, that Mattina walked into the sitting room of Number Twenty-four Kowhai Street and said aloud, 'God in Heaven, what am I doing here?' And thought, Why is everything so green? The drapes, the green vinyl suite with its swivel chairs, the lawn outside, the trees, even the sky has a tint of green.

A Dorothy Townsend, a neighbour home from her morning's work in the carnation fields, had given Mattina the key to Number Twenty-four. 'From Albion Cook, the real estate agent,' Dorothy said. 'And welcome.' Her glance carried a hint of 'They say most Americans who come here are cranks or they think they're going to reform the world or. us, get back to the land, organise protests under *our* sun — we're quite happy, thank you.'

Slightly alarmed, seizing the point of view, Dorothy wondered, Are we quite happy, thank you? The country awaited further discoveries of oil, to make itself independent; wells were drilled in the greenest pastures while the grazing Herefords looked on, licking their flanks, rolling their honey-filled eyes. Mines everywhere. Gold, precious stones in the Coromandel, scheelite up Central, coal on the Coast, while the memory-mines remained overgrown, inaccessible to all but those able to mine centuries of time; and those who at least tried, tearing at the undergrowth and the over-growth with a desperation that drew blood from themselves and the surface of their own limited memory. . . . And is this me, my point of view? Dorothy wondered. I and my family are from the distant north: we did not belong here *originally*.

'Welcome,' Dorothy said again, 'to Puamahara.'

'The home of the Memory Flower,' Mattina added, hesitating to offer certain knowledge of the legend, putting a question in her voice, sensing the delicate balance between guest, a stranger, and host.

'You know of the legend, obviously.'

'I read of it in the brochure,' Mattina said, almost apologetically.

'We've only lately heard of it ourselves,' Dorothy admitted. 'And of course they've seized on it for tourist promotion. We — my husband and son and daughter and I — are from England, the Midlands.'

'Oh.'

Later, Mattina looked out on the rectangular space of garden where a tall lichen-encrusted orange or grapefruit tree entwined branches with two equally old lemon trees to form a hedge dense enough to almost hide the rest of the garden where tall trees lined the boundary of the next property. Mattina could see the mountains only from a side view across a neighbour's wooden fence. It was now noon. The scorching light of the September sun robbed the mountain slopes of all apparent vegetation, making them appear as castles and cliffs of rock with taller castles beyond these against a smoky mist of mountain sky. In the distance, masses of cloud swirled and swept around the harsh rock walls, battlements and towers, while the arrow-slits shone golden as if fitted with bars of light.

After a momentary musing on the scene, Mattina said again, abruptly, 'God in heaven, what am I doing here? Why am I gazing at mountains, creating or appraising distance and nearness, harshness and softness, when I am thousands of miles from home. Where is everybody?' She was aware, suddenly, of an air of desertion, as if the whole world had gone elsewhere, leaving her at the mercy of the mountains, the distant western beaches, the sky, the sun, and perhaps even the kowhai bird. She opened the front door and walked along the concrete path to the letterbox and the street. She flipped open the box, letting a pile of yellowed leaflets and a wet newspaper drop among the clump of wilted spring flowers beneath the box. The flowers were minute green-tipped white bells of exquisite frailty — what were they? She recognised daffodils by the path — or were they jonquils or narcissi? And what was the name of that spring blossom-tree with sweet-scented purple flowers? Her knowledge of plants was limited. She was not used to trees with giant blossoms as big as creatures with folded winglike petals — such, she thought, were for the tropics, the Hawaiian islands, the Bahamas, not a New Zealand that she and Jake had known only through that recording of bird-song sent to them by a friend who'd stopped overnight in Auckland on his way to Sydney. The record, half bird-song, half stern commentary on the morals of the birds, became a family amusement with Jake mimicking the commentator's disapproval,

21

'The male blackbird is an *unsatisfactory provider*.' Mattina could not recall hearing the kowhai bird.

The purple-blossoming tree bordering the street filled the air with sweetness and the scent of fresh rain; the mountain air felt damp, chill. Unsatisfactory provider or not, a blackbird sang his heart out from the next door television aerial. Looking up and down the street, Mattina noticed the fallen gold flowers from the trees planted at intervals by the sidewalk. Well, she thought, they're likely to be kowhai trees in Kowhai Street.

'Settling in?'

Dorothy Townsend again, checking her letterbox for the day's mail. Waving and smiling as she called. She walked across her lawn towards the boundary.

'We were strangers too,' she said. 'Perhaps we'll always be strangers.'

'How do you like it here?' Mattina asked curiously, wondering why Dorothy Townsend should be so anxious to proclaim her origin.

Dorothy smiled. 'It's different from the Midlands,' she said. 'And don't forget, if there's any help you need. . . .'

She stared at Mattina's scrubby jeans and rumpled sweater, her sneakers, and the scarf over her head, not in the English way where the head, face and chin were lumped together, the way the Queen wore her scarves, but the Hollywood actress way with a sprightly bow at the neck . . . definitely not the English way. Dorothy's tenuous point of view held for an instant, bearing like foam on the breakers, the resting wings of the homesickness that had pursued Dorothy, Rex, and now and then, the children, Hugh and Sylvia. The West Midlands! The Malvern Hills! The seaside, *real* seaside holiday, once every three years! How could distance bring such weight of longing to their lives?

'Oh, everything's fine,' Mattina said. 'I need to know about the trash, food, and so on.'

'Albion Cook will have left a list of instructions. There's a dairy around the corner if you want to buy milk. We put out a milk bottle under the letterbox and the milkman delivers every day — you buy tokens at the dairy. The rubbish is left on the verge, in a regulation blue plastic bag, every Friday morning. Early. Make sure it's early or they'll miss you!' Dorothy's voice held a tone of longing, deprivation, almost of desolation.

'A *blue* plastic bag? Must it be *blue*?'

'Oh yes, they'll take nothing else. *Regulation blue*. We had green for a time until they changed; now blue's here for good.'

Mattina felt confused. Dairy? Rubbish? *Regulation* blue?

'We're a quiet family,' Dorothy said, 'We keep ourselves to ourselves, but don't be afraid to ask for help. And enjoy your stay. Oh, another thing, we sometimes play music in the weekend. It's alright though — it's religious music. We have young people in for meetings in the garage. My husband is a Full Gospel businessman.'

'Oh?' Mattina said, feeling more confused. 'Thank you. It's kind of you.'

'And sometimes Rex sleeps during the day. He's a shift dyer.'

'Oh?'

'I expect you'll get to know us in Kowhai Street.'

'The kowhais are the trees, I guess,' Mattina said.

'Yes, New Zealand trees. And there's native bush along the east of Gillespie Street, towards the mountains. You'll likely see it in your stay here . . . two months, is it?'

'Two months.'

'You'll certainly get to know everyone here. And our street has a neighbourhood watch scheme where you look out for the others in the street, report anything suspicious day or night . . . it works, too.'

'I'm sure it does,' Mattina said, feeling increasingly bored and tired. 'Has Puamahara so much crime?'

'You'd be surprised. Everything has changed. Burglary, rape, murder. . . .'

Mattina frowned with disbelief.

'It's true. Oh, and would you like some carnations for your house? I get the rejects but the rejects are often better than the others. Flaws in the blossom, a slight imperfection of colour, a misshapen petal, features you wouldn't normally notice.'

'I'd love some flowers,' Mattina said.

'I'll leave them on your doorstep if you're out.'

'Of course.'

Mattina thought as she entered the house that she and Dorothy Townsend were not unlike in appearance: both were small and dark, but where Dorothy's cheeks were rosy, her skin fair, Mattina's skin was sallow beneath her suntan. Dorothy was much younger. Mattina felt she had seldom spent so much time paying attention to trees and flowers. She couldn't remember when last she had given them any thought. What else can I expect, she said to herself, in the town of the Memory Flower? And now I have been offered as much as I want of rejected carnations, and perhaps never know why they have been rejected. Who knows, she thought, feeling tiredness overcome her and rebelling against a stupid confusion in her mind, we could all be rejects in a rejected world and never know or dream that simultaneously the chosen flourish elsewhere in a perfect world. On whatever fanciful notion her journey was based, in a world where criteria for perfection were lost or secret or out of reach or unknown, she felt contented, now, to be in New Zealand for two months, to remain as the constant receiver of rejected carnations.

Her movements now were pursued by sleep. She found the electric switches, and made her first cup of tea in Puamahara, from curled dry teatips out of a small rusty tin. Coffee, her preference, was nowhere to be found. Then, not bothering to unpack, she lay under a blanket on the bed in the middle room and slept for hours, waking to early morning sounds of the trash collectors banging the trash cans far below in New York streets, of police sirens, of the street-workers drilling their canyons in the middle of the street. . . .

Tossing her head, as if she scattered dust from a garment about to be put on for a fresh day, she shook the sleep from her and glanced at her watch. It was five in the afternoon, the same afternoon. The noise had been the milkman wheeling his laden trolley from house to house, clattering the empty bottles. Half awake, Mattina went out to her milkbox to collect the full bottle that replaced Dorothy Townsend's empty bottle, put thoughtfully in Mattina's box. Sharing the box was a bunch of carnations, about ten, different shades of pink, red, apricot, their stems strong and sharp-ended with one or two unopened buds each deeper in colour than the opened flowers. Mattina breathed the sweet, spicy fragrance. Milk and carnations: a wholesome welcome to Puamahara.

Half past five. Ordinarily, whiskey time. An old-fashioned or whiskey sour. Nothing in the cupboard but a half empty bottle of frothy sherry that could have been dishwashing detergent or strong urine. Time to shop for food at — what was Dorothy Townsend's name for it? — the *dairy*.

Taking the blue canvas shopping trundler from the alcove in the hallway, and her coin purse of shining New Zealand coins adorned with flowers and birds, and the notes with the worried face of the British Queen, Mattina walked to where she hoped the dairy might be, and as she walked she sidestepped the many cracks in the pavement, also the humps, and then the surprising number of snails also going somewhere; she noticed the neat uncomplicated shape of the houses, like dolls' houses built for people, and the confectionery-colouring of the wooden walls and the roofs of corrugated iron or tiles, and the front paths leading directly from the gate to the front door with a branch path at the corner, leading presumably to the back door; and the garages, single or double, many of aluminium, glinting like cooking-foil. And except for the car-cemeteries on the front lawn of the end house on the corner of Gillespie Street, all the lawns were

24

neatly clipped and all the gardens had spring flowers, daffodils, narcissi, and many others that Mattina could not name; and blossom trees, cherry and plum, and larger trees as at Number Twenty-four Kowhai Street, with blossoms frilled and flounced like dolls' dresses caught up in the branches. Mattina recognised the now wilted forsythia; she remembered the Hudson Valley in early spring, gold with forsythia even when blocks of ice still lay on the borders of the river and in the side pools where the drifts of bright green moss had still not surfaced. The Hudson Valley was remembered as a place of journeys between New York and Lake George, where Mattina and Jake had their summer place.

She arrived at the corner dairy, a small store next to a butcher's that was closed, its window display, a marble slab, gleaming empty. In the dairy, two women were buying a newspaper.

'That's the last one,' the storekeeper said.

She turned to Mattina.

'I'm sorry. No more *Western News*. There's been a rush on them because of the murder, the old woman murdered, discovered a few hours ago. Burgled, murdered. In Puamahara. In Kowhai Street, second from the end into Royal Street. Madge McMurtrie, the invalid.'

'That's awful,' Mattina said.

'You're American? Or Canadian?'

'American. I'm here for two months. Study, research, and so on,' Mattina said, sounding informative but giving little real information.

'Then you'll know about murder, coming from the States. We have a lot of Americans these days — refugees from the violence and the nuclear bombs and missiles and Star Wars. No-one is safe in the streets there. Where are you from?'

'New York City.'

'I'm told that's the worst. A murder a minute. Like that piece of music on the radio, only there you talk for a minute.'

Mattina stared, dazed.

She bought her groceries, speaking slowly as the woman had difficulty understanding her words while she herself had to ask for some words and phrases to be repeated. What strange English, she thought.

'And you've come all that way from all those murders to be in the middle of one. Face to face.'

'I'm at Number Twenty-four, Kowhai Street,' Mattina said. 'Mattina Brecon.'

'I'm Hene Hanuere. My husband Hare and I run the shop but we're giving it up in a week or two. Going up country. It's no good here. Two break-ins in the first week, and the kid brings in her school friends and they help themselves. And Hare's so softhearted he gives away the groceries.'

She looked curiously at Mattina.

'What are you researching?'

'I'm interested in this land, in Maharawhenua itself, in Puamahara, the story of the land memory, the Memory Flower. I guess you know it in the Maori language.'

Hene looked embarrassed.

'I get by with English,' she said. 'It's the language I've always spoken. It's the younger generation that are speaking Maori. I'm learning, you know, it's not so easy when you've been brought up Pakeha, but it's coming back. The trouble is, it's been away so long.'

She smiled, at ease now. 'We're all changing back now. It's strange, you know. Like someone you turned out of your house years ago, and now they've come home and you're shy, and ashamed of having turned them out and you have to get to know them all over again and you're scared in case you make a mistake in front of the young ones, for the youngest ones know it all. You know, it's been lonely without our language. People from overseas sometimes understand this more than those living here.'

'I think I understand,' Mattina said. 'Separation from home, family, country, language . . . the power of distance . . . but you do hold the land memory?'

Suddenly shy, Hene became again the storekeeper with Mattina the shopper and the stranger.

'If you'd like to order a local paper, the Puamahara *Western News* or the city paper, *The Times* . . . but there are usually plenty. It's only today there's a rush, with the murder.'

'Was the murder actually today?'

'Last night, they think. Someone found her about noon. I'd be careful if I were you, Mrs Brecon.'

'It's Mattina.'

'Yes. I keep your newspaper, then?'

'I'll have it delivered, I think.'

'Just as you wish, Mrs Brecon. Arrivederci,' she called as Mattina left the shop, and Mattina responded, 'Arrivederci.'

The universal television goodbye supplanting all other languages.

5

The penultimate Madge, being dead, has no point of view unless (which is likely) she transmitted part of her self to the relatives who visited her or to the eighteen-year-old man (on leave from the Manuka Home) who burgled her house and murdered her. In the town of the Memory Flower she deserves a chapter written in the course of daily work among memories.

She was Madge McMurtrie, the penultimate Madge. Madge and Dugald McMurtrie had retired two years ago to Puamahara, and one year later Dugald died of a heart attack, and two months after that, Madge was diagnosed as suffering from an inoperable cancer that was predicted to end her life in eight or ten months. After time in hospital Madge chose to return to her home at Number Eighteen Kowhai Street, to make herself comfortable in the sitting room of the L-shaped house where (as in Mattina Brecon's home) the front window faced the street and the rear windows the mountains. The local hospital (known as the Ghost Hospital because although fully equipped and furnished, it had the staff to accept only a handful of patients) sent a nurse daily to attend Madge. Meals on Wheels brought her midday meal. Neighbours came in from time to time. About three weeks before the murder, two members of Madge's family came from a distance to visit her. Madge was not aware that the hospital had summoned her niece, Olga, and her great-niece, Sharon, and for days after she learned of the visit ('they're eager to see you. They're very fond of you. They just learned, by chance, of your illness'), Madge lay in almost the final luxury of her point of view. She arranged other relatives in their various categories, listened to what they might say and what they chose to leave unsaid. She watched dreamily the tracing and intertwining of the maps of love and greed, the cities of love and greed rising in detail before her, with the faces of her relatives at each window of each building. The schools of the cities were filled with her nieces and nephews and their children born and not yet born; the administrators were her family, the traffic controllers, the police force, the librarians in the library, all were her family, and the Mayor was her son, long absent and silent, and the dream-city was Puamahara. The family owned Madge's fantasy of construction as much as it owned them. Madge supposed that as her reward for accepting the otherwise unacceptable gift of death, she now had special insight. Others, knowing that rewards are seldom earned, and suffering brings no reward but that given by the sufferer, felt that Madge was now slightly deranged. Yet her view of her family and their fierce possession of one another, of their goods (and soon, hers), of their surroundings and institutions, of the very facts of their lives — birth dates, marriage dates, meals, the age at which each walked and talked and read and 'understood' the world — these gave her no agitation or discomposure now but a satisfying sense of an equal power and passion of insight into the make-up of her self and her family. She was experiencing completeness of point of view, of self.

On the afternoon that Olga and Sharon came to visit her, Olga showed the kind of compassion she could afford; that is, she had enough to unload anywhere at any time and still leave a rich supply for her own maintenance. One may doubt that such compassion is 'true', that 'true' compassion combines with action to empty the heart of all light and warmth and comfort, leaving the donor wondering if there will ever be a replenishing of supply, and half hoping there will not be — 'or how can I get on with my life? Better keep what compassion I have.'

Therefore Olga in rosy health asked kindly, softly, if there were anything she could do to help. She had brought flowers, white polyanthus in a black plastic pot. 'You can watch the flowers opening each day,' she said, adding, with a hint of offering a teasing challenge, 'It's a *perennial*.' She had read, among one of the number of packaged observations that bypass thinking, that 'living plants' were 'good' for the terminally ill.

Madge, watching the threat to her point of view, felt a surge of envy for the plant. Year by year in the corner of the garden. How could it be that in the vegetable kingdom a few selected plants were immortal with a period of only apparent death?

'I know it's a perennial,' she said sharply, feeling ashamed, and realising that she was now beyond the furiously traded exchange of knowledge that in her lifetime and that of many others had accounted for measurement of personal success and esteem within the family.

She turned towards Sharon, her sixteen-year-old great-niece.

'So you're my great-niece? Or is it grandniece? Your parents sent me a photo of you when you were a baby.'

'She's like you, Aunt Madge. Everyone says she's most like you,' Olga said anxiously.

'Everyone? Madge thought. Extravagant claim, surely; besides, it seemed to Madge that everyone was dead now. All the Madges, except her, the penultimate, and the last Madge, whereabouts, person and surname unknown. She was sure that somewhere there was a last Madge.

How untidy Sharon is, she thought. Baggy skirt, loose blonde, tousled hair. Was that McLeod face really hers, Madge McLeod at six-teen? Her and Dugald's children were stillborn or died in infancy, except the son, born late in an irritable season. And there had been grandchildren. Madge couldn't remember herself at sixteen. Faces were now a succession of scenes, like films, rather than fixed views.

'Do you dance too, as I used to dance? Highland dancing? Do you wear a kilt?'

Sharon looked embarrassed.

'You know times have changed,' Olga said hastily. 'Sharon's a good dancer, as you used to be, but it's modern dance now.'

'Tap's coming back,' Sharon said.

'No highland fling? No Seann Truibhas?'

'Oh, some do it.'

'Is she good at languages?' Madge said to Olga, as if Sharon were an infant.

'She's learning to speak Maori,' Olga said proudly.

Madge frowned.

'You mean she does the haka?'

'No. *Real* Maori. They're all learning it today.'

'How peculiar,' Madge said. 'How worrying for you.'

'Things are different now,' Olga stressed. Her distance was unmistake-able. Madge felt herself being disposed of because she belonged to another time of highland dancing, of Saturday night socials at the Scottish Society, and the Maoris in their place, the haka as something for the All Blacks to perform before the test match with the South Island or the Springboks. She belonged to another time; yet that was no longer so; time had gone from her; at least the polyanthus and its sister and brother perennials had the burden of time forever.

'And have you liked living in Puamahara?' Olga asked. 'I'm sorry we didn't get to visit you before.'

'It's a nice house,' Madge said, 'Dugald and I made sure of that. We did it up. It's carpeted wall to wall.'

A flush of enthusiasm flowed into her pale cheeks.

'And it has a dining nook, and ranchsliders for the morning sun and the mountains. We were going to have an overhead garage door put in. And aluminium joinery.'

Both Olga and Sharon looked impressed. Their faces filled with sym-pathy as they realised that soon Madge would be leaving her treasured home with its wall-to-wall carpet and ranchsliders, and all prospect of an overhead garage door and aluminium joinery.

Madge's sigh turned to a groan of pain. Recovering, she looked again at Sharon.

'So you're the image of me at sixteen? Our mother brought us up to be well turned out. When Dugald and I played bowls (after he retired), we were always well turned out, though some of them are now wanting to wear green instead of white, and some are asking for yellow. I still prefer the white, because if it's clean everybody knows it and you feel it's something to be proud of. Dugald and I like it that way.'

In her enthusiasm Madge had moved into the present tense. She became aware of the lapse, but what did it matter, she thought. She had no obligation, now, to remain within her 'correct' time. The tenses belonged to her.

She noticed that Olga's glance had a kind of insistence. Had she missed a clue? Madge wondered. Sharon, apparently bored, was at the window looking out at the garden and lawn and the mountains beyond.

'It would be nice to live in Puamahara,' Olga said. 'Now that Sharon and William are growing up. Tom and I are thinking of moving out of Auckland, south somewhere . . . even as far as Puamahara. . . .'

'There are plenty of houses about. The prices aren't what they used to be, though,' Madge said.

Then she realised that perhaps Olga was hinting. She had always felt that death-beds were great targets for hints. Did Olga and Tom want the house, her and Dugald's home? Fair enough, but it had already been disposed of to their distant, silent son. He had the right. Madge responded to Olga's insistent gaze by murmuring (why not use the last, the most forlorn power?), 'Dugald left me a nice nest-egg. His family used to say he had a long sock somewhere.'

Sharon was at the bedside again, listening, watching, frowning.

'I don't understand your language, Aunt Madge,' she said.

'I speak the language of another age,' Madge replied, knowing that indeed her time had left her, her own words had left her and were no longer used in their old meaning. These were the desertions you didn't anticipate. You knew about the body and the mind, the growing irritation with the world, the anxiety to lose it and the terrible feeling of grief that you were losing it, but you forgot about the ordinary seemingly inanimate states and objects and concepts that died anyway, withered in your hand. Like time and your words.

Olga laughed, 'Oh yes, "long sock". Never fear, Aunt Madge.' (Never fear!) 'Even I use words that are out of date. And where have all the *creeks* gone, and the *paddocks*?'

She leaned forward, her eyes glistening, almost accusing, for the dying are targets also for accusations.

'They now say *streams*. And *fields*. And the Minister of Agriculture has been talking of the *New Zealandisation* of Fisheries!'

'Oh, Mum, don't go on about it,' Sharon urged. 'At least you can still understand what people are saying. And the language is never dead anyway, it's the people using it that can't keep up. And you're not so bad, Mum. These days you even say *tena koutou* or *haere mai* without saying *Hairy My* and looking nervous.'

'Creeks,' Madge murmured. 'A lost word.'

'You see,' Olga said. As if the blame were with Madge and others of her generation for losing the words creek, paddock, footpath and others that were dying and being replaced. And why hadn't Aunt Madge discovered sooner that she had cancer?

'I must tell you,' Madge said, 'that I'm not one of those rich aunts with money for bequests.'

Olga looked embarrassed at the sudden change of subject. No long sock, then.

'Oh. You don't think . . . you can't think that's why we've come to see you after all these years?'

Madge smiled with a hint of mischief in her glance.

'Of course not.'

Madge (the penultimate Madge) then took the diamond-studded ring from her finger.

'My wedding ring,' she said, 'Perhaps Sharon would like it as a keepsake?'

Sharon looked puzzled, repeating the word, 'Keepsake?'

'Yes, a keepsake from my death-bed.'

Sharon shuddered. 'Death-bed?' Great-aunt Madge was talking like a Victorian novel.

Madge frowned with annoyance. Which language did the young speak, then? Surely they knew of *keepsake*. Of *death-bed*. Perhaps such words were also gone from the language?

'Ooh,' Sharon said impatiently, suddenly speaking words that Madge did not understand. They sounded like Maori. Sharon was certainly fluent. Madge wondered how it was that in her own lifetime she had collected so few Maori words into her vocabulary.

'Here, take my wedding ring, Sharon. I'd like you to have it.'

Sharon took the ring and twirled it, remarking on its glitter.

'Real diamonds?'

'Real diamonds.'

Olga watched, pleased and proud.

'Wear it,' Madge said.

Sharon pulled the ring on to her engagement finger. She laughed, 'Oh, thank you Aunt Madge. You're a dear. I'm engaged now!'

Great-aunt Madge couldn't have guessed that Sharon, sixteen and still at school, was already pregnant.

After she had removed the ring Madge resisted the feeling of loss of a bond, and then she felt desolate as if she were widowed again, as if the first widowhood had been a shadow. She knew that other women of her generation chose to be buried wearing their wedding ring — then why had she given it so lightly to someone of another generation who did not speak her language? In Madge's day the loss of a wedding ring was a calamity, a *harbinger* of misfortune. Well, she had merely invited the misfortune after already experiencing it. Her sickness, however, was more than misfortune. A wedding ring was a trivial possession to lose when she had been slowly giving up her life to a sickness that behaved like a predator enjoying a prolonged meal; leaving her, after each intensive feast, with so little strength that she could scarcely move her body, her arms, her legs.

Sharon had accepted the ring as if it were her right to have it, her *entitlement*; the sickness also asserted its unquestioned right.

'I promise,' Olga said, 'that Sharon will look after the ring. Sharon's a real McLeod.'

Promising to visit again, they said goodbye, each bravely kissing Aunt Madge's corpse-like cheek. And when they had gone and the district nurse had been on her rounds, Aunt Madge, helped by morphine, settled into her usual dreamlike state, the utter fatigue and weakness melted by the warm stream of light flowing from east to west as she lay; from the mountains to the sea. She knew that her strength was going the way of her time and her words and her love and her hate and her own greed; her wedding ring, her home in Puamahara, and perhaps even Puamahara itself, the town of the Memory Flower, what a fuss the Tourist Department had made, lately, of the legend — everything flowing from her, from the town, from the land; yet she felt little anger of grief now over her loss, the loss of her self. She had been surprised, though, at her renewed pang of grief over the lost words: but what use were the words when the point of view, the self that spoke, explained, described, had gone?

Madge was in a similar state of dreams when the intruder broke into her home, struck her unconscious with a lethal blow, then, panicking, seized a purse from the dressing-table and fled; and it wasn't until the next morning that the body was discovered. The body. No longer the penultimate Madge who used to laugh, 'There can't be many left, one more Madge perhaps, one more Lily, Ethel, Mabel.'

A death in Kowhai Street. A point of view resurrected only by those who use words to record the real or imagined memory. The penultimate Madge with the lost language of another age, the keepsakes, paddocks, creeks, death-beds, machines used innocently for sewing, not for gunning, a face as a cosmetic mask, a box as a chest of hope, and big tree never kauri or matai . . . in Kowhai Street, Puamahara, Maharawhenua.

Tena koutou.

Haere mai.

E pare ra.

6

As Mattina Brecon returned to Number Twenty-four Kowhai Street she noted the police car parked outside Number Eighteen and the staked ribbon encircling the house, giving it the appearance of a bizarre birthday present. There were more than the usual number of cars, she supposed, pausing in front of Number Eighteen, then continuing towards the schools on the left or to Tyne Street on the right: Mattina had studied her map of Puamahara. She was familiar enough with scenes of accident and murder. Also, she and Jake had been in Paris at the time of the Turkish plane disaster when sightseers picnicked in the forest beneath the winter branches draped with shreds of clothing, pieces of arms and legs, hands and feet.

So the old woman was dead. They had caught the alleged culprit. The horror would diminish day by day, and soon few would remember, and then the fact would be a small group of words in a police report unless, again, the keepers and recorders of memories real and drawn from imagination, set down or spoke in words the story of the time; words of whatever language the writer or speaker felt at home in.

Walking towards her front door, Mattina saw by the boundary wall at Number Twenty-two a tall stooped figure as thin and tall as the hoe he was using to chip at the grassy edge of his concrete path.

'Hi,' Mattina said, leaving her trundler on the path and crossing the lawn, 'I'm Mattina Brecon. I've come to live here for two months.'

'I'm pleased to meet you,' the old man said. His voice was frail. His hair, still plentiful, was silver. 'I'm George Coker. I've lived here alone since my wife died fifteen years ago. You'll excuse me if I don't stop hoeing but I must finish this today.'

He did not explain the urgency except to remark, 'I'm ninety-three.'

He continued to chip at the trespassing weeds.

'I shouldn't be doing this,' he said gleefully. 'I sometimes fall and can't stand up. But the work has to be done. If I were younger I'd help with your weeds too. And I have my roses to care for. And the grapes along the back fence.'

'Take care,' Mattina said, without anxiety. Having had grandparents who lived determinedly until nearly a hundred, and having a mother of equal tenacity in her eighties, she realised the value of iron among the lustrous ductile solids of age.

Jet-lag again. She felt so tired. As the telephone was already connected in her name she wondered if perhaps she might call Jake in New York, or John Henry in Cambridge. Certainly not Big John Henry — her name for the lover whose mistress she'd become for a brief period ten years ago, and whose heart attack on their planned romantic weekend on a small island off the coast of South America had given both a shock that Mattina's useful cheque book could not soothe, for while it paid the hospital bill, the airport private room, the first-class flight home where Big John Henry's wife waited all-forgiving, all-loving to claim him, it had never been able to settle the still unpaid-for dose of reality, and Mattina's humiliation at the desperate way she used money (rather than the usual dishonesty, charm, blackmail, promises in blind faith), to buy and keep someone's love. The thought of telephoning Big John Henry who had long ago gone from her life was the result of chance memory or fancy that thrives in foreign soil, pushing up through supposedly sealed areas of the past.

Mattina phoned no-one that evening. Finally surrendering to jet-lag and tiredness she fell asleep in the middle room that became her bedroom, and when she woke it was morning with bird-song in the garden, and, beyond, the sounds of motorcycles revving, cars starting, and a train grinding slowly, heavily, on the midtown tracks towards the north; and from the neighbouring property at the back, although it was only half past seven, someone mowed a lawn while next door the workers had begun their hammering and sawing to complete an addition to their house, while the concrete mixer with occasional syncopated rhythm clattered and turned emitting a pebbly groan. More noise, Mattina thought, than she'd ever heard from their apartment in Manhattan; and through all, the birds 'valiantly singing' as in the midst of battle.

Slowly, Mattina 'placed herself' in her new surroundings between the mountains and the sea, the Tararuas and the Tasman Sea. In Puamahara in Maharawhenua in the North Island of New Zealand. Eight o'clock. Breakfast, juice and coffee. Then bed and sleep again until a decent New York hour of waking, ten o'clock, when she dressed, drank more coffee, ate a slice of toast topped with yellow butter and rich sour marmalade, then sat by the empty fireplace and looked out at the back garden and the mist-wreathed mountains. The day before, she had seen three distinct terraces of peaks like sky-gardens cultivating cloud and mist; today one only was visible, as if the other two had been a privileged dream granted for her first day in Puamahara. Two months. Am I really here for two months? she asked herself. Her occasional enthusiasms often ran cold, and now, after the wearying flight across the Pacific, the two-hour

35

queuing in the Auckland Customs Hall, the flight south, her arrival, her beginning acquaintance with Kowhai Street, the murder, she wondered if the intention of her journey could be sustained. She felt attacked by the forces of distance; she wanted to curl up and sleep herself back to New York city and Jake and John Henry. In New York the world was so people-packed and vehicle-packed that it formed a breakworld protecting the inhabitants from the vastness of its ocean, its recurring tides, floods, tidal waves. Here, in Puamahara, the absence of the noise that in New York acted as a sound barrier, resulted in isolated sounds rushing in bringing the flotsam and jetsam of discord, with each sound insistent, forcing her to trace its origin. In surges, in the element of her acclimatisation, trains, cars, people, barking dogs, electrical tools, planes, helicopters renewed their presence, all in the midst of the continuing bird-song, and within the wave of the wind that had sprung up during the night and now made flute-like sounds from the wide-mouthed but narrow-throated chimney, faintly human cries in the cracked brick of the fireplace. And now a fat dark-blue fly with palely membraned wings and nodding head buzzed at the windowpane.

There's no escape now, Mattina thought. I'm at earth level. And as if to agree, a small grey bug with parallel slats like window-shades, crawled across the carpet at her feet.

'There's no escape,' she repeated aloud, this time referring not to what she thought of as the invasion of 'pure' world, but to the pain that seized her. She had told no-one, not Jake and perhaps not even herself, of her continuing bouts of sickness, vomiting, lassitude, lack of appetite; nothing apparently serious, yet from time to time her recognition of her state struck a signal wire in her brain, bringing a flash of fear of the unknown, of what lay in store for her body. She blamed the pollution of New York, the air that choked her and stung her eyes: almost everyone in New York city had their bottle of eyedrops to ease the pain from the hostile polluted air. 'Noo Zealand,' she had been told, was different, 'pure'.

And sitting looking now at the back garden and now beyond the wide front window and the lawn and trees to the street, and seeing the clear new sky arched so close as if the town had its personal sky, the occasional clouds drifting like varying shapes of washing set free by the wind, Mattina already felt the freshness and vigour of the sea-mountain air. She looked at the undusty trees, the huge blossoms from the blossom-tree pinning the corsages against the sky, the golden newly washed and oiled spring flowers. A few people passed in the street — a woman wheeling a baby carriage, two women with shopping trundlers or trolleys. Most of the women she had already met or seen wore clothes patterned with flowers and leaves, of all colours. She supposed that the flowers here were like the sheep, valued and cared for. In an old newspaper in the house she had noted that separate whole pages were devoted to the life and care of sheep, and of plants and flowers — care of the newborn lamb, eradication of disease, medical research on sheep diseases; the health of plants in the nursery; flowers hardy and tender. No such attention was devoted to human beings. Fantastically, this might explain the women's clothing as garden camouflage! From the house directly opposite Mattina's, an elderly man appeared holding a pair of elongated shears like giant hair-clippers, trailing a bright orange electrical cord. Suddenly the air was filled with a high-pitched whining sound as the front hedge was sheared. Then, returning his machine to the garage at the end of his driveway, the neighbour wheeled a motormower from his garage and with a rising and falling wail pitched above its bass drone, the mower chewed at the lawn, not always completely controlled by its driver, with the blades of grass flying out at both sides like green snowflakes in a blizzard.

Mattina shut the window to drown the noise. So this was the town of the Memory Flower. She was certain now that it had been a flower: a weed would have been killed long ago. She thought of the uncomplicated two plants in the corner of their apartment sitting room. They had not even the complication of a name! Just indoor plants. Some kind of palm with leaves like plastic and needing little attention except for occasional dusting, wiping, drinks of water and the removal of dead leaves. They'd had, once, a night-blooming plant, a wedding gift supposedly blooming once every twenty-four years but two years ago when it and the marriage were twenty-two and young John Henry had his eighteenth birthday, someone poured detergent or drain-cleaning fluid over the plant and killed it, bringing grief to Jake, Mattina, and John Henry who'd become linked to the plant and its and their future blooming, and almost every day someone would study the plant, inquire about its health and look forward to its flower. And when it died, Jake said never again would he link his life to a plant. Yet he spoke wistfully. Words were enough, he said. Words covered everything.

Again, Mattina surprised herself by thinking about plants and flowers. 'Already I've spent most of my time in Puamahara talking about or musing on vegetation. In New York such thoughts never entered my head. I know, however, that those of our friends who left New York City for a place upstate or in the wilds of New Jersey, slowly had their loyalty to New York obliterated by the plants they grew, that climbing and creeping and sweetly

37

flowering made a ground cover over their memory of the city. And here I am in this traitorous country at once becoming a traitor to the life I have enjoyed as long as I can remember. Why, when I was four years old my grandmother used to take me into the pub and sit me on the counter while she ordered and drank her whiskey. She took me everywhere — East Side, West Side, Greenwich Village, Staten Island on the ferry, to the parks, the art museums, even to Fire Island.'

Mattina felt a pang of loneliness at her reminiscence aloud; the kind of loneliness that rises from a serene contemplation of what has been lost and will never be recovered except through memory.

A strange land indeed, she thought, not knowing whether she referred to New Zealand or the United States of America, to Puamahara or New York City. Wouldn't Jake smile? she thought. To know that I'm even planning to grow my own vegetables, that the women of Puamahara are plants walking, that my neighbours in Kowhai Street likely dream of themselves as trees!

Rousing herself from her daydreaming (a practice unusual for her) she decided to try to get to know the residents of Kowhai Street, and as the neighbour opposite was about to finish his lawnmowing, Mattina, dressed simply in a dark gown with her dark hair drawn back by a grey ribbon, supposing that while not wearing patterns of tropical flowers and whirls of leaves and fruits she looked Puamaharian enough to say, 'Hi', walked across the street and down the driveway to the open garage where the neighbour was stabling his mower.

'Hi. Good morning,' she said.

The neighbour turned.

'Oh, hello.'

'I'm your new neighbour for two months, Mattina Brecon from New York.'

'I'm Hercus Millow. Would you like to come in for a cup of coffee? I'm just about to make a cup. Mowing is thirsty work.'

He paused, then frowned. 'I don't know how much longer I'll be able to look after this demon lawn, and the hedge that won't be disciplined. I don't suppose you have this kind of problem in New York City — you are from the city?'

'Oh yes. Manhattan. We don't have a lawn. And I'd like a cup of coffee.'

Hercus Millow, whitehaired, tall, with a skin that might have been his last layer it was wearing so thin that his tributary veins showed clearly beneath the tracing-paper texture, directed Mattina towards the front door.

'These steps are like mountains to me now,' he said, standing aside to let Mattina go in first.

'I haven't lived here so long myself. I'm almost a stranger.'

'Indeed?'

Mattina noted that the residents she had met had spoken of themselves as strangers. And even the murdered woman, Madge McMurtrie, had been spoken of as a stranger. Perhaps strangers never became at home in Kowhai Street?

'I shifted here after my wife died,' Hercus explained as he set out a plate of buttered currant bread, and spooned the instant coffee into two china teacups. 'Milk? Sugar? I come from the Hutt, down the Coast.'

Each time someone spoke of a place it was with such transparent love that Mattina felt unprotected, unable to cope with feelings she was sure were unfamiliar, yet she too had 'places' and spoke of them lovingly. Here, people spoke of places in the way Jake spoke of the treasured literary classics and of the words he hoped to use to write his novel. As Hercus Millow said, 'The Hutt, down the Coast', he shared the places with her, as if to say, 'You know, the Hutt, down the Coast, marvellous places, there are none in the world like the Hutt and the Coast.'

'They must be special places,' Mattina observed, whereupon Hercus Millow laughed, and said, deliberately reducing the miracle, but deceiving no-one, 'The Hutt? Mostly industrial now. With a river that floods from its normal piddling size. And so you live in New York?'

'Just now I'm interested in Puamahara and Kowhai Street. The Memory Flower is a romantic legend, don't you think?'

Hercus smiled.

'Oh, the legend. Yes, we've all heard about it now. They've only recently made a song and dance about it. The town of the Memory Flower. Goes down well with overseas visitors, gives them a feeling that when they're in Puamahara they've arrived somewhere.'

'What about the townspeople?'

'I doubt if they have time to think about it much. The town has an ageing population — it's said that people come here to die. You see all the retired old blokes and biddies lining up for their super every second Tuesday, jamming the checkouts in the market. I'm one, of course. No doubt there's a concentration of memories in Puamahara; the fear of their loss, too, of withering and going out of shape.'

'I'm researching material about Puamahara,' Mattina said vaguely. 'I work for a publishing company.'

Before she could explain her work as reader of non-fiction manuscripts,

Hercus Millow's smile changed from cynicism to delight.

'Oh, you're writing a book about us, about Puamahara?'

'Surely,' Mattina said, trapped. 'Not really.'

'You're a writer?'

Why not, Mattina thought, if that will satisfy them.

'More or less.'

'You're writing about us, then?'

He laughed aloud, then said, 'I could tell you a few things about Puamahara and Kowhai Street. I wouldn't mind being in a book. Take those people over the road, next door to you, the Townsends. They came from England. They're still almost strangers. Very quiet, scarcely a word, the two children like mice, not a word out of them, either, and they were born here and have gone to school here and are now in High School. The boy sometimes mows my lawn when I can't manage. The old mother came out to live with them; she's shifting to a flat in Gillespie Street, I hear. And then my neighbour on one side is Ed Shannon and his wife and son — they keep the computer shop in the Mall. On the other side there's the James, Jo and Gloria and their daughter Decima (she's in the Manuka Home). Jo is a piano-tuner. And then next to you there's George Coker, and then Dinny Wheatstone, Miss Wheatstone, retired, I think. I don't know what she's retired from; a bit funny peculiar, calls herself an official imposter; obsessed with the idea.'

'Oh? You certainly know your Kowhai Street,' Mattina said, impressed.

'Dinny Wheatstone's quite harmless. And then next to her was Madge McMurtrie, dying of cancer. Whoever murdered her may have done her a good turn?'

His glance was questioning. He didn't believe what he was saying. Mattina felt a stab of anger against words that could be so arranged to seduce the speaker, the writer, the listener, the reader, into believing that a truth had been created or discovered; against the magnetic power that held the words together so that few dared separate them or examine them, but used them, again and again.

'It's the kind of thing they'll say,' Hercus said, 'to get over the problem of thinking about it, and having to compare ways of dying. There's a heck of a lot of dying in Puamahara — all those homes for the elderly. The Veterans' Home, the Religious Home, the Lodge Home, the private homes charging the earth, and all quite specific about those they'll have and not have — a choice of the frail elderly, the ambulant elderly, the seventies, the eighties, the nineties, up to the hundreds with a special lounge for the party and to receive the telegram from the Queen, Betty Mountbatten, née Betty Windsor.'

'And how do you spend *your* time, Mr Millow?'

Hercus did not answer at once. He spaded a slice of currant bread on the palm of his hand.

'As I told you, I'm a stranger here, having come from the Hutt. I don't get about much — my leg. I use the old car for shopping. And I've just bought a racehorse.'

'A racehorse! How exciting,' Mattina said.

'A two-year-old filly, in training just now but she goes into the Maidens in about six months. We call it Phoebe's Bliss after its mother, the famous Phoebe. Our original choice of name was already taken.'

'Taken?'

'On the register. You'd be surprised the assortment of names. So we came up with Phoebe's Bliss. She has to qualify though before she's in the Maidens.'

'I'll be in New York City when that happens, I daresay,' Mattina said.

'New York. I've never been there. I've been in other places, during the war. North Africa, Italy, Germany. I was a prisoner of war in Germany.'

'I'd like to hear about it some time,' Mattina said, surprising herself by her lack of eagerness.

'I usually get around to talking about it, you know. It's one of the clearest memories I have. Last week — now last week's gone for ever. But the war — for me, it's still here. Other chaps experienced it this way. It's still here, but distant. Some experience it as now — they're the ones gone crazy.'

Talking about the war, Hercus Millow showed his excitement. His eyes gleamed, he leaned forward: the war, the old fire, yesterday's fire warmed him through his lonely widowhood, his lameness, the constant pain in his leg, the prescribed pills that fuddled his mind and caused him to walk sideways, now and then, like a crab; walking towards the war.

'I'm satisfied in Puamahara,' he said suddenly. 'It's not the Hutt, but it will do me until they carry me out feet first.'

'I'll see you again, Miss Brecon,' he called when Mattina, tactfully dampening his enthusiasm for the war but promising to visit again to hear of life in the prison camp, explained that she was hoping to make an introductory visit to others in Kowhai Street.

Outside the white gate by the mailbox E. and R. Shannon, Mattina decided on her next visit. A woman backing a white car from the driveway leaned from the window.

'Can I help you? Have you come about the computer?'

'Sorry?'

'Oh, my husband has clients calling at the house sometimes. We have the computer shop in the Mall.'

'I was just passing. Exploring. I'm staying at Number Twenty-four.'

'From the States?'

'Yes. Mattina Brecon.'

'I'm Renée Shannon. You must come over and tell us about Miami. I've always wanted to go to Miami. The Everglades.'

'Surely,' Mattina said. 'I'd love to come over.'

'Don't forget then,' Renée said as she steered the car from the driveway. 'I look forward to seeing you.'

Mattina walked to the corner of Kowhai Street, crossed to the house now known as the 'murder' house and skirting the staked rope arrived at Number Twenty. On impulse she walked up the drive to Dinny Wheatstone's front door and rang the bell. She saw the curtains move and had a fleeting glimpse of a face, then the front door opened and a small woman with greying hair and intensely blue eyes opened the door. She wore a floral-patterned house dress, big red roses on green-leaved stems against a background of white clouds shaped like torpedoes. Her face was expressionless as if to conceal a wealth of expression.

'Good morning,' she said, with a sudden good-morning smile.

'I hope you will forgive me for coming by like this,' Mattina said. 'I'm at Number Twenty-four for two months and I'm meeting my new neighbours in Kowhai Street. I'm Mattina Brecon from New York.'

'I'm Dinny Wheatstone — really Dinah, but everybody calls me Dinny. I'm a stranger here myself.'

'Oh? You've recently moved here?'

'I've been here twenty years. Will you come in for a while?'

Mattina hesitated.

'Don't worry. I'm harmless.'

Mattina drew her breath sharply. 'I'm not scared of you,' she said, laughing nervously. 'Remember, I come from New York. I've seen everything. No offence meant.'

'None taken,' Dinny said, obviously also a prey to the powerful small words hunting in twos or threes.

Mattina's confidence ebbed as she followed Dinny into a large book-lined sitting room with a piano, a music case housing a violin, and one opened, containing perhaps a clarinet, in one corner. Paintings hung above the fireplace and around the walls, two being portraits of the same man, one a watercolour named *Mount Taranaki*.

Dinny answered Mattina's questioning glance.

'I'm kept quite busy, or I used to be. I'm making tea?'

'I've just had coffee,' Mattina said. 'But. . . .'

'But. A great word, that, don't you think?'

Mattina looked uneasy, 'Sure.'

Dinny went to the small kitchen and a few minutes later returned with a plate of freshly buttered date scones and a pot of fresh tea. She laughed.

'Yes, I make date scones. You'll likely hear about them. This happens to be my morning for date scones. And in case you're wondering, yes, I do wear floral dresses.'

Mattina said nothing. Then, 'Music, books, paintings . . . you must have had an interesting profession — were you a teacher, perhaps?'

Dinny looked sly. 'To tell the truth,' she said, 'I used to play the piano, the violin, the clarinet. I used to paint. I have written three novels, all unpublished. My latest is in your letterbox, put there early this morning. I'd like you to read it. Please. I know — don't ask me how — you're interested in closeness and distance. That's since the Gravity Star was discovered. But closeness can obliterate; and we novelists end up flattening the characters with ourselves — I once saw a lizard skeleton that had been trapped all year beneath a carpet but when it crept there it was an alive lizard. Well,' she smiled gleefully. 'Aren't you impressed?'

'I am indeed,' Mattina said.

'The truth again is that I'm not as clever as I make myself out to be. I'm an imposter. I suffer from the imposter syndrome. Perhaps you have heard of it?'

'No.'

'It's where you are so anxious to determine your level of ability, which in some cases can be quite high, that you simplify your search for your own truth by adopting the sincere belief that you are an imposter, your accomplishments are nothing, after all — either you dreamed them, others invented them, or you've deceived yourself. And then the only way to heighten the importance of your ability is to proclaim yourself an Official Imposter.'

Mattina, glancing at a row of books on the shelf beside her chair, picked up one entitled *Central Heating: a novel by Dinah Wheatstone.*

'You said you were never published?'

'I published those myself.'

'You wrote the books.'

'Yes, as an imposter novelist, not a real novelist.'

'But we're all imposters one way or another, aren't we?'

'There you are, back to the easy words again, making false claims to level everyone, trying to steal my glory,' Dinny Wheatstone cried accusingly, adding, 'The fact is, very few of us are real imposters. And it's different from play-acting. Imposterism or imposture comes from the core of your being because there's nothing else there. Your central being never develops a self; that's not a disadvantage entirely, though you do have to fight for your point of view, almost as if you were dead.'

'And there's no cure?'

'No. I was born that way. I didn't come out of the closet, so to speak, until I was fifty. And now I'm sixty and a fully fledged open imposter and I spend my time marauding among other people's points of view.'

Mattina wasn't sure how crazy Dinny Wheatstone might be, although at the same time she felt that Dinny made a good deal of sense. Mattina's New York friends included a wide range of the interestingly eccentric.

'How did you know I might be interested in reading your novel?'

Again Dinny Wheatstone smiled slyly.

'I know,' she said. 'I also heard you were a publisher's reader. Apart from that, I know quite a lot — I get it from the air — yet it really comes from the core of my being as I'm not cluttered up with my own being, and can admit quite a fund of impressions.'

'And you still paint, and play musical instruments? And are you writing further novels?'

'Since I discovered that I'm really an imposter and it's not just a fancy, I've been reluctant to continue. Still, one never knows. . . .'

She's crazy, Mattina thought.

And as if to justify Mattina's opinion, as they were saying goodbye at the doorstep, Dinny looked about her secretively and lowering her voice as if fearing eavesdroppers, she whispered, 'Kowhai Street is a street of imposters. Imposters and strangers. And I'm the Official Imposter with leave to occupy all points of view.'

At Number Twenty-four Mattina retrieved the package from her mailbox and scarcely glancing at it, placed it on the hall stand and went to the small kitchen where she drank a glass of milk for lunch and looked out at the mountains, for the kitchen had the best view. She thought about Kowhai Street, its shape, the way each house was separated from the next by fences and the way all lived, as animals, within their territories; one or two or three to a household; sharing as best they could, sometimes colliding like stars or bees or, simply, people; with those living alone covering vast distances within and without, untroubled by invasion but also unread by glancing eyes, untouched by other skin, their listening-space undented by the voices of others. If she were a novelist, like Jake, Mattina thought, she could mix a fine people-brew within Kowhai Street, to observe the result. Should she perhaps have told the neighbours she was making a film of Kowhai Street and Puamahara, that her investigations were the preliminary work, with cameras, crew, producer, director, following? Or would Kowhai Street fear the eye where it appeared to tolerate the ear? A street of strangers and imposters, even the stranger dead, the penultimate Madge, and the stranger mad, Dinny Wheatstone.

Impatient with her unhabitual musing, Mattina set out to explore the main street of Puamahara.

7

Mattina walked along Gillespie Street towards Tyne Street, the main street. Gillespie Street, a secondary State Highway, had rows of brick and stone flats in twos, separated by two garages, with occasional shops between the flats; and a dairy, a garage selling bread, pies, balloons and toy windmills, and gas, or as it was known here, petrol; two veterinary surgeons, one on each side of the street; two nonconformist churches; an old people's home with a soothing name . . . and on the corner of Tyne Street, a brightly painted black and gold Post Office resembling a hamburger or fried chicken parlour.

Tyne Street was busy, noisy, with cars and large trucks laden with a variety of goods — glossy new cars strung like an open necklace along the length of the trucks and glittering in their sunstruck gaudy colours; sheep crowded in double layers, their glazed eyes staring through the slats as they trampled, turned and jostled, bleating and stinking, their excrement draining through a pipe outlet that emptied its foul trail into the street while pedestrians hopped and leapt aside to avoid the splashing.

Joining the queue at the Post Office Mattina took a leaflet on postal services, bought a booklet of stamps, and in the adjacent bank she changed travellers' cheques. Next, she crossed to the Mall and noticing the computer shop, Computer City, beside Bathroom City and Furniture City, she approached the man who was operating a small computer while a stick figure darted to and fro on the screen dodging bullets and, when struck, falling apparently dead while a new stick figure sprang from the corpse to begin its life of dodging bullets, and now and then, deadly rays and pen-size missiles.

'Are you perhaps Mr Shannon?' Mattina asked.

The man, about in his thirties or early forties, stopped pressing the computer keys whereupon the stick figure waiting to be shot at, began dancing up and down letting out a cry with each leap, 'Help, help, help!'

'Yes, I'm Ed Shannon.'

'I met your wife, Renée, this morning. I'm Mattina Brecon, your new neighbour in Kowhai Street. I'm from New York City.'

Ed Shannon rubbed the sweat from his face and said, 'Whew.' He smiled. 'The planners of the Mall forgot or ignored the warmth of large areas of glass heated by our burning sun; only the windows fronting the street can open, the rest are stationary. It's worse upstairs. Oh. Pleased to meet you. You must tell us about San Francisco. Renée's keen on

Miami but I'm all for San Francisco.'

Mattina noted the pride and fear in his voice as he spoke of 'our burning sun', and the way his words, 'San Francisco, Miami' appeared to give her the ownership and responsibility of the two cities.

Ed Shannon glanced around the shop. 'What do you think of this set up? I suppose you see plenty of this in New York?'

Mattina was again surprised by the Puamaharian's certainty of the inclusiveness of the United States and its cities, particularly New York City: from computers to murders, the States had everything, a world of gadgets, goodies and horrors. The repeated words, 'You'll have this in the United States, of course,' like a cultural doffing of the cap to the Master, irritated her with its exposure of the sense of inferiority that she'd heard had gone from New Zealand. It seemed to her to be alive still, perhaps with changed forms and expressions, more subtle but unmistakeable, as in the cities where the gaping-eyed wonder at the material goods of the United States had been transferred to the gaping pride in the highrise towers of Auckland and Wellington and the continued remark made with the utmost satisfaction of accomplishment, 'Auckland is getting to be like New York!'

At the same time, Puamahara in its layout seemed to Mattina very much like smalltown U.S.A. Cleaner: obviously someone was responsible for cleaning the sidewalks and streets of empty packets, plastic bags, drink cans, milk cartons; except for Tyne Street where the responsibility perhaps fell on a national body. Plastic litter was everywhere in the world, on earth and in the sea, but in smalltown U.S.A. it was likely to be piled in drifts behind stores or sharing waste lots with abandoned automobiles where grass and weeds, grey-stalked, stunted, beaten by winds of pollution, hadn't a first chance. Here in Puamahara vacant lots were quickly dressed, it would appear, in coats of green furry grass and weeds studded with masses of yellow-button flowers.

Mattina felt there was an American air, also, in the glittering store displays, the advertising lures; here, the faces of the shoppers reflected more eagerness, a hunger for the 'goods' — the word that in early American usage meant only the stuff, the material, for clothing. Here, the shoppers stared in the windows as if appraising works of art, things of beauty; the gleam of the 'goods' was hypnotic — washing machines draped with blue and red satin ribbons, other appliances labelled 'award winning' — for smoothness, freshness, fingertip control.

'You'll come and visit us then?' Ed Shannon said.

'Oh yes, of course, of course. Thank you. I don't guarantee I'll be able to answer all your questions about the States.'

Ed Shannon looked embarrassed and said hastily, 'Oh, it's not that people in New Zealand don't travel to the United States — they're back and forth every day. Not like the old days. But Renée and I — and young Peter — would like to know what it's *really* like. You know what I mean.'

'I guess I do,' Mattina said, not admitting to him that most of her life had been spent on the trail of *really* and its parent noun.

'Puamahara is a great town,' she said, unsuccessful in her attempt not to sound patronising and hollow-brained. And promising to visit the Shannons she left the crowded Mall and once into Tyne Street she was again among the windows praising smoothness, freshness, lemon-scentedness, the desire to wash the earth and its contents with instant freshness, and sun, lemon and pine 'conditioners'. Now here was (in Jake's words) 'Little ole Noo Zealand' trying to wash its and the world's guilt away in award-winning machines.

In spite of the cattle and sheep trucks in Tyne Street, and the obvious need to infuse some acceptable fragrance, Puamahara, in Mattina's opinion, was demeaning itself by trying to adopt the fragrance of elsewhere to conceal the apparent or invisible bloody deeds. Becoming impatient with her criticism she said aloud, 'Well why not let Puamahara and the world sink and slide into their smooth futures!'

She then joined a line of shoppers walking the corridors of the Blissway Market where soothing, smoothing music gently oozed from the primrose walls; and when she had bought her supply of food and household cleaners, wipers, scrubbers, polishers, removers, deodorisers, unblockers and fresheners (jasmine-scented), she hired a taxi from the adjacent office and was soon home at Number Twenty-four. It was now mid-afternoon. She felt that one shopping excursion to Tyne Street was enough for many days. She noted as she unfolded the *Western Mail* that the murder of the penultimate Madge was still in the news, with an account of the life of the alleged murderer, and the reference to Number Eighteen Kowhai Street as 'the murder house'. A feeling of sadness at the evident passing of a fragile innocence came over her at the thought that murder had coincided with her first enjoyment of lemon-and-rose and sheep-scented Puamahara. She had overheard a shopper in the Mall say, 'When murder like that happens in a place like Puamahara, that's the end.'

Again, the small words linked in deadly persuasion. And the people, stick figures, accepting as truth an habitual arrangement of words. Mattina wondered if perhaps she had arrived in Puamahara in time to dance up and down crying out, 'Help, help, help!'

Part Two

Wheatstone Imposter

8

That evening Mattina opened the typescript left by Dinny Wheatstone, and began to read:

'The human race is an elsewhere race and I am an imposter in a street of imposters. I am nothing and no-one: I was never born. I am a graduate imposter, having applied myself from my earliest years to the study of the development of imposture as practised in myself and in others around me in street, town, city, country, and on earth. The imposture begins with the first germ of disbelief in being, in self, and this allied to the conviction of the "unalterable certainty of truth", produces the truth of disbelief, of deception of being, of self, of times, places, peoples, of all time and space. The existence of anything, of anywhere and anytime produces an instant denial only in graduates of imposture; in most others who remain unaware of such a state, particularly in themselves, there may be little or no knowledge of their reality, their nonentity.

'My qualification for writing this short narrative about the residents of Kowhai Street, Puamahara, is chiefly my imposture which as a result of my nonentity, is accompanied by an uncanny perception of human life, love, death and the process of time. I do not claim it is an accurate perception but it is wholly presented as a vision. I know you all, I know your past, your present and future, yet I have not created you, I have merely "seen" you. All graduates in imposture perceive in this way. It is the reward or penalty for being no-one; yet always there is no guarantee of truth. In an imposter, all points of view are burgled because the imposter has no point of view. Locked within the language of my imposture I further bind myself with every word I use, and yet I acknowledge the treasure of my deceit because it is within the human country of birth, meeting, parting, and death — the sanctuary of the imposter. And although the inevitable deceit also of language has built for us a world of imposture, we do survive within it, fed by the spark, at times by the fire of the recognition of the hinterland of truth.

'Complete imposture, I repeat, leads to nothingness in which one inhabits all worlds except the world of oneself.

'I am a literate person. I attended school, studied various subjects, read much and was not encouraged to question, until at the natural time of life when urgency arises, I, using the language, said Where, Why, How, Who, When, What? Indeed, at school I chanted a rhyme, a mnemonic:

I kept six honest serving men
They taught me all I knew;
Their names were Where and What and When
And How and Why and Who.

I questioned all replies, demanding proof, and proof came dressed in words, was identified by words; even the marvel of proof within music, painting, dancing, science, all art, came always dressed in words, while that mass of proof attainable only through the listening, watching heart, the language of feeling, that too became words, continuing to build the language of imposture.

'Perhaps I should not complain. We all inhabit the world. It is as natural to believe this as it is natural for us, standing on earth, to believe the earth is motionless, a secure foothold, although we have learned that it spins itself like a top observed as at rest within its spinning, surrounded by vapours of movement. We are all deep in imposture, surrounded only by intimations of truth; our foothold is not in truth.

'Do I appear to be writing a treatise? Let us enjoy our world until it and we come face to face with truth; our capacity for enjoyment is deep and not easily destroyed.

'I too have learned lately of the Gravity Star, the discovery of the star that annihilates the concept of near as near and far as far, for the distant star is close by, puncturing the filled vessel of impossibility, overturning the language of concept, easing into our lives the formerly unknowable, spilling unreason into reason.

'After this preamble let me begin. Do not be surprised to find yourself, your future, your past, within this small book. I'm writing of Kowhai Street, Puamahara, in the Maharawhenua. I have seized control of all points of view, although Mattina Brecon, the character from New York, trying to entice the point of view to herself, became unwilling to surrender it. I shall apportion it as I think fit because, as I have said, it is my only power, my true self that is no self. I speak now. I "tell". Generously I give the point of view to others. It is words that take charge of the telling. . . .'

9

Ed Shannon was a tightly built, composed man who looked well in shorts and wore them summer-long. His speech, too, was controlled and well clad, without stray meaningless exclamations and asides that are part of the usual patterns of speech — ah, I see, you know, eh, sort of, kind of, and the fact is. His words came fully manufactured in precast phrases and sentences. He was an ambitious man, not so young — in his early forties — but eager to seize an opportunity that would let him and his family penetrate deeper the suburban glories offered with future higher salary and status. He hoped that his management of the computer centre would lead soon to a senior management post, and thus, at a party or conference, he had learned to steer himself through avenues of influence and possibility (political, clerical, editorial trees) to the prize bloom of each evening, usually the guest of honour, from a branch up north or from Aussie.

Ed was devoted to his family, his work, and his home computer. Anyone with a view into the make-up of the human personality would not have been surprised to learn that Ed's apparent confidence, air of security, of personal pride, affirmed a host (with himself as guest) of fears — fear of making mistakes at work, of losing his job and having to go on the dole, of not being able to meet the mortgage payments, of finding that Renée had been unfaithful to him, that Peter had failed at school, and, even in this crowded house of fear, that the Council, deciding to widen Kowhai Street, might claim a strip of his land and thus lower the value of their property. He was afraid of seasons, of holidays, of possible impotence, of the bill for repair of the car, of being in a court case and having the facts printed in the *Western Mail*; of growing old. Fortunately, none of his fears was consuming, each simply passing by in a procession distant enough for him to retain his appearance of confidence and security, but close enough for him to perceive the prospect of his world suddenly changed, in disarray, and to cry out at night in his sleep.

Renée Shannon was a more tousled personality, draping loops and hooks and multiple strands of feeling, and like some highly charged synthetic material, attracting an accumulation of whatever she touched, so that every now and then, if only to discern the true pattern of herself, she was forced to brush away, springclean the clutter of events and people, her feelings and the feelings of others, and begin again. She had come from up north where the world was busier and noisier and she thought of Puamahara as a 'dump'; and when, in her springcleaning mood, she felt she was buried in daily occurrences and feelings, she looked about her and said vehemently, 'Puamahara is nothing but a dump', Ed, knowing her to be no less ambitious than he, would frown but give no other sign, unless perhaps the pores of his skin rallied closer to reject the assertion, or his body stood taller, while the always passing fears crept in, the way ants used to do in Renée's beloved Auckland, rippling up and down, irritating. Ed hated the thought of living in Auckland because he had never lived there. He preferred Aussie. But what was wrong with Puamahara? It was cosy. He could find himself appointed area manager with responsibilities as far as Wellington and beyond to the South Island. Puamahara had more than Renée gave it credit for. In her moods she'd exclaim, 'It's nothing but a home for geriatrics.'

Young Peter, in the standards at school, ten going on eleven, was quiet, an ordinary boy, although at that age unusually thoughtful: 'Mum, can I mow the lawn?' And ten years from now, Ed would think, listening to Peter's politeness, he'll be a hulk, bearded, untidy, unemployed. . . .

The remaining member of the Shannon family, the computer, had a special corner in the sitting room, taking more space with disk drive, the disks, the printer, the cassette recorder, the programme packs, than the three-piece suite with its two recliner-rockers deep-buttoned in dralon, cramped into another corner. 'If I'd known the space the computer would take, I'd have had an extra room built on,' was Ed's answer to Renée's complaints. 'This corner's as good as any, in the meantime.'

And so most evenings when Ed came home from work, he didn't sit reading the evening paper or watching news on TV, he could hardly wait to plug the extension lead into the 'power board' ('four outlets individually switched, pastel-coated'), his hunger for electricity outlets appeased as he gazed greedily at the four sets of holes like faces (the faces of stick figures!) in the soap-coloured plastic board; switch on, and settling himself (arranging the back cushion as if he were in the driver's seat), bring life to each appliance in its proper order; then, running his finger along the upended row of floppy disks set at arm's length, extract his choice for the evening which had become his usual choice as he ignored the Murder Mystery, Haunted House, Duckshooting on the Moors, Torpedo Shooting, People-Shooting (enemies, of course), ah! The opening strains of 'Jesu Joy of Man's Desiring' merged with the theme from 2001, as the Flight Simulator Course appeared on the screen while, placing conveniently his two manuals — Flight Physics and Flight Manual — his various maps of the airfields of the eastern seaboard of the United States and additional practice-fields of California, with his printed diagram of the controls of his twin-engined Piper plane, Ed chose his flight for the evening. Each time he sat at the controls he realised the programme demanded more skill than he possessed, and then he was quick to tell himself that in the big jets the pilot worked with a co-pilot, navigator and flight engineer, with each taking charge of part of the controls. 'How do they expect my eye to dart here, there and everywhere?' he asked himself when again and again his faulty airspeed, his failure to perform a simple act, nose up or down, to adjust wingflaps, note the engine revs, caused him to overshoot the runway and crash into the bright sea beneath the bright sky. Often he crashed after becoming airborne and smoothly traversing the blue computer sky above the emerald fields bordered with computer trees. It was too much. Especially since Peter, who was far from being a genius at school, could fly for miles and suffer nothing more than an occasional loss of airspeed.

S-P-L-A-S-H! CRASHED AGAIN!

Ed was learning slowly. After a time he was proud to be able to choose not Fair Weather Mode of Flat Seas, Clear Skies, Windless World, but Reality Mode where he submitted himself to Possible Fire, Engine Failure, Excessive Turbulence, Clear Air Turbulence, Fog, Snowstorm, Iced Wings. . . . What did it matter how unreal or real, how false or true his flight was, if in the end, he always crashed, prompting from the sound effects accompanying his attempt at flight, the siren-sound that caused Renée to cry out, 'Turn it down, Ed, the neighbours will think there's been a disaster.'

It was agreed that Ed could use the computer for two hours each evening, either earlier or later, depending on the programme times on television and on Peter's homework. The addiction to the computer made Renée uneasy, for although it was part of Ed's work, its diverting of attention from her and Peter and their daily activities appeared to Renée to emphasise an absence in her own life. She was not wholly unhappy with this, for in her apparently crowded day it was like a clearing in the forest or a parking space where formerly there was none. She was reluctant to fill this space, although she knew from family experience that once its existence was known or felt, others would be eager to advise her; as if, entering her presence as though it were a house and observing a large empty room, they exclaimed, 'This mustn't be allowed! Not an empty room!'

Peter's interest in the computer also made Renée uneasy. Other kids had them at home, he said. And used them whenever they wanted. Their teacher had said it was a good thing, computing. 'We want the whole of the country to be computer-literate by the twenty-first century,' the teacher had said.

Proudly, Ed had shown Peter how to work the computer; no son of his would be 'computer-illiterate' — that was the phrase the experts used, and any phrase they used had to be noted. These experts! They had always hung around New Zealand like ants round a drop of honey, and the ones most listened to were the ones from overseas. It wasn't good enough, not these days, everyone was saying. Ed too. He was surprised that Peter, such a dreamer, had learned so quickly to operate the computer. A funny kid, Peter. It had seemed as if he could never get facts right, yet here he was airborne for hours in Reality Mode, making processions of colours, sounds, shooting the enemy with missiles, bombs, guns, bows and arrows, flying out there in Space Wars with Space War weapons, picking off the enemy aliens, the inhabitants of other planets different from earthlings, strange creatures with eyes for brains or hands for brains, with different-coloured skin, multicoloured hair, voices that flowed like waterfalls and made marks on space, language that grew stationary like a tree and could not be picked until it was ripe; creatures with different weapons, speech-weapons, scent-weapons, listen-weapons, where a sentence in their alien talk was their army, a song their weapon, their thoughts like laser beams. Peter could destroy them, though, with earth-weapons, for that was how the game was programmed. It was obvious that Peter enjoyed being in Space.

Renée's contribution to the family business was her help with the stock and accounts. Although she seemed never to be able to organise her surroundings, she could make beautiful lists. Her dreams, however, remained in Auckland. Had they been living in Auckland, she told herself, everything might have been different. Auckland 'turned her on', she would say, using the out-of-date language of the sixties, for although she was now thirty and her teenage years were spent in the seventies, she and her friends had adopted the sixties as 'their time', just as Ed, thirteen years older and an infant of the nineteen forties, thought of himself as a 'forties' man, talking of the war and Hiroshima, the peace, the housing boom, the dreamdays before decimal coinage, as if that were his 'real' time. He talked of the multinational companies taking over the country's bread and ice-cream as if he had been part of the deal. Yet he'd moved readily to computers. As a forties man he had simply chosen his time, as Renée had, and now Ed was fond of saying the country was in ruins, it had been in ruins since the takeover of the bread and ice-cream.

The computer was a drug. Both Ed and Peter had dark circles under their eyes and their faces were pale from close scrutiny of the tiny (but deadly) weapons and the equally tiny stick figures representing the human race, while Ed's face had a permanent frown from trying to work out how to get his plane airborne in Reality Mode.

In the world of Puamahara, three weeks had passed since the arrival of Mattina Brecon. The turmoil surrounding the murder gradually lessened as the town concentrated on the murderer 'with a mental history', his capture tempered with compassion but serving a gourmet helping of We knew it, We always knew it, We warned them, Something has to be done in future to protect us from him and others like him.

Mattina was beginning to believe that her journey to savour the atmosphere of the town supposedly containing the Memory Flower, the land memory, had been her excuse to leave Jake in peace while he finished his novel. She felt she was making some progress in her research when she accepted Renée's invitation to Saturday dinner.

'Look, do come over at about half past five and have tea with us. . . .' Renée's words trailed. She hesitated, disconcerted by one of those threads that may start without warning to unravel self-confidence; you see them trailing, undoing, and they're so strong they can cut through skin.

Mattina smiled.

'I'll be pleased to come over,' she said.

Mattina thought, I might get further clues; as if it were a cheap detective novel, after all. Renée thought, Now we'll settle that argument about the Everglades. Crocodiles or alligators. And Ed will learn at first hand about Silicon Valley.

People as proven unreliable dispensers of information are still the first option in the urge to find out. The information comes with voice, body, mind, clothes, the capacity to argue, agree, to make love all in the interchange that is reason enough for putting aside the small-printed encyclopaedia, for what's two inches of black print against a mobile unpredictable dispenser of knowledge that refuses to be packaged without a supply of all human feelings and possibilities? (I, Dinny Wheatstone, author of this imposter record, divine the activities of Kowhai Street, the street of the Gravity Star among the ordinary extraordinary people, while I study the primer of possible impossibility, the meaning of the meaningless, as if the Gravity Star irons all displayed meaning into nothingness, obliterates the significant signs and print of the alphabets of all language, leaves a smooth language of nothingness and also of possible impossibility for a new world to walk on, making new footprints, or talk of making with new tongue-prints.)

Later, in the Shannon house, Mattina looked with interest at the room where she, Ed, Renée, Peter, sat in dark-painted, carved wooden chairs at the round wooden dining-table. In one corner an accumulation of shapes (presumably the computer and its accessories) was shrouded with what looked like an old bedspread, while in another corner the three-piece suite was arranged in the pride of its red velvet, 'real synthetic velvet'. (Here the possible impossibility already gapes, like a split truth.)

Through the open door into the kitchen, Mattina could see the white-ware shining to attention, the straight-backed stove, belly forward, the beheaded white-bodied refrigerator. She felt grateful that in her New York home the kitchen was out of sight along a corridor. (The glance like a little dog will go anywhere, tracing the shape of objects as if shape were scent, exploring without rest among the white polished goods. Among old handmade utensils, irregularly shaped pottery, knotted wood, there's a point of rest, an ease, a homing-place.)

Although Mattina did not identify her unease at seeing the modern kitchen, she glanced quickly away from the gloss and polish to the faces of the family, and whatever their faces may have held, whatever secret explosions past or to come, in their lived-in home of skin, with their used eyes and lips and hands, they gave the sense of rest denied by the clean surfaces of the kitchen whiteware.

Mattina noticed the dark circles under Ed's eyes, and the pallor of Peter's skin.

'I guess you go out in the mountains in the weekend,' she said. 'I've heard all New Zealanders are great mountaineers. But if you'll pardon me, you're not tanned, are you?'

Renée tried to direct attention from Mattina's embarrassment at having made a 'personal' remark, by serving the roast lamb, green peas, roast potatoes, with a jug of freshly made mint sauce.

'New Zealand lamb,' Renée said self-consciously. 'The experts are always trying to make us eat some other food but we like good old lamb. It's hard, you know. Sometimes it seems as if everyone in the world is trying to change the ordinary New Zealander. We're fair game for every jumped-up expert.'

Mattina was polite. 'Oh,' she said. She was tired of hearing about experts, New Zealand lamb. And scenery.

Renée spoke directly.

'We're really dying to know about San Francisco (that's Ed) and Miami (that's me).'

Mattina smiled at Peter.

'And what about you, Peter?'

'Same as Dad, I *guess*,' Peter said winningly, adding, 'And the same as Mum too. The crocodiles.'

'Or the alligators.'

Mattina said nothing. Her own knowledge of Silicon Valley came only from reading newspapers. As for alligators and crocodiles — she knew some were freshwater, others saltwater creatures. She was impatient with this roundabout way of getting information — surely an encyclopaedia would have informed the Shannon family! She understood, however, the excitement even in an age of world travel, of meeting and talking to those who had been there, seen that, talked to those who . . . why, she herself had made a career of being there and talking to *them* in all parts of the world; and her impulse to visit Puamahara had been her longing to be linked *at first hand* with the town of the Memory Flower.

Renée, Ed, Peter waited for her reply.

'I'm sorry,' she said. 'I know little about Silicon Valley. Or about crocodiles and alligators. What I know is probably as much as you know. As for my facts about California and Miami . . . even they may be no more than yours.'

Renée looked disappointed.

'We thought that you, coming from America. . . .'

'I should think you also know more about computers than I,' Mattina said, 'though I should have thought that here in Puamahara you'd not be bothered with such things.'

'We're not backward by any means,' Ed said sharply.

'She didn't say we were,' Renée said quickly.

'I meant,' Mattina said carefully, 'Puamahara is such a paradise, in a way . . . that computers seem out of place.'

Renée did not voice her thought, 'There they are again, the Americans trying to decide what we should and shouldn't have. Even if Puamahara is a paradise, why should we be deprived? I suppose they think we'd be happy lolling around in the sun all year.'

Instead, Renée said, 'We like to keep up, you know. We might have lovely scenery but that doesn't make us less intelligent.'

Mattina said quickly, 'I felt computers might spoil your atmosphere.'

For the tourists, no doubt, Renée thought.

She said, 'We're so far away here,' without entering the everlasting argument of far away from what, from whom, which distant people and places? Not knowing of the Gravity Star and the possible impossibilities of space and time.

Renée served dessert, formerly known as 'pudding', lemon meringue pie with fresh cream.

'It's from the lemons in our garden,' she said.

'I have them too,' Mattina said. 'Everyone has lemons and oranges and grapefruit. I thought they grew only in Auckland.'

'Puamahara,' Ed said proudly, 'is one of the horticultural areas of New Zealand.'

'I know,' Mattina said with equal pride. 'It's the *centre*. That's why the Memory Flower grew here, in Puamahara and Maharawhenua. Here is where the history of the land was discovered and recorded. You could say that here in this fertile district, your past, your present and your future have been programmed.' She smiled at Ed. 'To use your computer language.'

'Oh yes,' Renée said. 'We've all heard about the legend. The Tourist Corporation has done it to death.'

'We have it at school,' Peter said. 'And it does make us special, in Puamahara, doesn't it, Mum?'

'I suppose it does,' Renée looked, wondering, at Mattina. 'I didn't really believe that was why you came here, to Kowhai Street in Puamahara. But it's true, isn't it?'

'It is, you know,' Mattina said. 'Ours is such a vast country, so varied in climate, in geography, and when one part of our land is asleep, the other is awake; we have three time zones. Where, in our country, would we know where to search for the Memory Flower? The earliest people — '

'The Red Indians,' Peter said eagerly.

'The Indians would have known, and do know, but it may be too late to ask them; but you are a small young land — '

'We are old,' Peter corrected. 'Old as old.'

'I mean your colonisation was later. When I heard of Puamahara as the place of the Memory Flower I wanted to come here, to a land of one time zone, yet as your tourist brochures say, with a variety of features — glaciers, plains, mountains, sun, snow, hot springs and geysers like ours in Yellowstone Park; a desert road; a country small enough for everyone to be neighbours; a family place; at least, that's what I thought. With everyone, all races, sharing the Memory Flower.'

'I wish we had time zones,' Peter said. 'Like you and Australia.'

'I thought,' Mattina said slowly, 'that I'd find the Memory Flower, the land memory growing in the air, so to speak, with everyone certain as could be of the knowledge of the programme of time, learning the language of the memory, like the computer language, to include the geography, history, creating the future. . . .'

She frowned. 'I'm not so sure, now. . . .'

'Oh, we're doing all that,' Renée said vaguely. 'Aren't we, Ed?'

Ed wasn't sure what to say. Like most New Zealanders he was sensitive to criticism from 'aliens'.

'We could be . . . could be . . .' he said wisely.

He leaned forward.

'But what exactly do you *mean?*' he asked.

Mattina smiled. 'It sounds crazy, I guess. It's the idea you get about other places. But I do feel that having the memory at hand, even if it is buried in legend, is having access to a rare treasure. Such memories are being lost rapidly and everywhere we are trying to find them, to revive them. Puamahara in the Maharawhenua could be the place for pilgrims (I guess I'm a pilgrim) to be healed of their separation from the Memory Flower.'

'Little old Puamahara!' Ed said, slightly mocking.

'Just fancy,' Renée said.

'It's too up-in-the-air for me,' Ed said. 'But we do wish you all the best with your stay here, your research, if that's what you're doing.'

'It's just Kowhai Street,' Mattina said. 'The street I'm living in. And its people. Somehow, it's different from my other research. There's the Gravity Star; and your heavens are brilliant day and night.'

'Yes. Instead of Miss New Zealand we have Miss Skin Cancer Queen. . . .'

'And are you studying us?'

'Everyone here, I guess. It's not exactly *studying.* Just knowing.'

'Will you put in the murder? Poor Madge McMurtrie. Yet she was dying, she would have died soon. And that youth . . . from the Manuka Home.'

'Let's not get into that,' Ed said. 'Everyone who comes into the shop starts off with the murder and what if and so on. I'm sick of it.'

'It's like on TV,' Peter said turning to Mattina. 'And Dad's got a murder game just like that with everyone wondering who did it and why and then the murderer being caught, and Dad doesn't mind playing that game, do you, Dad?'

'It's only a game,' Ed said sternly.

'But you like playing it, Dad. You're always playing it when you're not flying. And you talk about it.'

'I tell you,' Ed said fiercely, 'it's different. It's not real. It doesn't happen.'

Peter spoke obstinately. 'But it did happen, Dad. It happened in Kowhai Street. And Kowhai Street's real . . . isn't it?'

'That's enough,' Renée said sharply.

'And sometimes Dad plays the murderer, too, don't you, Dad?' Peter persisted.

'That's enough,' Renée repeated. 'As your father said, these games are

61

not real, they have nothing to do with real life. You know that, Peter. All those people and the clues and the houses and the streets and the murderers and the victims (there are six each to choose from), they're only a game.'

'And Dad's not flying either?' Peter asked, while Ed, blushing, stared from Peter to Renée.

'Of course the flying's real,' he said fiercely. 'Pilots use the simulator to learn to fly.'

'Then how can you tell which game's real and which isn't?'

Mattina rescued them.

'About California and Miami,' she said again, 'I'm sure you all know more than I.'

'We've all seen Miami on TV,' Renée said. 'The Everglades. Those movies where they all get around in a high boat. . . .'

'A wherry,' Peter said. 'And they hit out at the crocodiles.'

'The alligators,' Ed corrected.

'It's all swamp,' Peter said. 'Swamp and vampires. And in Miami it's all killing and drugs.'

'I'm not so sure,' Mattina said mildly, thinking that now the dessert had been praised and eaten and praised, and they'd had a cup of tea, it might be time for her to leave.

'I think perhaps. . . .' she began.

'Of course,' Renée said promptly, 'I see you're anxious to get back to your work. First, you must see over the house.'

'If you want to show it to me,' Mattina said hesitantly, realising that part of the hospitality in Kowhai Street was 'seeing over' the house and garden.

'You two can get to your computer,' Renée said, 'while I show Miss Brecon the house.'

'Mattina.'

'While I show Mattina around.'

Later, at home, Mattina went over the details of her inspection, remembering the conversation.

'We had ranchsliders put in . . . we wanted louvre cupboards; they're not real louvres but they look attractive. And we had to choose between Gordon's Tiles and the newer kind of colour-steel . . . we chose the newer kind . . . we've in mind for later an in-ground swimming-pool — they're better, I'm told . . . we were given that love-seat for Christmas. . . . Aren't the flowers lovely? We like freesias . . . Ed knows someone who's into bonsai. It's useful to grow bonsai in a big city, don't you think?'

Mattina hadn't said, 'But you're in Puamahara,' because it was clear that Renée's thoughts often strayed elsewhere, north.

'Oh, and I haven't shown you the bathroom. We've put in a whirl-pool bath; and mirror tiles. The new kind, not the old kind.'

'Oh.'

'And you will have noticed our carpet's shagpile?'

'Sure.'

To Mattina's surprise, Renée had then burst into laughter.

'I'm no fool you know! You can't believe that I'm entirely serious about this? Being shown the house and garden used to be a set piece for visitors, and now it has become a sort of nostalgic joke as well as a good piece of entertainment — like the Main Trunk Line and the old Railway pies and cups and saucers . . . and the British Empire . . . we're great at entertaining ourselves, you know, and we do enjoy our homes.'

And when they were standing at the front gate, Renée looked up and down the street and into the sky and said, 'It's so nice to be living under the sky. There might be inequality, real poverty, and all those new finance houses where the windows are curtained with dollar notes, and the bankers and foreign exchange dealers wear clothes patterned with polyester dollars . . . truly . . . this country is at sixes and sevens and I think Puamahara is a dump and I'd give the earth to be living in Auckland . . . but so far we all have our fair share of sky, especially in Puamahara. Just look.'

And Mattina, looking up at the sky, had agreed, and thought she must remember to imprint the sight of it, its closeness in comparison with distant Manhattan sky. She felt gratified to know that for two months she too had her 'fair share of sky'.

10

Between the Shannons and the Jameses, Hercus Millow, the retired sergeant-major, lived alone and spent his time gardening, following the horse-racing on the radio and television, and in the evening reading or watching television. Now that the winter was over and the blossom-filled days of late October were nearer, and the sweet peas and the climbing beans were budding, Hercus, wearing his summer hat, a fawn panama, and his grey walkshorts, liked to rest on a canvas 'executive' chair against the sunny side of his house and look through his binoculars at the detail of the mountains. He had the appearance of a passenger on an ocean liner; one might not have been surprised to hear him cry, 'A ship! A whale! A wreck!'

And as he sat changing unattainable distance to palpable closeness, and back again to distance, he'd murmur to himself, 'Now there's the trig station, there's the trampers' hut; perhaps a hermit lives up there among the wild pigs. I wonder what it's like up there alone with that beaut view over the Tasman, maybe to Taranaki, to the misty headlands of the South Island. One of these days I'll get a good pair of binoculars, see into the *real* distance, bring the mountain peaks down here into Kowhai Street, near and sharp as if before a rainstorm. And is that cloud of mist really the snowfall of early October?'

Then bringing his view closer, into Kowhai Street, he'd study the houses opposite, looking clear into the front sitting room to the frosty-faced televisions, the parrot ornaments, the family photographs. His binoculars, one of his relics from the Second World War, and then the best of their kind, were old-fashioned now, and although they focussed well they'd none of the new type of high-powered lens that could bring stars and planets and comets almost to touching distance. They were steam-age binoculars. Today, Hercus had no doubt, they'd be built with a radio, a clock, a thermometer and calculator, all in one. His camera, too, was of another age: an empty magic box that dared not be looked at by the sun or the night or the wind. Cameras now were as daring as astronauts, yet full of delicate mechanisms that snapped if you touched them. Regretting but accepting the passing of the camera with no innards, the magic box and the simple binoculars, Hercus knew that to satisfy his full viewing curiosity he'd need to borrow the new-style camera and binoculars owned by his friend living at the War Veterans' Home in Power Street.

And as he sat in his canvas chair or limped around his garden, his two cats, Prime Minister and Leader of the Opposition, flanked him in true military — or parliamentary — style. Anyone observing Hercus might think of him just as an old man with a limp, sitting in his garden or his sitting room looking out at the Eastern Mountains; but he was not a man who had settled into retirement with house and garden and memories of a happy marriage in another town. He still thought of himself, as we have seen, as a stranger in Puamahara, at home only with the many watercolours and oils of flowers to remind him of his wife, the painter, whom he had nursed in her prolonged illness. He felt he could never be used to the design of Puamahara, the landscape. Puamahara had no river, the sea and the mountains were too far away; his friends in the Hutt were out of touch with him or had died in the War Veterans' Home.

He was Sergeant-Major Millow. Through several hours of each day and night he was the commander and the prisoner in the German camp; looking out at the fallen kowhai blossom, the flower-filled peaceful landscape, the blessed sky, he wondered and knew why these were not etched as deeply in his mind as his landscape as a prisoner and soldier. He knew the commonplaces, many of them fallacies, about the comradeship of war. He knew that in times of suffering, memories are formed that as the years pass have the capacity to spread under the seismic impact of their own stress, causing other memories to disappear and new details of the time, new scapes, to reappear in the present. The details of the prison grew as clear as the plants in his garden; he remembered the leisure hours of football, makeshift tennis, handball, and the event of each day, the exercising of the dogs. Dogs were walked at all hours, all breeds from Pomeranians to Alsatians, with some of the men owning guard dogs more handsome than the German dogs. A few, disliking dogs, preferred to sail their yachts in a puddle when rain-water was plentiful. Hercus Millow, listening in Kowhai Street to the barking of the neighbourhood dogs, heard those of the prison camp, remembering the affection that each man had for his pet, the account each gave of the walk, of the prepared meals, and how in the evening when reality burgled the fantasy and would not be ejected, each tried to banish it by talking to his named pet, reaching forward to stroke the invisible coat. One prisoner kept a horse, another milked two cows each morning and night, sharing the milk, butter and cheese with his friends.

'After all, I'm a farmer,' he said.

'Don't let your imagination run away with you,' his neighbour mocked, stroking the Airedale dog that muzzled and licked his hand.

'Here boy, good boy, good dog.'

'Hey don't you steal my dog,' someone called. 'He's mine. Here's your little runt with the short legs. The Royal dog.'

Again and again Hercus intervened in the passionate quarrels that erupted over the livestock. And each morning some wag holding his nose complained to the officers who, with Hercus, shared separate sleeping quarters, 'The stink of the zoo in there. I think we should have restrictions on the number of animals we keep. Hey, cockie, why don't you send your cows back to the farm? Not to mention your chooks!'

'Twenty-five thousand miles away, is that how far we are from home?'

'About that. Almost as far from the moon and sun.'

'Go on. After the first thousand miles, distance seems the same; even after the first inch or centimetre.'

'Wouldn't it be beaut if they abolished distance?'

'They?'

The prisoners, soldiers, the civilians, forever in the grip of 'them'.

'I should say,' said the scholar among them who made a daily trade of the serial he wrote on scraps of paper and cloth, and who recited long passages of prose, 'that you'll have problems if you interfere with the perception of distance. You'd interfere with time. You'd have yesterday and tomorrow breathing down your bloody necks; not to mention the Ancient Greeks and Romans. And you'd find yourself in ancient cities, and among mountains, some vanished, some still standing. Also,' he said with a blissful smile, for in prison camp or not he'd at last found use for a word first known to him five years earlier when he was fifteen; and he knew that some may live a lifetime before they use a cherished word or phrase with special meaning to them, 'Yes,' he said, his face still showing its blissful smile, 'You'd have the Ancient Romans and Greeks. You'd have cities and rivers of today in your backyard; and you'd have the *Carpathians*, the *Carpathians* in your garden. The Carpathians?'

He began then to quote in a chanting tone, 'The Carpathians are a great mountain system, extending from Bratislava to Orsovo, in crescent form . . . the region is wild and fertile and well wooded with oaks, beeches, evergreens, firs, and wild animals are found, including the wolf, bear and lynx, the chamois and ibex; the bearded vulture is found there. . . .'

He smiled again. 'Yes,' he said, 'We could touch the *Carpathians*.'

Hercus had a stroke after his wife died. Lately, he'd fallen and had been unable to get up, and he'd banged and yelled and thumped the ground, but nobody heard him, in Kowhai Street and Puamahara, although in Kowhai Street everyone knew everyone else and most had blue and yellow discs pasted on their letterbox or front windowpane: 'This household is a member of Neighbourhood Watch. We care.'

Caring was in fashion as a topic to be talked about, Hercus knew. There was also talk of 'parenting'. In every street there were groups who sat talking about 'caring' and 'parenting' and 'opening up' and being 'open' and 'grief' and 'grieving', with a new set of rules for grieving. And still no-one had heard the cries when Hercus fell.

He did not think he was afraid to die. He didn't believe in an organised religion or in life after death. He believed that when you died you died. Kaput. Like the young man trying to imagine the Greeks, the Romans, the Pyramids, Pompeii, the Carpathians, the Andes, in the same world, Hercus couldn't manage to work out events like the resurrection or even the dead (natural death or killed in action, buried, cremated) reappearing as new; it was impossible, unbelievable, that is, as long as you had only ordinary human concepts to work with. Hercus had no doubt that if human thought suffered an overturning process then the way would be clear to know the formerly unknowable, imagine the formerly unimaginable.

He knew his death was not too far away; he had no means of measuring its distance, nor even of scenting it, as an inland traveller sniffs the salt in the air as he nears the coast. He felt that he would die sooner rather than later; and again he could not visualise the distance in time for sooner may be one second, later two seconds distant. He felt that after he died, sooner and later would have no command over him and no reference to what he might become or where he might be.

'Hercus,' his friends said, 'you've too much time on your hands.'

Hercus grimaced and looked at his hands.

'It's better than blood,' he said. 'Or is it? It's true I can't get about, with my leg. My home is my world now. And *soon*, perhaps it will be my armchair, then my bed.'

He spent his day like many other Puamaharians — reading the morning newspaper, when he'd sit facing away from the mountains, with the sun on his back; and in the evening sitting in the small porch facing the western sun; backing his and other's racehorses; watching the midday soaps on TV; pottering about the garden; or ticket in hand, matching the latest Lotto numbers; or searching through the Golden Kiwi results; or on Tuesdays waiting for the Bonus Bond results. The rest of the time it was a trip to the R.S.A. club (with his nephew driving the car); feeding and caring for the cats; and staring at the mountains. All layered over the continuing life in the prison camp. A seemingly quiet, measured existence, enough money to buy food, pay rates, electricity, telephone bills, television licence, and the monthly visit to the doctor on the west side of town, near the lake.

Also, Hercus liked to read a book. A few propped up one another on his bookshelf, books he knew and liked to reread: *A Child's Garden of Verses. Letters of Robert Louis Stevenson.* A book of poems in Scottish written by Hercus's great-great-grandfather. Also, a handful of paperbacks — Neville Shute, C. S. Forester, Nicholas Monserrat. Hercus did not read as a habit or daily meal. His reading was described as 'picking up a book'. He had once described himself as 'a great reader'. That had been then. Now, between other activities, he would sit down, glance at his bookshelf, and 'pick up a book', and then, reading, he felt a sense of loss that a world still treasured had retreated from him, of regret that the retreat had been at his own command, as other daily activities pressed upon him; then a sense of confusion at the routes once offered and the routes once taken in the morning world of tireless strength of mind and body. He almost wept, then. Letting the picked-up book fall by his chair, he sat recollecting the moments when his life had matched in wonder the reading of a satisfying book.

Also, he listened to music on the radio, not making a choice, accepting what the station offered, and when he became aware of the music, feeling an odd sense of displacement as he compared the music of 'then' and 'now'. He even smiled amusedly, noting that the 'old' national station that once kept strictly to 'Where E'er You Walk', 'Bless This House', 'I'll Walk Beside You', and brass band music, now played a 'musak' selection with no announcing between, with songs from the fancier hit shows — *Evita, Starlight Express, West Side Story*; and themes from the television programmes old and new.

Only the news had Hercus's full attention. The news retained for him its wartime urgency. He turned up the volume for all the world to hear as, listening closely, he identified enemy and ally and marvelled that although the Second World War had finished forty years earlier, the announcers, while not identifying 'the enemy', still used the language of war — referring to 'allies': 'Western Allies'.

Not that I'm a pacifist, mind you, he'd say to himself, and then contradict himself by acknowledging that anyone who declares or fights wars is mad. Plain mad. Hercus felt that his own ability to 'see through' the military mask had been born in his early thirties when becoming a soldier and an officer in a hastily amassed colonial army that set out to fight for 'the mother country' he saw the youngsters of nineteen and twenty, starry-eyed, wrapped up in whatever patriotic garb (and garbage) was tossed to them to keep out their fear. They'd all seen too much in the war, but Hercus, being older than the men he commanded, had been able to withstand the mask of glory, the imposter war, while the younger men, transformed into imposter soldiers, came home full of anger and hate not at the declared enemy but at their own country and themselves. They had been promised freedom and peace, an end to evil ideologies, both visible and invisible; they felt betrayed as if they had travelled a great distance to extinguish a fire, then returned to find the same fire burning in their own backyard, flourishing everywhere. They'd helped put paid to Hitler's evil in the mistaken belief that Hitler owned it: their disillusionment came when they realised that wars won or lost are instruments of reminding, not of forgetting, and so on their return they could not wipe their hands and their backsides and say 'That's that', and get on with the everyday pleasures and comforts of living in God's Own Country; they had to keep guard over what they felt they had won in the war; they had killed men and women and children, laid waste to lands, forgetting or too young to realise the nature of evil. In reality, they fought a war to keep the munition companies solvent; and because they feared the 'enemy' would occupy their land and the lands of those elected as 'allies', dominating all citizens with brutal forms of moral, racial, religious slavery; and because, if you are asleep and the alarms start ringing, persisting long enough with their shrill siren note, you overcome inertia, wake up, and prepare to fight. The spread of Nazism had sounded all alarms. And now the climate of future wars favours either complete inertia or perennial wakefulness, with little chance of survival but much chance, during wakefulness, of exploring the human spirit and its capacity for good and evil: an exploration within World Government.

Hercus hoped for peace within World Government, yet he remained pessimistically satisfied that his death would be sooner rather than later. 'I don't want to be around again when they start,' he'd say. And so he, like many other residents of Puamahara, chose the approaching inertia of death, prepared for by the gentle 'even tenor' of their daily life, defined as 'a settled course of progress'.

(I, Dinny Wheatstone, imposter novelist, know, however, that an even tenor, an apparently 'settled course of progress' conceals both inertia and artistic endeavours: seasonal quiet, a world without colour, is guarded by the Housekeepers of Ancient Springtime.)

11

The destruction of love can be brought about most swiftly when one love constantly demands of the other, 'Do you love me? Do you really love me?' while the other, at first replying, 'Yes, of course I do' and being met with 'Are you sure?' has no place to go but away. And now Mattina, sitting at Number Twenty-four, musing on each of the residents of Kowhai Street, wonders if her questioning might destroy the answer. 'Who are you, really? What do you think and feel and remember in this town of the Memory Flower? Tell me, tell me!'

She suspects that her desired acquisition of so many lives in a short time may be influenced by her growing certainty that her own life may soon end. Perhaps, she wonders, I'm fighting a war against death, with lives for ammunition. I'm still the rich woman whose possessions will buy privilege, entitlement.

During the next week, Mattina met the James family — Joseph and his wife Gloria, but not their fifteen-year-old daughter, Decima, in the Manuka Home out of town. The James's house, next to Hercus Millow's, was set farthest back from the street with a clear view of the mountains and within earshot of the Gillespie Street traffic. As Mattina walked up the rose-bordered path (each rose tree clipped of lower limbs with only its head standing tall against its upright stake; the small knots of beginning buds like tightly controlled curls) she was surprised to hear no sound of piano tuning, and when Gloria invited her into the sitting room, Mattina was equally surprised there was no piano in sight.

'Joseph has a workshop at the back,' Gloria explained. 'He doesn't even play the piano very well. Most tuners are not pianists. I'm not and I'm a tuner — I sometimes do work when Joseph is rushed. At least people are no longer surprised, and they don't even call me a "woman piano tuner", although there was an article in the *Western Mail* when we first came to Puamahara, "Woman Piano Tuner for Puamahara". Joseph has perfect pitch, of course.' Her 'of course' contrasted strangely with her pride in herself as a piano tuner; as if to say, 'Women piano tuners don't have perfect pitch. . . .' She spoke the words 'perfect pitch' as if they were an unassailable answer to all arguments, a fact given, perceived and maintained through all fantasy, unshaken by vagaries of time, weather, fashion, politics, events of family life.

'It helps with his work,' Gloria said. 'Although these days we don't need perfect pitch — the latest electronic tuning instrument does it all: tests, listens, judges, and if the result isn't perfect, the computer gives a menu of further adjustments and commands.' She was half-smiling as she spoke.

'I'm impressed,' Mattina said, 'by the number of homes with pianos. And even in Puamahara — and it's a small town — there's a music store selling pianos.'

'Oh, we used to be a great piano country! The early settlers, the families hoping to find paradise with acres of land, a mansion, servants, leisure, all brought their pianos and sheet music. The early battles to get land at all costs were fought by furniture — pianos and writing-desks — as well as by people. When we were growing up, many homes had an old piano with stiff yellow keys, broken strings, borer-riddled wooden frame. Some maintained their pianos. In the fifties and sixties there was a surge of interest with the cheap small Japanese pianos fitting into the smaller homes. The smaller instruments are in fashion now — guitar, violin, clarinet; and most of the kids have recorders. And these days in many homes you're likely to find the old piano in the spare room, piled with washing and toys — the New Zealand equivalent of the English coal-in-the-bath. And if you ask, "Does anyone play the piano?" there's usually someone of my age who says, "I *used* to play." The new generation of players is good, as deserving of attention as our athletes. In music, we've reached the equivalent of the four-minute mile, and beyond, if you see what I mean.'

'I think I see,' Mattina said politely, amused to find that sport seemed to provide most of the comparisons and metaphors. Already she'd heard repeated talk of 'first and second leg', 'having a good innings', 'going in to bat', 'scoring a try', when the topic had no reference to cricket, horse-racing or football.

'It's good of you to invite me to your home,' Mattina said, aware that she had invited herself.

'I've heard you're studying us,' Gloria said. 'The news is up and down Kowhai Street. What with the murder and your arrival. . . .'

'Oh,' Mattina said.

Gloria was one of those clone women that Mattina had observed in Puamahara — well-built, big-boned, with a large face and neck, heavy legs, fair skin or dark skin, frizzy sandy strawberry-blonde or grey or black hair; and very blue or very brown eyes. Scottish, Irish, Eastern European, Scandinavian, Polynesian, Mattina was not sure. The mid-westerners of America had a similar appearance. Farmers. This clone of

New Zealand women appeared to be physically strong, matronly, capable of working at carpentry, sculpture, ditchdigging; of holding a family together by force of her outer and inner strength. Both Maori and Pakeha appeared to have this strength.

I'm generalising again, Mattina told herself. Yet both men and women in New Zealand appear strong, calm, generous; I suspect there might be an overlooking, in the midst of such strength, of their natural talents for gentleness, delicacy, subtlety.

She decided to ask about the James's daughter.

'Your daughter doesn't play the piano?'

Before her question could be answered, Joseph came in from his workshop. He heard the question. He stood beside Gloria, giving the impression of containment, of their being knitted together with no prising apart or momentary dissolution that is a daily feature of parenthood, followed by rewelding often with a different, stronger adhesive or, as in knitting, a different pattern and thickness of wool. There was a static quality about the closeness of Joseph and Gloria. Perhaps the bonds that might not be broken forcibly by family turmoil, could wear thin and, set in the same place year after year, begin to cut deep?

'We have one daughter, Decima, as I said,' Gloria replied. 'She doesn't play the piano. She has been diagnosed as suffering from autism and now lives out of town in the I.H.C. home, Manuka Home.'

Mattina, startled by Gloria's unexpected frankness, said, 'Oh. I've heard of autism. It's. . . .'

Gloria smiled and said with bitterness, 'It's *fashionable*. Or it was. The fashions of medicine and treatment are ruthless. No-one does much for Decima now. Experts visit from overseas, there's a flurry of interest, plans are made, the experts leave and we're back to the same old institutions with a few inspired staff and the puzzled remainder struggling to survive in the wake of expensive experts and the excitement of hopes that are seldom fulfilled.'

'My husband has a cousin who's. . . .' Mattina began, and stopped, aware that this wasn't the time for such exchanges.

'It's worse now she's older,' Gloria persisted. 'They don't busy themselves any more about her life. Like pop stars, the autistic lose attention early. Pop stars, puppies and kittens. And how can a pimply youth or young woman compete with the new generation of six- and seven-year-old angels?'

Joseph, taking his packed bag of tuning devices, stared, his face nakedly helpless, at his wife.

'Isn't it silly?' he said unexpectedly. 'I still carry the old tuning bag when I don't use half the instruments. Our new imported tuner (from your Chicago),' (glancing at Mattina to give her the responsibility of owner- ship of a city), 'is more accurate but not as good as the ear because the ear makes allowances modified by the brain, and this instrument,' (pointing to an accordion-like box on the table beside him), 'hasn't the experience of a brain. Brains travel over distances of time and space; instruments stay home. This tuning device remembers, oh yes, because it has an allotted memory, but it can't say, "I remember" because it isn't an "I", it's a nothing, with no self. And although it's known as a third or fourth generation tuner, it has no ancestors and no ancestral memory. Nothing happens to it. And that's why it can't really *listen* to the notes of the piano. When computers cry — well that will be a different matter, though most likely it will be saltwater programmed to turn on as a specific response, and not tears performing all the duties of tears upon a loved human eye.'

He paused. He had shifted the burden of their daughter and their daughter's burden to a place where words no longer mattered; and even beyond the notes of music, to the rests on the other side of music.

Gloria persisted.

'Decima has never·spoken,' she said, almost directing an accusation against Mattina, the intruder, the unknown. 'Just think. Fifteen years. Oh my God!'

She jerked her head upward and breathed deeply.

'Fifteen. And unknown. That's the pity. Unknown by herself or anyone. I never realised how important it is to be *known* and to *know*.'

Joseph lightly grasped her hand and kissed her on the cheek, then, with a reinforcement·of Gloria's accusing glance, he turned to Mattina.

'We're pleased to have met you,' he said. 'I hope you are successful in your research.'

Then burdened with his leather bag and his tuner he pushed open the side door into the garage. They heard him starting the car.

'Yes, we have internal entry,' Gloria said, interpreting Mattina's glance at the door to the garage.

'Oh?' Mattina said, wondering when she would be used to the real estate language constantly spoken by the people of Kowhai Street. Internal entry. The car as part of the household. Like the chickens and cattle in other lands; but with deadlier breath.

'Yes, internal entry.' Gloria spoke with an abstracted air.

'And we're being clad for Chrïstmas. Waitara stone. The garage too. Life must go on. You won't be here for Christmas, will you?'

Later, as Mattina was leaving, Gloria said, 'I hope you didn't mind my talking about our Decima. Some people do mind.'

'You're welcome,' Mattina said.

'And you must call on us again. We're so pleased to *know* you.'

Her underlining of *know* was like a knife scored beneath the word.

Returning to Number Twenty-four, Mattina sat in what was now favourite place — the armchair; looking out on the garden, the citrus trees and the mountains. One month only remained of her visit. For a town where a legend was born, Puamahara was, she thought, as dull as could be expected, simply because such towns are the birthplaces of legends, where people live their ordinary lives; legends, like poems, spring from unrippled waters, undisturbed earth in a winter season.

12

Mattina's thoughts returned often to Gloria James and her emphasis of the word *know*, her reference to her daughter as *unknown* and *unknowing*. The life of Gloria James appeared to depend on a concept and its word, and the fragility of this dependence was horrifying, but was it not merely the usual dependence of anyone upon the language, spoken or written? Mattina's earliest memories were of her own passion to *know* what she thought of as the *truth* about people and places, loosely termed the *world*. Her life, she realised, had been so smooth and in a particular way remote from the inner view of people, as if she had sailed along a dark stream beside a procession of sheer cliffs where she had been unable to find a clinging-place for her fingers or toes, and, later, had been unable to read the surface of the cliffs with scars, faults, hardy and delicate plants and flowers absent from the smooth surface. Her life had been showered with entitlements of wealth, privacy, a private education, selected friends, a nanny like a near signpost along the distance to her parents, a port hostelry from which she returned to herself without making the complete journey to her parents. Even her marriage to the promising young novelist, Jake Brecon, was an entitlement, a prize expected and believed to be deserved, as was their beautiful clever son John Henry. Mattina and Jake shared this preoccupation with discovering the 'truth', but when Jake was about to explore and imagine and discover within his writing, Mattina's nature was that of a surveyor who records rather than creates. She realised now that her travels to foreign lands had not been simply to acquire real estate, nor simply to *know* about people of other lands: her aim had been to make a collection of people whose lives and 'truth' she had discovered and *knew*. She understood now her passionate need to study a handful of people who lived close to the source of the Memory Flower. These citizens of Puamahara would surely have brushed by the petals of the Memory Flower, touched the leaves, experienced the seasons that nourished the flower. Mattina felt that her visit was a genuine attempt to justify to herself her life of entitlement by learning the unmoneyed and unprivileged truth about a distant town where the people's entitlement lay in their being close both to the flower of memory and the seed of oblivion.

She wrote the names in her notebook:

Joseph James, Gloria James, Decima James.

Edmund Shannon, Renée Shannon, Peter Shannon.

Rex Townsend, Dorothy Townsend, Hugh Townsend, Sylvia Townsend.

Hene Hanuere, Hare Hanuere, Piki Hanuere.

Madge McMurtrie, deceased.

Dinah or Dinny Wheatstone.

George Coker.

Hercus Millow.

Then, hesitating, she wrote her own name. and Jake's and John Henry's, linking herself with Kowhai Street.

Then, continuing her strange mood, she opened the full middle page of her book and began to sketch *The Death of the Penultimate Madge*, imagining the scene as a Dutch interior, the room darkened, the floor tiled; the frozen ribbon of light through the small window; the characters grouped around the partly obscured body with Decima James forever unspeaking in the foreground, her long blonde hair trailing as if she faced an oncoming storm that would touch only her; Joseph James leaning over a spinet, listening to the music, his glance sideways towards Decima and her silence; Gloria turned to face Decima and Joseph; Renée Shannon pouring a glass of sherry for George Coker and Hercus Millow, the two old men standing side by side their frail bodies lanterned by the ray of light; Rex Townsend holding a tightly wrapped bolt of cloth, a dyed shroud for the penultimate Madge; Dorothy, her opened mouth indicating that she sang hymns for the occasion, although she made no sound; Peter, Sylvia, Hugh, all in their school uniforms their books under their arm, standing together, palely solemn, looking towards Madge McMurtrie; Edmund Shannon, startled, afraid at the door; Hene, Hare, Piki Hanuere, also standing at the door, each grasping green fronds of fern; Dinny Wheatstone framed in the doorway, her face expressing complete disbelief, her glance seeming to attempt to annihilate the group, the room, the time, the event with her weapon of disbelief, that is, knowledge rejected as homeless, in the full power of her imposture.

Mattina, making her quick sketch, smiled to herself, 'At least I'm not at risk of losing substance. For the moment, I'm the observer, the holder of the point of view, and even Dinny Wheatstone's presence can't erase my work.'

Painstakingly she printed beneath the hasty sketch, as a way of securing its life, *The Death of the Penultimate Madge*.

Just for a moment she felt the stifling, strangling surge of distant time, the yesterdays set free, marauding within the present, capturing the future. She felt afraid, confronted by the idea of a suddenly unlabelled world with everything she had ever known by name, by word, vanishing, all identity lost, yet remaining in place as an overwhelming unknown power.

Quickly she closed the exercise book, effectively excluding the group of people in the simply sketched scene.

And that night she slept without dreaming, and woke to look out at the Australian gum tree with its jewelled array of Emperor caterpillars; and up and up at the now constantly blue Puamahara sky.

13

For the next two weeks Mattina did not leave the boundary of Kowhai Street. She had bought a store of food, there was a corner mailbox, her milk and newspaper were delivered. All day, exercise book and pen in hand, she went from house to house talking to the residents of Kowhai Street, questioning them, while they, even with a suspicion of being flattered, accepted her role as researcher getting to know a segment of Puamahara, the home of the Memory Flower. Even those who became angry when market researchers or political canvassers appeared, welcomed Mattina; her questioning ushered them upon a stage where relatives and friends might view them, as if they might appear on television, ceaselessly interviewed like pop stars or visiting artists. Hadn't Mattina Brecon murmured something about a film later? And although some may have been unwilling to have their words seized, recorded for *use*, most overcame their objections, reminding themselves that if ever their intimate lives and dreams were used for a 'documentary', they were still superior to the insects, reptiles and other animals, and even, some thought, to the remote races who were filmed with the kind of commentary that equated them with 'lower' animals. Mattina felt that her examination of Kowhai Street was an attempt also to cancel distance between nations by starting with a small group in a small town, and although she assured herself her study was based on love, or a kind of love, it was also, as we have seen, obsessive, with herself as a stranger among strangers and (according to me, Dinny Wheatstone), imposters, trying to break the distance between herself and 'the others', and not, as she expressed it to the residents, 'between neighbour and neighbour'. She had therefore created herself as the dreamed-of centre of the circle, and when from time to time she sensed this, she excused her error, if it was an error, by reminding herself of the physical illness at work within her. Her certainty of it was uncanny; in the end, her journey to New Zealand may have been an act of panic, not a pious exploration of yet another foreign land and its people to add to her passionately collected items of knowledge.

She walked up and down Kowhai Street. She inspected and made notes about the houses, their architecture, their gardens, the sidewalks, known as footpaths. She exclaimed at the beauty of the kowhai trees, their bloom now fallen, their pale green feather-and-lace fronds arced like a mass of miniature fountains. She sought to trace the gas and waterpipe and sewer lines; noted the street lights, the concrete or wooden poles, the electric wires and telephone lines. She examined everything and everyone, filling her exercise books with notes, her cassettes with recorded sounds. She included the many dogs of Kowhai Street, the cats, the birds, the soil, the plants, the sky, the sun, the clouds and the falling rain and the winds that passed from highway to highway, up and down Kowhai Street. She observed the scraps of paper, the empty packets, the broken beer bottles and empty beer cans on the grass verge on Saturday and Sunday mornings. She listened to the sound of the radio, the loud jangle of music from the open kitchen window as George Coker made his breakfast and lunch; she smelled the smells of Kowhai Street, the burning rubber from rubbish fires in the houses fronting the State Highway, the drift of leaking gas from the garage on Gillespie Street, the spray-painting fumes from the car-yards fronting the highway, the drift of pesticide from the commercial gardens and orchards out of town; the daily lunch of stew from the old people's home; and also, fronting the highway, the freesias in the gardens, the bushes of daisies, the trellises of budding honeysuckle, even a hint of the fragrance of the blossoms in the orchards, for it was now late October and the runaway Time, influenced by this imposter typescript, seemed to have removed the guiding presence from each day, and there was only night and day and night and on the wall a calendar recording days of the week and on the mantelpiece a clock, perpetually wound, telling the hours. And passing from the obvious sights and sounds and scents, the movements of grass, of branches, stalks, traffic, people, animals, of gates and doors, Mattina arrived at the sensation lying beyond those easily identified and recorded. She moved downwards to a new distance that became incredible in its nearness, like an animal of long ago and far away breathing near her in the dark.

She experienced this still unreachable distance in the middle of the night when she woke suddenly, not knowing what had wakened her. The Puamahara night was dark and still except for the low rumble of the neverending highway traffic and the occasional flickering of the street light outside George Coker's, where it penetrated the tiny holes in the drawn blind gently moving now and then in a current of air blowing between the half-open door and the ill-fitting window-sash. The timbers of the house, like the bones of an ageing person had 'settled' and shrunk, as the years acting like a wine-press had squeezed out their substance.

Sitting upright in bed, Mattina listened. There was the sound of breathing, as if an animal were breathing rhythmically. She could sense the bulk, the waves of warmth coming from about half way between the window and her bed. She felt her heart turn over with fear; she held her breath and listened again, and again she heard the breathing. A large animal was in the room. She snapped on her bedlight and looked around into the path of the light and in the shadowed corners. Nothing. Had it been, perhaps, simply a mouse that she heard too keenly on waking? Perhaps she had passed through that momentary state when the still-clinging dreams are forced into seconds of reality before they dissolve or disperse wherever dreams like blowaway seeds are carried? Back into the night-earth of the mind?

Calmer now, still sitting upright, seeing no animal but still aware of the breathing in the room, she felt less fearful. She accepted the presence of the thing although she could not see it or explain it except with the conventional, 'I've been putting too much effort into this crazy research or search. Tomorrow I'll relax and take a walk to the orchards I've heard so much about. On the edge of town. I'll forget Kowhai Street. I'll take a rest from the human race.'

She switched off the bedlight. She fancied she saw eyes gleaming in the darkened room, and still she heard the breathing of the invisible creature, and felt the waves of its warmth.

And again she reached for the bedlight and closing her eyes and less fearful in the light, she soon slept, and in her dreams she heard the roaring, wailing, yelping, crying of many wild animals, as if she slept many thousands of years ago in distant northern mountains.

And next morning when she woke the presence was still in the room. It did not move and it did not follow her but it was there occupying space that had always been the province of Here and Now. From her intent scanning of Kowhai Street had she perhaps, she wondered, reached down through the surface of the day to retrieve a sample of a distant time in a distant place?

Well, it's crazy, she told herself. She of all people to find herself with an invisible creature collected from the depths of the storehouse of time or of her own mind. She decided that if she phoned Jake in New York he might be too far away to understand the drift of her conversation; besides, overseas calls were full of echoes: you spoke and it was you who answered.

It could be that the creature occupying her room was not the only arrival in Kowhai Street. She termed the presence a creature although she· felt it could be looked on as a thought, a memory, a time, or just a shape occupying a new kind of space. Whatever it was, it was warm, either warmed by the sun or by its own blood; and alive.

14

The invisible being stayed as a presence in Mattina's room. She told no-one. A feeling of panic came over her when she asked herself what on earth did she think she could learn from Puamahara that she could not have found in Manhattan: it too had its memory flower.

Then almost two weeks before her departure she accepted an invitation from the Hanuere family to spend the afternoon and the night, if she wished, at their home up the river a hundred kilometres north of Puamahara. They had sold the dairy, they said, and were shifting north, although Hene and sometimes Hare stayed to train the new owners. Up the river, Mattina and a party of the Hanueres' friends from Wellington would have a meal, enjoy a few games to raise funds for the old people to buy their pensioner flats instead of renting them from the government; and in the evening they would catch up on news, sing, entertain, be entertained, and sleep.

'Do come,' Hene had urged. 'See how we live when we're not in Kowhai Street. See the way of life of our people.'

Mattina hesitated.

'But I don't know the language.'

Hene laughed. 'Neither do I. I'm learning. And the best way to learn is on the marae. And don't worry, it's quite informal.'

Perhaps, Mattina thought, she might learn more of the legend of the Memory Flower, for the Maoris were the people of the land who held or harboured a source of memory which the latecomers, the other immigrants, were only now learning to seek and share. Mattina knew that New Zealanders of all races had reached a self-consciousness of an identity they had been struggling for years to find and capture, and now they had captured it, they dressed it in fashionable ideas and feelings and drew attention to it and congratulated themselves on their discovery, on its presence; and fortunately, the sensitivity of growth and maturity was tempering and softening and lighting with imagination what may have caused (and did cause) shame, guilt, denial, the refusal of ignorance to *know*. There were people of many races in Puamahara. One noticed them as one did not notice, say, in the United Nations city of New York. People in Puamahara turned to stare at unfamiliar dress and accents. It seemed to Mattina that every wave of fashion in everything — people, new forms of art, poetry, language behaviour, dress — had set out ten or twenty years earlier, and now washed about the shores of New

Zealand; also, there was still the flowing colonial wave from 'elsewhere' — even casting up visitors like Mattina herself who came to 'study' the distant foreigners. There was now, however, another wave often more hoped for and talked about than real, but visible in the land itself, flowing from the land and having been there for centuries concealed often by the more visible waves from elsewhere. It was now flowing in its own power, inwards and outwards, reaching the shores of the Northern Hemisphere.

A station wagon already packed with guests arrived outside Number Twenty-four. Mattina, with a paper bag of food that she felt might be welcome, and her handbag (known as her 'pocketbook'), but not the requested sleeping-bag, stood by the mailbox and stared self-consciously at the crowded van.

'You sit up front with Piki and me,' Hene said. 'Hare's at the back with the others. Hey you kids. Take care of those kittens.'

Hene then introduced her relatives from Wellington.

'The kittens are Ngeru and Boy George,' Hene said.

Looking back into the van Mattina saw two thin black kittens each wrapped in a piece of blanket and being cuddled by each of the two little girls.

'Are we all set? You lot OK in the back?'

They travelled the long straight West Coast Road through bleak plains where the wind, roaming unchecked by the usual mass of huge dark-green trees, buffeted every car and cycle, and the van rocked from side to side as if it were a flimsy boat on a vast sea. They passed through a faded city of stone houses with hundred-year-old trees arched above the streets with their branches entwined, and in the parks many-trunked old trees with their heads far in the sky and their branches covered with dark-red blossoms. Then, beyond the city, along the winding path of the river, they travelled an uneven makeshift road, and soon stands of bush replaced the stone city and the polluted flotsam-filled river became clear blue and green and curved closely against the earth like a greenstone necklace; the hills now rose tall, big-boned, angled, showing hints of green, burned in places, elsewhere matted with golden grass or tussock with darker bush shadowed in the steep valleys. On the tip of one slope a head-shaped boulder was sculptured from the rock; one could imagine the face staring north-east to the volcanic peaks and mountains of the interior of the North Island that, like all interiors, was steeped in legend, as if once the glance of the sea is left behind, the glance of the unknown secret places of the earth and sky intensifies and is directed upon those who live in the interior and upon the traveller, the stranger, who leaves with a heart imprinted with the glance, and an urge to return again and again, and to tell of the journey, beginning, 'When I was in the interior . . . of the North Island of New Zealand . . . of the Andes . . . of the Rocky Mountains . . . of the Carpathians. . . .' The coast-dwellers absorb their own secret though the eyelid of the watching sea never closes upon them, but when its eye can no longer follow them, its immediate fury is diffused across the seas of the world; different, indeed, from the eye of the interior which smoulders even in the traveller's absence, day and night, century after century.

The day was sunny, the sky pale blue. They arrived at a small village set beside the river between two steep hills rising from a small plain that was partly cultivated with fruit trees and vegetable and flower gardens, while the land nearer the river held about six dwellings, old, with corrugated iron roofs and weatherboards from which the paint had long ago faded and peeled. The houses were bare bones, unclad, untiled, with old-fashioned sash windows, the cords hanging broken.

'Only three families live here now,' Hene explained. 'But more are returning. We don't realise how unique it is until we leave it for the city. The Pakeha has nothing like this way of living — not here in New Zealand. I believe it's like a small English village without the post office, the pub and the general store.'

She pointed to a new stone structure backing on to one of weathered stone, with moss around the lower walls.

'There's the new kindergarten. And the old building's the church. The kindergarten belongs to the government,' she said with some bitterness. 'And those small pensioner flats — they're the government's too. I told you we're raising money to buy them. As for that kindergarten — the design is not of our choosing. We have our language nests now. Kohanga reo. Also we didn't want the Plunket Rooms here, with nurses coming to tell us what to do with our babies.'

Then she pointed to a group of young people working in the gardens.

'We've rescued them from the Court, from prison. Soon Hare and I will be working full time helping the young people. We rescue Pakeha kids too, and we bring them up here but after a few weeks the novelty seems to wear off and they get homesick, not always for their home but to be on their own, not always in a group the way it is here, the way it is with us. Some of my people don't like to be in a group but usually it's the Pakeha way. I've seen them come here invited to stay, and they're on cloud nine; then they get restless, they want to be somewhere else, they've had Maoritanga for the time being, thank you, and yet if you happen to be among a group of people at a function you hear the same people holding forth about having 'been on the marae' and how wonderful it is, and how much they learned — which they did — and others look enviously at them — well, we're all a bit that way, I suppose; some people are hard to understand; even the elders of my own people don't seem to understand what *I'm* doing.'

She looked shrewdly at Mattina.

'Forgive me for being frank,' she said. 'Funnily enough, it's visitors like you who get to know more about us than many of those who live here. The novelty, I suppose. The tribes of the far south on that TV programme *The Beautiful World*, eh? We're distant enough from the rest of the world to be thought not to have feelings and lives of our own: both us and the Pakehas are at the long end of the poking stick — Look, they move, they speak, they walk, they think. Isn't it so, that the further away you are, the less you are known, the more easily you may lose your state of being human? For some of us, we've already lost it in our own land. I know it's hard to think of separate individuals in a country thousands of miles away just as it's hard to think of separate numbers among millions — the millions wipe out the handful — where's three dollars among three billion? There was a time, you see, when this country and both Maori and Pakeha and others were nothing because we thought we were so far away — far away from the rulers, the seat of Empire; but now we're ourselves, and we can't be ignored or made nothing and no-one, because the distance has gone.'

Hene looked thoughtful.

'When we do become far away from ourselves we become nothing. And if we are far from God, it's not God who does the abolishing, it's us.'

'Oh,' Mattina said, not wanting to get into a discussion on religion. She was rescued by the announcement through a megaphone that the two competitions had begun — guess the weight of a sheep, and drive ten nails the fastest into a block of wood.

'This is to keep us busy while the hangi is being prepared,' Hene said. 'And raise money too.'

'Let's guess the weight of a sheep,' someone said.

Hene, her cousin Riki, and her cousin Rua, in her seventies, known as Aunty Rua, came to the small pen where an 'older' ewe with a ragged dirty coat stood chewing her cud as she watched the watchers guessing her weight. Now and then she stamped her foot, voicing her authority

84

and impatience. Her mysterious glinting eyes like polished stone looked everywhere and nowhere; her long nose sniffed disapproval. Unlike many other captives, the ewe did not butt at her enclosure or trot round and round in panic; gathering more than its own fortitude, indeed, drawing from the fund of all animals that are bred to be killed and eaten, the ewe neatly tucked in her forelegs and sank to the ground on the scattering of straw, without relaxing the glittering suspicion in her eyes.

'It'll be harder to guess her weight now she's sitting down,' Riki said.

Each wrote their chosen number of kilograms on a sheet of paper, which they folded and dropped in a cardboard box.

'The next time we do this,' Hene said laughing, 'is at the General Election. Guess the weight of the sheep.'

There was some bitterness in her voice.

'The country's in a turmoil,' she said to Mattina. 'We're in the kind of state where we now believe everything they tell us and absorb like blotting paper all their fine promises.'

As soon as they had made their guess, the contest closed, the sheep was weighed, and no-one had guessed correctly. They fell silent as if the weight they offered had been returned to their mood, threefold or sevenfold or some other magical number. Then each brightened as the imagined complication of winning became more burdensome than that of losing. Only Hene said practically that she would have added the ewe to their small flock next to the vegetable gardens. The ewe would have been named, introduced to Geraldine the nanny goat and Oscarine and Kaiwai the cows.

The food for the hangi was lifted and served. While most of the company sat inside at the long tables, several including Mattina and Rua sat outside in the sun, on the long wooden seats ranged against the wall. By the time Mattina had her paper plate filled, the pork was lukewarm but the kumara and potatoes were like hot pebbles. The dark green vegetable called *puha* was tasty, gritty and strong like aged spinach, and all the food was smooth and slippery with juices and melted fats. What bliss, Mattina thought, as she picked up the pieces of pork with her fingers and sucked in the juices and the tender strips; and listened to the rushing of the river near where the dark green wing of the hill cast its shade and shelter only so far as not to disturb the sun-filled marae. The shrieks of the children; the barking of the black dogs that looped here and there chasing thrown sticks; the sweet taste of the meal; the old houses, their timber grey as if they were the most ancient trees; the walls encircling the houses like large faded aprons; beneath the commotion of eating, talk laughing, the animals, the river, Mattina felt the presence of a yesterday's silence that brought a hunger to the back of her throat: a world-hunger.

She looked at Rua sitting beside her and smiled.

'Not like America, eh?' Rua said.

Mattina again became the researcher, the foreigner.

'It's marvellous here. And Hene tells me you teach flax weaving?'

'Riki and I both teach,' Rua said. 'Riki is our cousin, as you know. He was kept in a mental hospital from age fifteen, and only last year someone noticed him there — thirty years later! — and said, "Hey why aren't you out in the world?" And of course Hene and Hare came to his rescue, and now he lives here, teaching weaving and making baskets, kete. He's a good boy.'

'Can you tell me something about flax weaving?'

Rua smiled. 'First,' she said, 'you must *know* flax. I know flax and flax knows me. You understand the sort of knowing I mean?'

'I do,' Mattina said, with rising excitement at the recognition that here was *her* kind of knowing; and that of the James family; and Hercus Millow; and of the others in Kowhai Street; the knowing that included but was not dependent on the Memory Flower or the Gravity Star; that by itself could banish distance, nearness, weight, lightness, up, down, today, yesterday, tomorrow.

Without binoculars, cameras.

Without the Memory Flower, the Gravity Star.

'The important thing to remember is that flax *knows* about you, your life, your secrets, and when you plant it, it's there watching you, knowing you; you can hide nothing from it. If it won't grow for you, you can be sure you have hurt it.'

'Oh,' Mattina said uneasily.

'Flax is always alive. See this kete?'

She held up a woven flax basket where she kept her sweater and pocketbook.

'This is alive, listening to us now. Yes, you must have a special feeling about flax to be able to grow it, cut it without making it bleed, scrape it without hurting it, and weave it without going against its wishes.'

Mattina was impressed. There was a warmth in Rua, a wisdom that could not be ignored. The others felt it too. From time to time the children came to climb on her lap and be hugged, or one of the men came to sit by her and talk earnestly about his or his family's problems, and leave laughing and making a gesture of triumph as if Rua's conversation or silence had given him new life and hope. She was like a public mother. No wonder she knew the secrets of flax and flax knew her. And seeing her surrounded by two or three generations, Mattina realised that in her time at Kowhai Street she had met only the two generations of families; no doubt if she stayed longer she would meet grandparents, uncles, aunts, cousins, brothers, sisters, and read them and know them as she was learning to know the parents and their children.

Later, after tea, scones and cakes, Mattina followed the others to a large room where, behind the scenes, members of the family had been arranging mattresses around the walls. She too chose a mattress and made herself comfortable, leaning on a pillow, with a rug over her, and when Rua chose the mattress beside her and began to point out and define the routine, Mattina felt an unaccountable gratitude, a feeling of having been honoured. Rua explained that those staying the night would sleep there on the mattresses.

A group of young men and women stood in the middle of the room. Self-consciously, almost defiantly, they explained that they were off to town and would be back later; they wanted a little excitement, they said. Mattina noted the sadness in Rua's face as she watched them leave. Someone brought in a television set, plugging it at the end of the room near the long table and, like a birthday cake revealed at last, it was at once surrounded by children clamouring for *The Giant Man*, their favourite programme, the tale of a doctor, who, accidentally irradiated, swelled to giant size in moments of stress. During the programme those who did not watch it talked quietly among themselves in an atmosphere of nostalgia, of sadness, yet of peace, with a sense of being at home; Mattina, a stranger, felt she had arrived at an important place which while being hers alone she also shared with others in the room. The slight embarrassment of bunking down with a group of strange adults and children in another land in a public hall as if they were evacuees from earthquake, fire and flood or battle, vanished rapidly. Mattina even dozed a while, lulled by the murmur of the talkers and startled now and then by the shots and the sound of police sirens from the television; and the shouts and shrieks of the children.

She hadn't slept this way since her teens in a summer camp in the Adirondacks, and then each child was at the mercy of the others, while here, with a mix of generations, there was little danger of bullying or being bullied. The experience, although novel for her, was usual for the group; she could sense their ease in being at home in an accustomed place, taking up the routines known since earliest childhood, no doubt feasting on a rich succession of memories, not all of happiness as the tangi or funeral rites were celebrated here, and while at first the rebellious teenagers among them had looked embarrassed, scornful, impatient, their faces had shown clearly the force exerted by the scene and by their own swelling tide of memories, and although they escaped for an hour or two into town, they returned later to join the group, some dancing, others singing, others like Mattina and Rua, watching, absorbing, talking, sleeping.

Time to leave, Mattina thought as she watched Hene rounding up those from Puamahara who were not staying overnight. Hare was staying with Piki and the two children with their kittens that were now fast asleep; and Riki; and Rua.

Saying her goodbyes, Mattina found herself gushing with thanks and warmth. She stopped suddenly, aware that she sounded like any tourist, excited and gratified by being shown and sharing a few hours in the life of 'people of other lands', while realising that if she were 'any tourist', she would return untroubled to her safe apartment in New York City or her summer house at Lake George and when friends came to dinner she would describe her travels and her meeting 'people of other lands, the natives of the area', listing her acquisition of sights and sounds and people as if she had spent a morning at a January or July sale in New York or Boston.

She knew, however, that her visit was not like that. Suppressing her excitement, trying to convey her sincerity, she said slowly, 'I'm so *thrilled* to be here.'

Their response was friendly and polite. Later, she comforted herself by recalling that even the astronauts spoke banalities on their first moon-walk.

Hene drove the van home to Puamahara.

'I love being up the river,' she said. 'We're glad to be leaving the shop. We ran out of goods. The big companies refused more credit.'

'I'm truly sorry,' Mattina said.

'No need to be,' Hene said. 'Hare has a good job in Telecom. And there's so much to do up the river. We've got to get the kids off drugs, glue, drink. We've got to make them feel important, to love them, give them satisfying things to do. It's rough. Half of us are out of work or in prison or mental hospitals. You know, I saw a TV programme, *The Forest Families*, about all those shy wild creatures, birds and insects and so on that have to be protected and helped to survive, but when I saw the title *The Forest Families*, I thought of those in the forest towns whose lives and homes have been almost wiped out, the people whose jobs have gone. A pity we're not a people with multicoloured plumage, building our nests in trees; and flying with our own wings; with interesting mating habits and walkie-talkies clipped to our legs; raising our young under the eye of the camera!'

'I'd be inclined to save both birds and people,' Mattina said, knowing her words were fatuous.

'Of course. It could be that in the end all this country will have left is a heap of rubble, polluted rivers, creeks and seas, an isolated struggling stand of native bush with one family of black robins, and one human being making her *Our Beautiful World* programme, shooting the scene from a camouflaged hideaway.'

'I see,' Mattina said.

'Well,' Hene said, 'it's not your problem.'

'Oh but it is, it is!' Mattina cried. 'If there's anything I can do!'

'H-h-h-h,' Hene said. 'No, we have to sort it out. You in the States have your own problems.'

She looked shrewdly at Mattina.

'Have you tried to sort *them* out?'

'Not exactly.'

'Of course not,' Hene said coldly.

Mattina understood but felt she could do little about her common human affliction of wanting to solve the problems of elsewhere, to inspect and report on the lives of elsewhere, even to live elsewhere.

They arrived at Number Twenty-four Kowhai Street. Mattina and Hene said a sleepy goodnight.

'And thanks for everything,' Mattina called out. Hene gave an answering wave. She called some words in Maori which Mattina did not understand.

Later in her bedroom Mattina became again sharply aware of the haunting presence, of the disorder of space and time. Its strangeness had settled within her as if it had always been there. She wondered if the presence might increase gradually its share of the invisible gap in the fabric of space and time, perhaps invite other presences, or even place her and the furniture and furnishings of the room in danger of falling beyond the fabric — where? She feared what might happen. She remembered that Dante had entered Hell through a doorway of the Antipodes — or had that been the exit?

'It's only rooms of time and space,' she told herself. 'They've always been there. Like most events, this presence had to make itself known at some time. One way or another. After all, walking on the moon required no more than technical skill, intelligence, and goodlooking thick-skinned young Americans; there was little spiritual or linguistic or extrasensory skill needed. And now that space and time are torn, like a caul at the birth of space-walks, there's no need to celebrate or even note the occasion with other than, 'Say, just look at this. What a view!'

Before Mattina fell asleep she listed once more, as if they were her possessions, the residents of Kowhai Street.

'I must be closer yet to them,' she told herself. 'I've barely two weeks. A miracle may happen.'

She smiled in the dark. Short of time or at odds with time, she said, we turn to miracles.

15

After her day among the Maori families, Mattina began to notice in Kowhai Street extra members of each family who, while they did not live with their relatives, came to visit more often than Mattina had been aware. Then one day the Townsends had a guest, and when Mattina and Dorothy met, as usual, collecting their milk, Dorothy volunteered that Rex's mother from England had been living with them for two weeks. How strange, Mattina thought. Why did I not notice her? Especially as I've set myself the task of recording and studying the people of Kowhai Street? People are not fences or sticks or stones or colours or stoves or chimneys to be noticed or not. Why did I miss seeing her?

'That will be lovely for you,' she said to Dorothy.

'She came out once before, just to stay,' Dorothy said. 'Now she's here for good.'

For good.

'That will be lovely,' Mattina said again, noting that she was becoming used to the easy repetition of blocks of words, and thinking that it would indeed be 'lovely', the children at last having a grandparent, the grandparent seeing her son and daughter-in-law and grandchildren, all living in the same country. Mattina felt satisfied as if an unwarranted gap in the human fabric had been closed. She remembered again her childhood in New York City and her excursions with her grandmother, and how they were the best of friends with secrets no-one else knew, real secrets that Granny took to her grave and Mattina buried and had now forgotten.

And so the next morning when Rex and Dorothy were at work and the children at school, Mattina, thinking to visit the grandmother whose arrival would enhance the lives of the family, eased herself through the gap in the hedge into the Townsend's property. (She had discovered that on older properties in New Zealand small towns, a gap in the hedge was used more than a gate.) Her knock at the door was answered by Mrs Grant, who recognised Mattina.

'Oh, you're the one from New York. I'm Connie Grant, Mr Townsend's mother. I married again, you see, and my husband died. He was a friend of my first husband. Do come in.'

Mattina walked through the small kitchen into the sitting room.

'Do sit down. Sit on that stool, here by the door.'

Mattina sat on the wooden stool near the kitchen door while Connie continued her drying of the family's breakfast dishes. Then suddenly she put the tea-towel on the bench and began to wail, 'I've lost me mop. I'll never have the place clean by the time Dorothy comes home. She's so fussy. And the children don't understand. They don't want a grand-mother. I'm so lonely, so lonely. My husband dead, my house gone, the furniture too, and now I'm in another country where no-one wants me. Oh my.'

'I'm sure everyone here wants you,' Mattina murmured. 'It will get better. It's just that you've lost so much, but here you have a new family.'

Connie Grant wiped her eyes with a handkerchief pulled from her apron pocket. Her face was thin and weary, her legs and arms like bird limbs. Her thin shoulders drooped under the weight of her world.

'I'll never get used to living here. They won't let me go home. And now they tell me they've bought me a flat, with my own money, mind you, and I'm moving in, two days from now, and I've got no things. Yes-terday Dorothy took me to see the flat. They say there's not enough room here for me to stay. Then why did they send for me? I clean the house, I wash the breakfast dishes. I'm fussy about the bathroom, but Dorothy gets angry at the birdseed.'

She pointed to the sunporch adjoining the kitchen where birds in two large hanging cages twittered and flew.

'It's the birds drop the birdseed and it's so hard to brush out of the carpet. Oh what'll I do? What'll I do? Will you help me find the mop?'

They found the mop behind the kitchen door.

'And there's the dustpan and brush too. Thank the Lord. I'd lost them. And thank you for coming to see me. I'm so lonely I cry myself to sleep in my little room. I've no-one and nothing left.'

Mattina gave her the tin of pound cake she had brought for their morning tea.

'Here's something for your tea-break.'

Connie took it eagerly. 'It will do for the children when they come home from school. There doesn't seem to be enough food in the house. I feel Dorothy and Rex think I'm eating all their food. And I know Dorothy suspects me of deliberately scattering birdseed on the carpet. "The birds have never done that before," she tells me.'

'Of course you don't eat all their food,' Mattina murmured.

'Come again and see me. Wait, I'll give you the address of my new flat in Gillespie Street. You'll come and see me there?'

'Surely,' Mattina said.

She returned through the gap in the hedge to Number Twenty-four where she made herself a cup of coffee and sat with her plan of Kowhai Street and Puamahara, moving her sharpened pencil from house to house, recalling the facts she had collected about each family. Yet Connie Grant's distress clung to her, giving an untidy aspect to her clean collection of facts.

The sooner I return to New York City the better, she said to herself. I thought everything would be clear as soon as I came to Puamahara, that I would live in Kowhai Street as in a cardboard street where the names and personalities and histories of the residents could be set out neatly with the bordering busy highways enclosing this one street at the other side of the world, that I would extract gold from each house and return to New York with a purseful of people whom I knew because I had mined their personal treasure, picked their bloom from the Memory Flower and from Puamahara; but that is not so. I have shared conversations, drunk coffee, eaten meals, gathered facts. I have discovered few secrets, few scandals. Kowhai Street, Puamahara, Maharawhenua and the world are full of people who pass their lives in not too much anxiety, pain or pleasure. In Puamahara, there's enough to eat, a place for most if not all to live, people to live among. There are churches, sports fields, schools, a library, perhaps a museum and art gallery, there are people being born and dying, yet I feel their anchorage is so slight that one morning the street and the town may wake to find all is adrift in the space of anywhere, or set on earth in places far from here, distant mountains or plains. There's no clear anchorage, no roots, the street is full of strangers with empty baskets of love, or so it seems to me; but only because I have not struck the most valuable of treasures: acceptance. I know they have not accepted me. It might seem so, but I am merely the American researcher, the visiting would-be expert to whom they have fed their information — it is I, not they, who is the creature studied for *Our Beautiful World* shown in prime time.

And thinking again of Connie Grant, the reclaimed grandmother who felt unclaimed as the lost property of two countries, Mattina herself felt oppressed by gloom, by the thought that her own journey might have come to nothing. And because her visit was soon to end she thought perhaps she should now thank those whom she had pestered with her questions. 'For they have indeed been kind,' she said to herself, aware that she was still far from the prized Memory Flower. Nor had she time to seek advice on the illness that increasingly worried her. She would leave Puamahara; she would leave ill, tired, with the old phrase, 'They were so kind to me.' How she had resented the final qualification given in a judgment of a president or dictator or ordinary citizen: 'But she — he — was so kind, he meant well, he was sincere, thinking of the good of others.'

'Always so kind.' Vague phrases that were more an expression of loss, of failure, an inability to grasp the essence of history taking place in the events of a day or of centuries; an expression of an intelligence inadequate to perceive the truth of what had happened. Mattina felt reluctant to discover that after all her planned journeys through the world, she might be the kind of tourist who could not perceive events, like those who passing through a country that is in great turmoil, emerge exclaiming to friends 'back home', 'Everyone is so happy. Conditions are marvellous. I never saw or heard of hunger, poverty, violence.' She was appalled that her two-month visit to Puamahara might result only in 'They were so kind to me. The people are full of kindness.'

A blanket sweetness surely not possible among a collection of human beings? But what if 'They were so kind' were indeed the one and only truth?

16

I, Dinny Wheatstone, imposter novelist intent on manipulating points of view, choose from daily life the commonplace facts of weather, accidents, quarrels, deaths, losses, gains, delights. Mattina Brecon is now experiencing the commonly haphazard daily life which she has little power to change or manipulate. She is reading my typescript. She has ventured into the world of Kowhai Street and Puamahara. She had hoped that within two months she might witness and feel a concentration of life that would reveal the secrets of Kowhai Street, the presence of the Memory Flower and its blossoming. She would then take from Puamahara an image of beauty and discovery to give her pleasure in the midst of the battle for breath waged in Manhattan's polluted air. Now in her last days in Puamahara she wonders if she might not have gained as much knowledge of people in distant places if she had merely walked two blocks to the Museum of Modern Art and browsed through the great paintings. At the top of the stairs, Van Gogh's *A Starry Night* would have spun the world for her to observe everything in its spinning; perhaps she might have then disputed the answer to the question, Who was the first on the Moon? Or found the answer without need of the question. Her need, however, has been to see and know the human condition in the flesh and spirit, to traverse the distance, accepting in jet travel the alarming distortion of distance.

Mattina landed in New Zealand without having her mind bathed in the enduring image of seas that extend, like the seas of eternity, between country and country; and because her flight's destruction of time and distance brought her here in a shredded state of mind where hours equalled years and the time became like a spiral ribbon striped with the past, present and future, she became unknowingly a focus of the Gravity Star. And Mattina Brecon, no novelist, had been able only to stand and stare at the passing time, and then, gathering her wits, to visit the residents of Kowhai Street and take notes about them as if they were animals in a zoo; and certainly to feel moments of interest, sympathy, compassion but never, during her weeks in Puamahara, to sense or capture the human force that feeds the Memory Flower. 'The force that through the green fuse drives the flower.'

17

During her last days at Puamahara, Mattina was given another chance: she accepted George Coker's invitation to tea.

'May I show you the house?' George Coker asked.

Mattina smiled. 'Everyone shows me their home.'

'Do they? Your place and mine are twins built by the same builder. Your place has been relined, rewired, replumbed, your roof retiled.'

Mattina flushed as if being given praise. In New York she and Jake had little idea of the construction of their apartment, the building terms used, the type of roof, slate or shingle. These Puamaharians were like birds, the way they poked and prodded at everything, even at the plants and trees, to make sure the identity was inescapable; and even when searching for a name mislaid, they'd say, 'The name escapes me for a moment, but I'll get it, I'll get it,' with a strong hint that this was no mere lighthearted metaphor, it told a tale of search, capture, imprisonment: the everlasting hunt.

George Coker set the tea cups and plates in his front room that was lightened by two wide front windows and darkened by heavy furniture, velvet antimacassars, and a sideboard with an array of inscribed silver cups and shields. Unable to contain her curiosity Mattina asked, knowing that New Zealand was a Rugby-playing nation, 'Are these for sport, football perhaps?'

'Oh, I won them,' George Coker replied, smiling. 'For egg-laying. I was a poultry farmer on the East Coast before I retired. And before that I was a writer.'

Mattina's interest quickened. 'A writer?'

'Yes, in the navy. I worked in the wireless room and wrote down the messages I received.'

'Oh.' An egg-laying writer, Mattina thought.

George Coker then talked about his family in the way the elderly sometimes talk when, near the end of their life, they assess the performance of filial duties in terms of 'goodness' and 'kindness', because these are the only two virtues left that matter.

'One of my daughters has been good to me. The other never comes near me. And after all these years, my son has started to come to see me. And we know what *he* wants. I'm more or less alone in the world now, except for my roses. I'm not about to be put in a retirement home. I've had two friends go there and die within a week, like plants picked from the garden and put in a clay pot. I'm very fond of my roses, you know. I can't garden as I used to do. I fell over the other day.'

He looked mischievously at Mattina, reminding her of her first meeting with him, and revealing that time had passed normally, with each week presenting its store of memories.

'You shouldn't garden, you know,' she said. 'Not at your age.'

He smiled, satisfied by her reply.

'I like gardening. My wife has been dead a good few years now, suddenly, after we came here to retire. I've still got the new twin beds we bought, and the new pink candlewick bedspreads. Good as new. We bought this three-piece suite, too, a corner suite you see with the wood insert for use as a table.'

'I see,' Mattina said.. A good phrase, she felt, affirming sight of what was visible or invisible. 'We'll see' was quite different, an authoritative phrase invoking the future.

Mattina first knew of George Coker's death two days later when she read the notice in the morning newspaper. He had been dead for one day and she had not known. He had died in his sleep. She was surprised to find the number of relatives listed in the newspaper — 'Much loved and mourned by his fifteen grandchildren.' With the death notice naming each, the youngest generation of Sarahs, Dianes, Waynes, Crystals, the older Marjories and Mabels. His son Henry. Not a Madge, although Mabel and Marjorie could have been, like Madge, penultimate. Deeply mourned. The funeral was to be from his daughter's home across town, near the lake. So one daughter had lived in Puamahara!

Mattina felt his absence, the unlit kitchen window at night, the roses in his garden surrendering to the convolvulus, and then, only ten days after the funeral, there was the sudden movement of cars back and forth, and then a van with two men shifting furniture from the house; voices in the back garden, deciding, conjecturing, judging. 'This tree will have to come out. And that by the fence always blocks the view. I never liked it.'

'He'd want the place sold at once,' a voice said, engineering the usual takeover of the wishes of the dead who, no matter what their legal power might be, have relinquished their say, their point of view.

A woman arrived that same afternoon and hung washing on the rusty circular clothes-line. The two men with the van brought other furniture into the house and the curiosity of Mattina and the others in Kowhai Street was satisfied when a sign was posted against the front of the house. Monster Sale. Auction on Site. Wednesday 1 p.m. The speed of the process took everyone's breath away.

The area in front of George Coker's house, different from Mattina's with her lawns and trees, was concreted like a car-yard, but with a number of plaster figures set in the concrete — four gnomes with red hats, red noses and blue flyaway plaster coats, one black and white bird with a long beak, two red and white rabbits begging, and one black and white dog, all with their paint faded and their bodies chipped in wing and limb. One gnome lay on his back, having been knocked from his foundation by Hugh Townsend's roving soccer ball. The rabbits were earless, the dog headless. George Coker had stressed to Mattina that the plaster figures had been set 'before his time'. It was there, on the concrete front yard, that the auctioneers would sell those of George Coker's possessions not already claimed. The house was to be sold later.

And so on Wednesday morning the auctioneers arrived and began arranging furniture and goods in the front yard. They set up a table in the shelter of the front verandah. Within the house there were again sounds of a vacuum cleaner while at the back someone mowed the lawn, at a half-running pace driving the huge whining, roaring mower up and down shearing twigs and branches and flowers (roses!), leaving the rose bushes with their foliage ripped away and the overhanging limb of the grapefruit tree wrenched from its socket. The back lawn shone in the sun. Then twelve o'clock. The noon siren sounded like an air-raid warning through Puamahara. There were screechings of tyres as workers on their lunch break sped home.

As suddenly as it had begun, the commotion ceased; there came the somnolence of approaching afternoon. Kowhai Street remained busy with cars parking the length of the street and a crowd from other parts of town waiting in George Coker's front yard for the auction to begin. Some sat on the low stone wall between Mattina's and George Coker's, many completing the mower's work by trampling what remained of the side flower-beds. Looking from her front door, Mattina saw Hercus Millow at his front gate, the Shannons, the Jameses, all watching; and past George Coker's, on the footpath, Dinny Wheatstone, the imposter novelist. Only the Townsends, settling their mother into her new flat, were absent. And although no-one could scan closely the faces of the others, Mattina could feel the anger, sadness, and the sense of unity against the vultures from other parts of town come to claim the remains of George Coker's life. Hercus Millow limped across the yard.

'Are you going in?' he asked Mattina.

'It's next door, after all,' Mattina said. 'I thought of joining the crowd.'

'I thought of it too, but no. The old man was a stranger.'

'I talked to him once or twice,' Mattina said. 'He was ninety-three.'

'I'm going to make sure that when I die no-one comes traipsing in and out of *my* house. I suppose they're selling everything to get at the cash.'

'It would seem so,' Mattina said.

'The McMurtrie's place is for sale too,' Hercus said. 'But no-one's buying. The agent will probably keep quiet about the murder.'

He smiled absently, back in World War Two territory.

'You've never seen so many houses for sale. People buying, selling, inspecting, negotiating; and all you need is your last prison cell.'

Oh not again, Mattina thought.

When the auction had begun Mattina walked next door to pry in the guise of observing. Most of the goods sold quickly. A triumphant stranger was busy hauling a refrigerator on to his truck. And there were the Shannons walking away with an armful of blankets; and Gloria and Joseph James examining the three-piece suite with the wooden inserts.

'It looks brand-new,' Gloria said.

They did not buy the suite. A natural hesitation, an inability to make up their minds, allowed an intruder from another street to make a successful bid. 'Sold for a song,' Mattina heard someone remark. Then noticing another pile of bed-linen with the two candlewick bedspreads looking so new, completely unused, she felt herself infected by the greedy hunger to own the bedspreads. 'I'm being corrupted in Puamahara,' she told herself. She had never coveted articles of household linen. She had enough money to buy hundreds of bedspreads. Yet her memory of George Coker and the way he had shown her the bedspreads, 'Two pink candlewick bedspreads, never used', returned to her with the sound of his voice, and for George Coker's sake she rescued the bedspreads to keep them in Kowhai Street, to use them during her last days in Puamahara. They would represent old George Coker's memory flower, for Mattina's afternoon at the auction had convinced her that the memory tree might be hung not with flowers but with items of household furnishing.

The Jameses bought a set of cutlery, and as they passed Mattina, Joseph said in an embarrassed way, 'We already have a set of cutlery. But this has scarcely been used.' Both use and non-use were valued.

The Shannons too retrieved their prize — an old-style milk-jug wreathed with yellow flowers, and as they left, they too seemed to feel the need to account to the watching stranger.

'It's Royal Albert,' Renée said. 'Our jugs always lose their lips, and our teapots their spouts. *Royal Albert.*'

'I bought the bedspreads,' Mattina confessed.

'We saw you,' Ed smiled. The watched watching. 'Good on you. They were brand new!'

'And pink candlewick.'

'Yes, almost new. Almost unused,' Mattina said.

'And have you seen over the house? The agent Albion Cook at the end of Tyne Street by the railway station is selling it.'

'I've seen most of it,' Mattina replied. 'But not empty.'

'No, not empty.' Renée echoed with a mixed tone of triumph and shame.

They walked together through the empty house on the old varnished wood floor.

'They've taken up the carpets,' Renée said.

'The relatives took the carpets,' Mattina said. 'A daughter was here, hanging out the old man's washing.'

'Oh?'

'Everything's gone, almost,' Renée said. 'And did you notice how the auctioneer also sold some of his own stuff, on the side? That other suite was for sale in their rooms last week. They've mixed their furniture with that of the old man's,' she complained. 'But they always do that. Let's get out. I think its horrible, all his goods on display and then all those imposter goods among the genuine.' Clearly the Shannons and the others were well versed in the procedure of auctions.

'I think his only real treasures were his silver cups and the photographs. Most likely his family rescued them.'

'Oh no,' Renée said. 'The silver cups went first. Before you arrived. Someone from the other side of town bought them. Said they'd use them for flower vases.'

Renée sounded shocked but Mattina felt she herself didn't care.

The sale had been sordid and the weather had changed; it was now threatening rain. She'd heard rain in the night and the gush of water down the drainpipe outside her bedroom window and she'd noticed the intense blackness outside as the store of darkness from George Coker's unlit house surged into the total night; the breathing presence in the bedroom added a density of time to the darkness. The presence was now so clearly defined that Mattina could have drawn a map of the room with a blank two-dimensional triangular space as if it were the outline of space furniture not anchored within the room. She felt that the presence, contained within two dimensions like a flat shape upon a map, might indicate not a breaking of the fabric of space and time but a levelling of the present, the beginning of the reduction of the room, Mattina, the house, the street and its people, perhaps Puamahara, Maharawhenua, to a two-dimensional existence, people-shapes and house-shapes, town-scapes, street-scapes, a worldscape without volume, with their present image of themselves an illusion only. The realisation of the possibility of such an existence, as if all were framed within a painting — Mattina, her bedroom, her house and old George Coker's house and goods and their buyers — caused Mattina to gasp.

'I asked you,' Renée said, looking curiously at Mattina, 'Were the photographs sold?'

Covering her confusion, her thoughts straying, Mattina said quickly, 'Sure, sure.'

She glanced at Renée, at Edmund, at the dwindling crowd of buyers. 'We may in the end be mere photographs,' she thought. 'Walking photographs.'

The next morning as she was dressing, the idea of the two-dimension returned. It couldn't be that she and everyone and everything could be reduced to mere cutouts without volume simply because some astronomer had discovered a Gravity Star that destroyed the concept of nearness and distance as opposites, setting them side by side and thus overturning all thought. Yet could it be? The ease of thinking it and believing it would be gradual, ensuring final conviction as walking on the earth brought conviction that the earth was flat and comparatively still. How did one know, how did one form the image of self and world if the possible were now the impossible, if distance were nearness, length were breadth, heavy were light, cold were hot and light were dark? Perhaps the only answer lay in the birth of a new language from a new way of thought. A world plunged into a swamp of absurdity, contradiction, when the dark shapes of various alphabets reached down their isolated forms, their hooks and arms and the cups and crosses and rods, to rescue the users of language who would then make the rescuers once again whole, meaningful, new.

I seem to have fallen under the spell of Kowhai Street, Mattina thought. She realised again that she had expected little, nothing and everything from her visit to New Zealand, that she had heard of the unusual turmoil within the country, the people's heightened awareness of their own time and being, paralleled by the almost sympathetic activity of the land itself — the eruption of volcanoes once labelled extinct, the repeated earthquakes described collectively as 'swarms'; gales and whirlwinds in places never before experiencing them. Such disturbances, while fostering myths and legends old and new and inspiring superstition and hysteria, revived the closeness of human beings to the elements. These, and the ferment of discoveries in space, of new and old stars, of moon walks and space weapons and satellites, could overthrow reason into unreason and unreason into reason with the change, one might say the necessary change, hindered by the slow development of a language that shifts at the pace of geological time, a new vowel each thousand years. The arrival of the Gravity Star, however, at the right time and the ripe time could plunge a person, a house, a street, a town into the abyss. Was that her discovery during her visit to the 'far country'? Mattina wondered. A shift of language, of landscape, of time and space? Or the rediscovery of the old truth that human beings everywhere had not travelled very far from the heath in *Macbeth* and the linking of 'events new-hatched to the woeful time' with the storm, the sun, and the night skies?

It rained the day after the auction, the rain splashing off the roof into the spouting and down the drainpipe. The gutters foamed with rain. The grass sprang tall, the leaves extended their tips like antennae, the colour of the flowers deepened, all drinking, absorbing the spring rain. Mattina sat at her front window looking out at the lawn, the trees, the flowers, the sky, the street, and at people and cars passing. She thought of herself back home in the Manhattan apartment with the windows tightly closed against the polluted air, and her looking down at the distant traffic and crowds or across to the screened offices in the buildings across the street — upstairs warehouses with more furniture and appliances than people, empty desks squatting near the windows, typewriters and computers unpeopled, filing cabinets flanking the walls; the grey clouded sky; the soot or smoke or dust or fallout from acid rain drifting against their apartment windows; the smell, invading the apartment, of sulphur or tar or burning rubber or oil or gas. She thought of how on the first opening of a tin of fish or fruit or meat, a gas-smelling vapour fumed in her face while its residue stayed in the taste of the food; the tuna tasted like automobile fumes. It was little wonder that she had been overcome by sickness, that even the food in Puamahara could not entice her appetite. For years, she felt, her diet had been automobile fumes.

Yet New York was *her* city. She would never leave it permanently. Others asked why she and Jake made no plans to leave New York before it was 'too late'. Too late for what? Too late following what? Too late before what? New York was *their* city in spite of everything. A city of murder, of intensity, of passion, of love, hate, greed, hunger — every human and inhuman emotion magnified itself in New York; thoughts, even fleeting thoughts, more quickly became action within and beyond the law; some said the cause lay in the food, the additives, some said in the polluted air. Most said that New Yorkers had a greater chance of surviving all if they never wanted for money; money purified, cleaned, switched off or on, made work, repaired, made swift, made simple all the pathways and processes that were the tangle of daily living in New York. Mattina knew. She lived and loved and hated in New York City. She recognised that even within the city's unpleasantness there were gifts not received in all her own world-roamings to 'get-to-know-the-people'. Also, especially in April, New Yorkers could see sky and stars, valued more because the sky and the stars in the polluted northern cities were visitors only, like birds of passage.

And one other treasure would stay as long as the city survived: the artists for whom New York had always been home. These were the true New Yorkers, most of whom were brought up in extreme poverty, whose stories have been told to one another at lunch and dinner, published in their books, stories overturning the heart in their poignancy and power, and in some with their inescapable longing for the ancestral homeland most do not remember or have never seen; yet all have memories of their own or those told to them by their family, of the huge room at City Hall where the immigrants wait to complete the required forms, where there used to be benches, pens, paper, to practise the answers, but where now the applicants must supply their own — pens now being like diamonds, and writing, severing everything they touch; the writers too, who hold them. The sign *Pickpockets* appears strange in the immigration hall of the new land. What is there to be picked but the currency of the past, of other lands, of memory? The room in City Hall is transformed from a bare fore-boding hall to a banquet-place of laden tables where guests, no longer home-less applicants for entry to a new country, feast upon dreams of their future and their past, and with the present as chief sustenance, go out into the grey polluted city and fumble to find the demanded exact coins that will pay their bus fare to an apartment they have rented on the lower East Side where the arms of the two rivers lie against the used land; or crossing the Brooklyn bridge or the Verrazano Narrows, they travel to the hinter-land. Those New Yorkers who began their life with loss and a great grief and later became writers, painters and composers, created a castle from their foundation of grief, where magnificent windows let in the light from

103

this and other worlds.

Mattina felt deeply the debt owed by New York City to its artists, once strangers from distant lands, who created a new dimension for the city, gave it depth, shape, and even were the city in reality a flat two-dimensional world, a scrap of paper or cardboard that could be torn to pieces, the shape and density given it by the artists lay unbroken in the world of the imagination, so that when outsiders looked at New York they saw not paper people in paper buildings under paper skies but real people of flesh and blood and depth in an adamantine city of height and strength, of all dimensions.

Not every city and town has been so favoured. With her growing affection for Kowhai Street, Puamahara, and for New Zealand, Mattina felt that if the naked reality of people and places were indeed flat, without substance, easily torn, then the work of the artists must be trebled or increased a hundredfold, to build the imaginative density which would reach into and clothe the naked reality, restore the dimensions destroyed by the extraordinary events and discoveries within an ordinary town and country.

Perhaps, Mattina thought, as she sat watching the rain raining on Kowhai Street, that may be all I have seen clearly from my stay in Puamahara. No secret lives of the people. The drama only of death in whatever form it may take; the ceremonies of lunch, tea, dinner, the inspection of dwelling-houses and the land; the nearness and distance of the sky, the sun, moon and stars, and the winds blowing from the mountains, from the sea, from the southern straits and the northern central land of mists, forests and volcanoes.

That evening a cable arrived from New York. 'All well. Have finished novel. Love from Jake and John Henry.'

18

The next afternoon as Mattina walked towards Gillespie Street she saw Joseph and Gloria James and a young girl in her teens arriving at their home, Gloria clasping the girl's arm as she hurried her in the front door. Mattina, deciding to breach all rules of sensitivity, walked quickly up their drive and knocked at the closed door. Voices, footsteps, and there was Joseph James opening the door slightly as if to a suspected intruder.

'May I come in and say Hi?' Mattina asked boldly.

Joseph James grimaced as if to reassemble his face from Joseph father to Joseph piano tuner, the last of the local tuners, he and Gloria in demand throughout the lower North Island. Mattina noticed he had grown a moustache which levelled his glance and behind which, as if in a secret pocket or hedge, he had stored the consternation, sadness, and any other distressing emotion to leave his face calm, businesslike. His voice was brusque. Mattina knew she was interrupting a family gathering, for the daughter, Decima was brought home, they had told her, once only in two months. Yet this would be Decima's only visit before Mattina flew home to New York; and Mattina felt an uncontrollable need to know, to share, as people do, contemplating the sick and the strange and thinking, Perhaps I, I alone, have some means, magical, intuitive, of helping the rare species from *Our Beautiful World*.

'May I come in?' Mattina persisted, adding, 'I'm shortly returning to New York, yet I've come to feel that Kowhai Street is my home.'

Joseph relaxed a little. 'I suppose it's OK,' he said. 'We have Decima home for the afternoon. She stays an hour, then we drive her back to the Manuka Home, out of town. She likes to come home but there's not much we can do for her, you see. Come in, then.'

He spoke the word 'then' with a lingering tone like a falling musical note, like the note Mattina had heard on the marae at the close of the karanga: a note that did not die or end but fell down and down, sinking through bodies and into the earth and deeper.

Mattina followed Joseph into the sitting room where Gloria watched as Decima packed a chunk of bread into her mouth; not chewing and swallowing, just packing and packing as a dentist packs cotton-wool into an open mouth.

Gloria looked alarmed.

'One piece at a time, dear,' she said. 'Chew it, swallow it.'

Decima gave no sign that she heard or understood, and continued

to pack bread into her mouth when Gloria reached forward suddenly
and snatched some of the bulk from Decima's mouth whereupon Decima
quickly clamped her strong teeth over Gloria's finger.

'Help me, Joseph,' Gloria called. 'Get her mouth. Open your mouth,
dear.'

As gently as he could Joseph forced apart Decima's clenched teeth
and released Gloria's bruised finger.

'You see, Joseph,' Gloria said, her voice quivering. 'There's no sign.
Nothing.'

Decima began to chortle and make circles with her arms.

Give her something to shake, a shakey,' Gloria said, explaining. 'She
likes to shake things. See, Joseph has given her that plastic cobra — see
its hood?'

'As long as she doesn't swallow it or strangle herself with it,' Joseph
said.

Decima glanced from Joseph to Gloria as she waved the plastic
snake.'

'See,' Gloria said, 'she hears everything, she sees everything, and if
I say "Sit down", she sits down, but she's lost to us, she could be thousands of miles away, in the Andes or the Carpathians, or she could be
in your home town, New York City, for all the signs she gives that she's
here and knows us. She knows her name. Decima. But she doesn't seem
to know where she is or who she is or that what she's doing is called
living. And she has no words. No word from her, not a word.'

Gloria spoke as if of a distant correspondent who never replied to
mail.

'No word,' she repeated.

'But she has no words to give,' Joseph said to Mattina., 'She has no
spoken language except for a few cries, chortles, laughter, other sounds
in her throat.'

He turned to Decima, the first time Mattina had seen either Gloria
or Joseph talking directly to Decima.

'You don't speak to us, do you?'

Decima laughed and shook her plastic snake, grabbing it by the tail
and describing a circle.

'That's the problem,' Gloria said. 'She is teenaged now, and she has
never spoken to us, no-one knows what's in her mind, she's as new to
us and others as the day she was born. Nobody knows her. She's *new*.
And look at us, being used up faster and faster each day with all our
words coming out and being spoken again and again. And look at her.

Brand new. But with a body growing, not new, used. That's the problem, isn't it dear?'

She addressed her last remark to Decima who nodded, almost as if she understood.

'Her language,' Gloria said, 'is all her own. She's one person alone in her own country, ruling it and ruled by it, and her own country has its own landscape and other features, and none of us can ever visit it. That's how the doctor described it. And Decima's country could be distant or next door.'

'Or both,' Mattina said.

'Both?'

'Like the Gravity Star,' Mattina said.

Gloria smiled. 'Oh you don't want to listen to Dinny Wheatstone, the imposter novelist, and her strange ideas.'

'It's not Dinny Wheatstone's idea, it's a real discovery.'

'Real?'

'Yes.'

'Well, if it's real. . . .'

Mattina did not explain. She glanced at Decima who now sat still, her feet together, her hands folded in her lap, the plastic cobra fallen to the floor and apparently forgotten. Decima's features and body were those of an adolescent girl. Her hair was golden like her mother's, long and silken. Where she may have once been a beautiful child with delicate features and large pale blue eyes, there was now a used cast to her face and body for her skin was scarred, probably from numerous encounters with furniture, falls from heights she insisted on climbing; as Gloria had said, Decima had no fear of physical danger. And her teeth gleamed wide, white and strong like those of a horse or an animal that gripped and tore at most available material — the wooden corners of furniture, clothing, bedding, books, the limbs and skin of herself and of others. The skin on her feet had hardened prematurely as her feet took the place of shoes, treading all surfaces hot and cold and rough without apparent pain.

It was hopeless, Mattina thought. What could anyone do unless one person like the tutor to Helen Keller, spending day and night with Decima, succeeded in destroying her distance as the breathing creature in Mattina's room had possibly destroyed space and time or as the inhabitants of Puamahara and the world would be torn like cardboard unless they themselves created both the stolen dimension and the new imaginative dimension?

Our Beautiful World. And the Gravity Star.

Apologising for interrupting the family gathering, Mattina said goodbye. Later in the afternoon she saw the James's car passing on its way to return Decima to the Manuka Hospital, on the edge of town.

19

When Mattina made her last visit to the Shannons, she was surprised to find the computer shrouded and unattended without even an exposed key exerting its power over Ed or Peter who now sat watching television while Renée transferred the evening pizza from the freezer to the microwave.

'It's pizza and salad,' Renée called. 'Real American.'

'I guess,' Mattina said, playing the part.

'Up to the table everyone,' Renée called in the tone of voice some use, that seems to address more people than are present, that might include any stray souls sheltering in the computer or in corners of the room, or indeed relatives harboured in the future.

Mattina, Ed, Peter, came obediently to their places at the table.

'Goodie, pizza,' Peter said while Renée, the attendant, mother, paraphrased unnecessarily, 'He likes pizza. We all do.'

When they had begun to tackle or, rather, to *address* their pizza, Renée put down her fork.

'We thought we should tell you, Mattina, as you're going home soon and as you're writing a book about us in Kowhai Street. . . .'

'Oh,' Mattina said, wondering about the idea of writing a book, and then explaining it to herself by acknowledging that ideas of 'writing a book' flourished so readily that, like a fly, they often settled in unwanted places.

'You mean my research? My husband's the writer, a novelist.'

'Your husband? You didn't tell us. Ed, her husband's a novelist.'

'Has be been on TV?' Peter asked.

'No, I don't think so.'

'Will *he* write a book about Kowhai Street?' Ed asked with an intensity that embarrassed Mattina. As if Ed's only existence now might depend on the flat pages of a book with his human essence converted into words and he himself closed forever unless someone chanced to open the book and read it, meeting Ed, with Ed now existing also in the reader's mind but nowhere else, not in any living dimension.

'The fact is,' Renée said, 'we've decided to make the move. We're shifting to Auckland. Out of Auckland, really. But Auckland.'

Mattina, waiting, glanced from Renée to Ed.

'You try to sell computers in Puamahara,' Ed explained. 'We all misjudged the market. At first everyone came to look, touch, try, but few bought. We hoped to catch the passing trade but we were in the wrong place to start with, at the back of the shopping complex, behind the fountain. The Auckland firm is closing the shop here and giving me the manager's job up north. Auckland.'

'Out of Auckland,' Renée corrected.

'Yes, but Auckland, if you see what I mean.'

'He's not one for Auckland,' Renée explained. 'But he still has a job. He's great with computers. He has a marvellous touch.' She looked wistful.

'And Peter's coming on, too. Do you know Ed can now fly blind into a storm? In all that turbulence.'

Her praise had a touch of wonder, as if her happiness in at last going to Auckland had showered all other activity with delight.

'I fly *only* in Reality Mode now,' Ed said basking in Renée's unexpected kindliness towards computers and his obsessions with them. 'Storms, night flying, battle stations with invaders from space, mountain landings . . . and all the while I alone am at the controls. No more slipping airspeed, no more nose up when it should be down; always — nearly always — the correct number of revs on the engine; wheels tucked away on cue. I fly the jets now, with full audio back-up. It's more real than real, isn't it, Peter?'

'Gosh, yes,' Peter said. 'More real than real. And Dad sometimes crashes on purpose, just to show us.'

The idea 'more real than real' captured Mattina's fancy. She could not place 'more real than real' within its dimension of comparison; Ed's computer flying as a 'hard-edge' painting in all dimensions. Yet if 'real' were the flat surface, was 'more real' below or above the surface? And where, then, was 'unreal' — airspace, earthspace, outer space, inner space? Or were the three compressed into one rich slab of cognition? And how then might they be separated?

'We'll be glad to be gone from Puamahara,' Renée said.

'You haven't been here long, have you?' Mattina asked. 'And all the plans you've made for redecorating! And the garden! And what a shame to leave the Puamahara sky, and the legend of the Memory Flower. Living at the source of a legend must be a special experience, surely? One you would not wish to give up?'

Renée laughed.

'Oh,' she said. 'The country is full of legends. Teeming with them, north and south. They used to be hidden under those legends from the Northern Hemisphere, but now that we've got our own slant on things, legends are everywhere. They don't often break into our *real* life. And, do you know, Auckland, where we're going, is built on volcanoes that may not be extinct after all. We're only now beginning to look closely at the place we're living in. The Maoris have been looking at it for centuries and their legends have long ago crept in out of the cold to be part of their lives. And now we're looking. You have to look at something, I suppose, besides your homes, furniture and gardens.'

Listening to Renée, Mattina recalled her own brief view of Auckland as a small city with tall many-windowed buildings, walls of glass reflecting an absent forest, clearly and uncannily, with the images of huge torn trees, bowers of leaves, severed tree-trunks, as if a forest grew in the sky and no longer on earth. And there were so few people in Auckland city, except those who were obviously tourists, harnessed to cameras, or businessmen like lizards in pale grey striped suits, going in and out of doors to bask in or retreat from the golden-dollar sun.

'Auckland's the place to live,' Renée said. 'Like your New York.'

'Oh, Auckland's not at all like New York. It needs more poets and painters and composers and writers, so many to a square metre, much more than it has, all built into the city's plans, to waken and put to sleep again the volcanoes, to give depth and height to the buildings and the people, to explore the forest in the sky, to make known that a forest grows in the sky.'

'What? Where?'

'No matter. I'm pleased that you're happy to leave Puamahara, and I'm sorry to say goodbye to you, and to Kowhai Street.'

'Oh we are too,' Renée said vaguely. 'Very much so.'

'The problem,' Ed said, 'is in getting a house that's not twice or three times the price of this. We've had an offer on this. And do you know they're turning our computer shop into a wool shop: wool is best for Puamahara, they think. Knitting and crochet are great favourites; knitting wool, needles, patterns, aprons and tea-towels with kiwis and Mount Taranaki printed on them. That sort of thing. A small line in souvenirs.'

'Who is setting up the wool shop?'

'A young couple starting on their own,' Renée said, as if she talked of a species foreign to her.

'They usually go into dairies, corner dairies,' Ed said.

'But wool's a great favourite,' Renée countered. 'Knitting and crochet are never out of fashion here. And tapestry. Much of the wool is nylon, though. With the rising prices.'

'Yes,' Ed said. 'The rising prices. We're sorry to see all our work, the cladding of the house and the rest, go down the drain. And I don't like to think of our house here being empty. I don't like empty houses.'

'But we won't be here,' Peter reminded him. 'We'll be up and away.'

'Up and away,' Ed echoed, steering into Reality Mode with the sky clear blue, the runway bright green, the cardboard buildings set neatly in place, the viridian trees scarcely moving in the light breeze. Number Three, Reality Mode, Calm Weather.

'We'll be away before you, perhaps,' the Shannons said as Mattina made her final goodbye.

ning Mattina set out to walk to the orchards on the edge of town. as now late October, the full gloss of summer, the grass shining on the verge of the highway, the polished black-and-white cattle standing in the paddocks on the boundary of Puamahara: staring cattle, swishing the flies away. Mattina walked by the Retirement Village, one of many in Maharawhenua, with its small brick buildings called *units* neat and square like the old-style transformers that were used to collect and redistribute electricity. (The Shannons had explained to Mattina that the end house in Kowhai Street was always difficult to attract buyers or tenants because the transformer outside disturbed day and night with its throbbing, whining, high-pitched sound.)

The brick units stood quiet as if untenanted. Each had a fringe of concrete in front, a trellis screening the trash can, and a small oblong patch of old-fashioned flowers blooming in dark red, yellow and brown velvet; and a few rose bushes on slim stems, topped with pink and red blooms.

Beyond the Retirement Village, more fields or paddocks. Then on the very edge of town, the Welcome and Farewell signs. Welcome to Puamahara, the town of the Memory Flower. Farewell from Puamahara. Come again. Then at the crossroads, three signs, the first pointing south, Manuka Home and Hospital for the Intellectually Handicapped; then north, Summer Garden Motel first turn on the right. Waterbed, adult video, spa pool. The next sign, pointing east to the orchards and the mountains, said simply, The Orchards.

There was no sidewalk along the mountain road, only a strip of grass against the hedges that were fragrant with white and cream flowers with a few thin bees at work in the flowers, pausing now and then, as if convalescent, in bed on the best bed-sheet of petal. Then more paddocks with dead oversprayed shrubs and trees, and decrepit old wooden buildings with fire-scarred chimneys; then stands of dark-foliaged trees, massive firs, their trunks tall, roughly barked, with rust-coloured needles heaped like a tide around them. Here on the open road with the State Highway left behind with its laden trucks rocking at speed north and south, there was an air of absence, of yesterday, in the broken-down wire fences and buildings, the roofless barns with their rafters darkened by fire or sun or ordinary weathering time. A circle of birds with fanning tails danced above the wire fence; their call sounded like 'sweetie, sweetie, sweet, defeat defeat'. A heavy-footed black-and-white bird lurched on to a fence post, balanced a moment, then flew away into the fir trees. ᴛ ʜ after the brief passage through yesterday and decay, Mattina came to rows of vines and fruit trees and a tree nursery; and then a gateway with a large white stone flower sculptured at the entrance, dividing In and Out traffic. The inscription read: 'The Memory Flower, Puamahara. It is thought to have been here that Puamahara, the maiden of ancient times, discovering and learning the secret of the source of memory was herself transformed into a flower known as the Memory Flower. The identity of the flower is not known. The early settlers claim it was an English rose or apple blossom. The Maoris say it was a flower of the bush. Others have named it as the flower known to bloom from the plant, *vegetable sheep*, used lately for its contraceptive properties. It is thought to be the same flower brought to England by Sir Joseph Banks and given to William Cowper, the English poet, and credited with effecting a cure of Cowper's depression. Welcome to the orchard of the Memory Flower.'

Close inspection showed that the Memory Flower had lost one or two petals, its paint was peeling, a hastily driven car had sheared its stem. Beyond the Memory Flower, however, the orchard trees were in full living bloom, rows on rows of trees as far as Mattina could see, apples, pears, peaches, in differing stages, some as blossom alone, others shrouded also with newly varnished leaves.

Mattina found her thoughts meandering with unusual fantasy. She tried to return them to her usual ordinary way of thinking. For many years now she had been aware of a longing to feel herself as part of a grand creation. Her love for Jake had its origins in that feeling, as had her brief love with Big John Henry and his recitations of great prose and poetry. She had spent her life on the verge of the creations of others. Her closest friends were playwrights, novelists, poets, musicians; and Jake was her novelist-husband. Her visit to the orchards and the place of the Memory Flower gave her the unique sense not of allying herself with a creation, but of being herself a creation united with the source of the Memory Flower. She was aware that such a feeling could be described as the seed of religion; but religion in its conventional sense was not for her. The orchards, the fountains of Ancient Springtime, the Memory Flower, had merged to banish the painful opposites and contradictions of everyday life. More than in the splendour of many kinds of love, in the gift of the orchards and the Memory Flower, it seemed that lost became found, death became life, all the anguished opposites reverted to their partner in peace yet did not vanish: one united with the other; each two were lost and found.

For a time Mattina sat on the wooden seat outside the shed used for displaying and selling the produce — fruit, vegetables, house-plants, pots of honey. Mattina felt as if she had walked for miles; she had not done so. Even here she could now hear the muted traffic of Puamahara; birds twittering and calling; a farm dog barking a deep steady bark like a chime; cattle lowing. Natural sights and sounds, she told herself; at the source of the Memory Flower. Yet as she retraced her steps down the drive to the entrance she felt, looking again at the stone — or was it plaster? — flower, and the detailed inscription resembling the print on a giant packet of cornflakes or detergent, that Puamahara had failed the Memory Flower. In the future, perhaps, she thought, the artists of Puamahara working side by side with the house-cladders, the plumbers, the builders of rumpus rooms, will create Puamahara's own orchard in the sky.

*

Mattina closed Dinny Wheatstone's typescript and set it on the bed-table. Her emergence from the typescript confused her. She felt that her hold on the passing time had been lost. Time whirled about her: the time-control of the script she had been reading. It's interesting, she thought. Episodic but interesting the way it has seized my own life and time. Dinny Wheatstone is a time-imposter also, writing the future with yesterday and today. It is now almost two months since I came to Puamahara, yet it is true that I have just arrived here. Is it possible that I have lived here for both spans of time, both within reality, that after my first week, when I began to read this manuscript, my three-dimensional existence became two-dimensional but no less real within the pages of Dinny Wheatstone's narrative while she, writing her story, also moved within the present and future?

She recalled then the detail that might help to explain: rather, it recalled itself to her. She sensed within the room the breathing presence that had broken through the fabric of time and space: an ancient distant presence that was new and close by, affirming the world of the Gravity Star.

'I have been in parentheses,' Mattina said. 'And emerging from this typescript, I leave in a few days for New York and my home.'

Part Three

The Memory Flower

21

It was indeed so: in three days Mattina would be on the plane to New York. She felt she should return Dinny Wheatstone's typescript 'in person', although her dimensional overturning and disarray had caused her to destroy mentally the meaning of the term 'in person'. The consequences of the reality or truth of the Gravity Star had to be accepted: the demolishing of logical thought, its replacement by new concepts starting at the root of thought, would cause the natural destruction of known language. A new language, a new people, a new world; and perhaps the end of known civilisation as human cognition, no longer supporting and supported by the words of the former languages, and for a time refusing to accept the apparently illogical, senseless, near-is-far, heavy-is-light, fights for the survival of both habitual processes of thought and their attendant languages. The threatening war was not Star Wars or atomic war, but war in a world suddenly deprived of its standards of sanity moulded within its written and spoken languages.

Even as Mattina realised the calamitous but liberating prospect of total change, she sensed that already those who ruled each country — presidents, dictators, prime ministers and their governments — would surely have drawn plans to deal with the new chaos as recognition of the new truth and its consequences spread throughout the world. She wondered about the nature of those plans. Governments, she thought, are hopeless at planning, simply because they are governments; maybe, already, behind 'closed doors', committees were awash with computer-printed papers being dealt this way and that by card-sharpers at the big game that each hoped to win simply because each was human with an indestructible fund of vanity, greed, hope, despair — all the virtues and vices of general and personal nature.

Our Beautiful World.

There was little to be done, she thought. A helplessness would encompass the peoples of the world as if a great fire (starting here in Puamahara, the home of the Memory Flower) were to spread throughout the language (and language reinforces memory, rebuilds its weakened foundations), leaving the earth littered with the ashes of words, of letters, phrases, loved and unloved in all languages; and because the human mind would have reached a new stage in its thinking, no fertilising thought would fall on the ashes to resurrect each word and phrase and letter into a new blossom in the new season. And how long could the people of the world survive, walking through the ashes of their languages, having little clue now to their thoughts and feelings, not knowing how to bring new languages to birth? Waste not want not. Least said soonest mended. Silence is golden. Mattina thought of all those words tired by use; and all that had often seemed useless, the words that propped up speech — after all, no doubt, you know, indeed, I guess, tacked on in a luxury of traversing a momentary desert of thought. . . all the he-saids, she-saids, he-thoughts, she-wondereds of print. She thought of Jake in New York, how he had scraped away to find spare words to build his novel, and how the search had tormented him; the words scarce, his typing ribbon red with blood. Dear Jake! Mattina experienced again the happiness of receiving the cable sent by Jake and John Henry. *Have finished novel.* No hint of the doubt and misery that had plagued Jake for twenty-five years as he dreamed of but could not write his second novel — he, the 'promising young writer' whose first novel had been such a success with critics and readers and fellow-writers.

'Here is a writer to watch,' the critics said.

And they watched.

And they watched.

And Jake wore his new mantle like the buoyant cloak of a young highwayman carrying out his daily raids on language and its working out of the sum of human possibilities and impossibilities; until a time came when, looking back, he could scarcely see the shadow let alone the substance of the first novel. He and Mattina had married on the wave, the plunder, so to speak of that first novel. And soon Jake's highwayman's cloak was in tatters and he had exchanged it for the cloak of a hopeful magician, a sage, who as each year passed, practised or dreamed of the secret rites and wisdom of a profession that did not respond to his advances. Perhaps that one book that perished like a prize bloom from too much scrutiny and constant attention, had left him in such a state of bereavement that he was unwilling and unable to accept the growth and nurturing of a new novel?

Now, at least, all was well. *Have completed novel. Love Jake and John Henry.*

And now with his novel completed after so many years, Jake would be one of the saviours, he and others, among the poets who had always accommodated near as far and far as near without throwing themselves into disarray; cementing near and far, light and dark, weightless and heavy, mixing the processes of thought with substance from the heart, as birds mix their straw with mud and saliva; with the writers the secretion is the devotion to language. Could such devotion given over the years gradually draw forth the new language to fit and be neighbour to the new ways of thinking? A more gradual revolution, a seasonal progression that would barely be noticed? Perhaps it had already begun, and the desert of wordlessness would not bring such devastation (there among the blooms of music and image and stone speech, of sculpture and the flight of dance?) and soon, almost without being aware of change, the new language would be in place with the new ways of thinking, the adjustments made; and oh! the view of the new horizons! The once inconceivable, impossible, now visible and accomplished.

In her disturbed state of at once meeting and parting, of being and not-being, Mattina began to think of her neighbours in Kowhai Street, and the way they had accepted her and confided in her, and how the idea of their being the subject of research had pleased them. At the risk of losing her sanity, Mattina, unable to deny or confirm her fictional experiences of almost two months, forced herself to weave them into her memory, as Dinny Wheatstone's typescript had done, as a form of truth composed of the real and the unreal. And so when she thought of George Coker and the auction of his goods and chattels, and the remembrance of his many grandchildren who never visited him, she accepted his reality; the happenings of Kowhai Street and Puamahara were nothing to him now; and everything. Precariously, Mattina made the equation of opposites. She thought of the Shannons and their move to Auckland, of Joseph and Gloria James and the child Decima living without speech in the unknown and known world, of Hercus Millow languishing with his platoon and their dogs in the prison camp, and using his binoculars to bring the distant mountains within his grasp; of the dead penultimate Madge, of Hare, Hene and Piki, and their new-old life up the river; of Rex Townsend, the Full Gospel businessman shift-dyeing the night away; of Dorothy, Hugh and Sylvia and of the mother, Connie, who had lost everything and could find nothing — how would the residents of Kowhai Street survive within the new order of thought, in the world of the Gravity Star? How could they find the new words when they may not realise they had lost the old? No doubt the government would soon speed the change by passing laws against the use of the old language and the old ways of thinking, using the old ways to describe the prohibitions! Whether through her two-dimensional or three-dimensional living, in print or in 'reality', Mattina felt she had achieved her ambition, the ideal of all her travels — to know the people of other lands, to acquire personal, human estate while adding now and then to her 'real' estate. Even after having her life and all points of view captured for the past two months by Dinny Wheatstone, Mattina was satisfied in being able to walk into any home in Kowhai Street and be treated as a welcome guest. They trusted her now.

'We are close now,' she said to herself, smiling, as taking the typescript of *Wheatstone Imposter*, she walked to Dinny Wheatstone's home.

'You have George Coker's empty house and Madge McMurtrie's, one on either side now,' she said as Dinny Wheatstone led her into the sitting room. Mattina glanced at the opened piano.

'I've been playing a Bach minuet,' Dinny said. 'Imposter music.'

'Oh?'

'Well, it's really a list of people who live or used to live in Kowhai Street, Puamahara.'

She saw the typescript in Mattina's hand.

'You've read it? Will your firm publish it?'

'It's interesting,' Mattina said calmly. 'Episodic. But it shows novelistic greed — you've taken all points of view, all time — it's an act of dream-light robbery. Yet I found it interesting.'

'You would, wouldn't you?'

'For various reasons,' Mattina began.

'Which reasons. Tell me.'

Mattina felt suddenly tired and weak. 'May I have a cup of —'

'Tea?'

'Yes, tea.'

Dinny went to her kitchen and as on Mattina's first visit, she brought a tray with cups and buttered biscuits which she called 'scones'.

'You know,' she said. 'The *stone* of *Scone*, but we say *scon*. We do spend a good deal of time eating. Here in Kowhai Street, in Puamahara, in Maharawhenua, in New Zealand. Don't you, in New York?'

'We're not great eaters,' Mattina said. 'At least I'm not.'

She did not explain that she had not been a 'good' or 'great' eater since she began to suffer the mysterious sickness.

'Yes,' Dinny Wheatstone said, 'I know. You must have medical tests when you return to New York.'

Mattina felt the pallor of shock in her face. She touched her cheek with the back of her hand. Her skin was cold.

'You know, of course,' she said, too tired to voice her resentment.

'Of course. But we New Zealanders are indeed great eaters. Eat, eat, eat. Other activity is often hard to come by, especially in Puamahara. Yet New Zealanders are also very *busy* people. And the times of quiet are limited.

22

It was midnight when Mattina was awakened by the cries. She sat up in bed, alarmed, listening to the chorus of screams, shrieks, wailings from Kowhai Street: a clamour such as she had not heard since the days of the riots in Park Avenue when thousands raging for freedom and equality of opportunity, attacked the department stores and carried away goods, clothing, appliances, books, records, leather jackets in particular; a riot of have-not trying to transfer identity by acquiring a mass of goods that clicked, spoke, opened, shut, played, cooked, heated, cooled, switched on and off, transformed, gave pictures, sounds, voices; and warmed, warmed.

In Kowhai Street the rage of cries continued without decrease, seeming to come from every home, and as Mattina listened, shivering in the chill of midnight, fear quelled her first impulse to investigate the fury. She tried to stay calm. She regretted she had not taken the flight home weeks ago after one day in Kowhai Street and the news of the murder of the penultimate Madge, for it seemed to her now that her life had grown increasingly strange in its shifting dimensions, and if she were to believe Dinny Wheatstone, the imposter novelist, the Gravity Star was exerting its influence, bearing its overwhelming unacceptable fund of new knowledge from millions of light-years and centuries of springtime. Mattina was aware suddenly that the breathing presence had gone from her room leaving a ragged spear of abandoned light dizzying around the room as the wake or wash of — the vanished star? An animal star? An illogical unknowing unformed star? It was crazy, an invasion of madness with all the classic symptoms appearing in the overthrown space. Had the Gravity Star or the implications of its existence seized Kowhai Street, and would it later seize Puamahara, allying itself to the first source, the Memory Flower containing the land memory, to begin its work of transforming being, thought, language?

If I were writing this story, Mattina thought, the words might have begun already to burn, and though still legible they would sink into the flames as if they desired their own oblivion.

Mattina wondered, do the people of Kowhai Street know of the demolition of their minds and their words — is that why they rage without ceasing?

She was calm now. She felt within herself a cleanness, an emptiness as if her mind and heart had become dark empty rooms disconnected from light with no switch to banish darkness. She groped her way, as if she were blind, to the bedroom door and out into the hall; opening the front door, she felt again the force of the cries and screams. She walked down the path to the grass verge on the street. The families of Kowhai Street stood at their gates or in their driveway, screaming and shrieking; the children too. Hercus Millow's two cats stood by his side howling with an unearthly note of searching and despair. The Shannons were calling as if from southern to northern mountain. The Hanueres made a plaintive lament. The Jameses were sobbing, the Townsends cried and shrieked. Only Dinny Wheatstone and Mattina were silent. And although the empty homes of Madge McMurtrie and George Coker had no-one at their gates, from each house came a succession of horrifying human cries as if from someone trapped within the walls.

Listening, Mattina realised that no part of the chorus had words of any recognisable language. The sounds were primitive, like the first cries of those who had never known or spoken words but whose urgency to communicate becomes a mixture of isolated syllables, vowels, consonants; yet within and beyond the chorus, recognisable as long as the human brain held some stem (of crystal, bone, iron, stone, gossamer), there came a hint, an inkling of order, a small strain recognisable as music, not a replacement of what had been lost but a new music, each note effortlessly linking with the next, like dew-drops or mercury after momentary separation from the whole; yet 'momentary', now, was centuries old, and even the midnight roses along the path to Mattina's mailbox were roses of an Ancient Springtime.

It was not entirely the cries that brought a renewed feeling of horror: it was the faces, the bodies, the clothes of the people of Kowhai Street. Mattina, feeling she had *known*, *invested in* each family, observed in the glare of the street lights, Hercus Millow, the Shannons, the Jameses, the Townsends, the Hanueres, all changed beyond belief. The surface of the road, the footpath, the lawns and front gardens had all changed. Everyone's clothes appeared to be in shreds as if each person had been attacked. Both day and night clothes were smeared with a mixture resembling clay, mud, with bright specks and clusters like sequins or diamonds that were also scattered over the road, the front lawns and gardens, and even on the walls and roofs of the houses. The people did not move from where they stood while they continued to scream. Their eyes were bright like animal eyes seen in the dark, small electric bulbs glowing the length of the street. Not daring to move at first, but aware that the changes had not overtaken her, her house and garden, Mattina, trembling, struggling against an increasing numbness in her legs and her arms, forcing her to cling to the mailbox for support, found herself staring directly into Hercus Millow's face; for though he stood several yards away, there was an apparent failure of the concept of distance to become reality, and Mattina found herself reading his face as she might read a telegram held close to her. His rage mixed with confusion; he showed a grief as at a loss so sudden and dreadful that neither he nor any of his neighbours had been able to predict its nature or prevent it. His face was a changing mask of hopelessness.

No longer able to bear his glance, Mattina looked up at the sky. She thought, surprised at such a natural event, 'Why, it's raining.' Yet the falling rain was not 'real' rain. Specks, some small as carrot seed (George Coker had shown her his packets of garden seed), others as large, mapped purple and grey, as beanseed, some like hundreds-and-thousands, others like dew-drops set with polished diamonds, rubies, emeralds; or plain dew-drops that flowed in changing shapes among the layers of seeds and seed-pearls and jewels white and brown and red pellets of clay and then earth-coloured flecks of mould; smears of dung, animal and human, and every 'raindrop' and mixture of jewels and waste, in shapes of the 'old' punctuation and language — apostrophes, notes of music, letters of the alphabets of all languages. The rain was at once alive in its falling and flowing; and dead, for it was voiceless, completely without sound. The only sound was the continuing rage from the people of Kowhai Street.

Gradually controlling her panic, her surprise that the rest of Puama-hara seemed to be sleeping peacefully enough, that the highways bordering Kowhai Street were, as usual, slightly less busy and noisy than during the day (their sound was strangely unrelated to the sound and quiet of Kowhai Street), Mattina returned to the house and protecting herself with the over-shoes at the back porch, she found the courage to walk across the road to Hercus Millow who, seeing her, stopped screaming and stared, his lamp-eyes glistening and glowing. The two cats stopped their wailing, and making small meows, sank low and crept towards the house as if stalking unseen prey. Their fur was coated with the new kind of rain, now with a scab of dung, now with a cluster of jewels, yet they did not lick obsessively or paw at their coats.

Mattina stood hoping that Hercus Millow might speak. Although his lips moved and his throat and tongue worked in an attempt at speech, the sounds he made were grunt, moan and, finally, scream. In the end he gave up trying as had the others in Kowhai Street. Having found their new voice, they accepted it and soon began to control it. They no longer screamed although some, out of fury and despair or helplessness, still made intermittent animal-like cries.

'What is it?' Mattina asked, pronouncing her words carefully in a luxury of untroubled speech and aware of the suffering in the eyes of the listening Hercus.

'What has happened in Kowhai Street?'

Hercus stared, whimpering in what she took to be an attempt to answer her until she realised that although he had appeared to be listening, he had understood none of her words. They were foreign to him. What had happened, what would happen, what should she do? And how would the other residents of Puamahara react when they discovered the plight of Kowhai Street?

She could now see Dinny Wheatstone, apparently normal in her imposture, leaning over her gate, watching and listening. And the Townsends, they too were muttering a new speech, their night clothes in shreds, covered with the new kind of rain. Perhaps, Mattina thought, because I'm from another country and Dinny Wheatstone is a crazy imposter, we have been spared transformation within Puamahara, this night as the Gravity Star shines beside the Memory Flower.

Then even as Mattina watched, one by one the residents of Kowhai Street, silent now, returned inside their homes, and after another glance up and down the street, at the roadway glittering with its newly fallen rain, Mattina went inside to her sitting room and sat at the table and drawing aside the curtain, looked out at the darkened shapes of the trees. She could see the halo of morning light on the farthest peaks of the mountains, as if beyond the peaks there were another world with another morning and promise of a day that bore no relation to Kowhai Street.

Leaning back in her chair, Mattina gripped the edge of the table as if to steady herself in the shock of an earthquake. Then she began to sob, without having spare breath, so that her indrawn breaths became groans; she rocked to and fro. Was this how it would be? Was this how any disaster would be, how she would behave when it happened? In a country of earthquakes there was constant talk of disaster, with the earthquakes, the volcanic eruptions, being used to mask other disasters more feared, perhaps more expected. Mattina had found that Kowhai Street talked often of First Aid, that most of the residents had their Safety Bucket containing medicines, candles, matches, materials for shelter and warmth, their solar-powered radio, tinned food; and so on; but what use now was a plastic blanket and a tin of Irish stew? And what was the nature of the disaster?

Mattina switched on her radio to the local station, the talkback show. Perhaps they would advise her, they would announce the disaster in Kowhai Street.

The same old talkback show: beat them, whip them, hang them, put them on an offshore island out of sight, they're cheating us, they're bludgers, love is what the world needs, more and more love; and castrate them.

No news of Kowhai Street. Mattina switched off the radio. Her sobbing over, her arms no longer gripping the table, she lay her hand on the table-cloth. She noticed a small cluster like a healed sore on the back of her left hand. She picked at it. The scab crumbled between her fingers and fell on the table into a heap the size of a twenty-cent coin. Examining it, she discovered it to be a pile of minute letters of the alphabet, some forming minute words, some as punctuation marks; and not all were English letters — there were Arabic, Russian, Chinese and Greek symbols. There must have ben over a hundred in that small space, each smaller than a speck of dust yet strangely visible as if mountain-high, in many colours and no colours, sparkling, without fire. It could not be possible that the bones of the world's written and spoken languages, at the onset of their destruction, had fallen first on Kowhai Street, Puamahara; that the residents of Kowhai Street, under the influence of the Gravity Star and the legend of the Memory Flower had each suffered a loss of all the words they had ever known, all the concepts that supported and charged the words, all the processes of thinking and feeling that once lived within the now shattered world of their words. The people of Kowhai Street had experienced the disaster of unbeing, unknowing, that accompanies death and is thought by man to mark the beginning of a new kind of being and thought and language that, in life, is inconceivable, unknowable. The people of Kowhai Street, still alive, were now unintelligible creatures with all the spoken and written language of the world fallen as rain about them. The only judgment likely to be made about them, should their plight be dis-covered, was a diagnosis of mass hysteria or insanity. They were alive, yet on the other side of the barrier of knowing and being. There might be those who would judge them as better dead, who might even wish to induce a 'merciful' death.

Mattina wondered what might happen if by morning all the world's words had fallen upon every corner of the world, if everyone had been transformed to a similar state of unbeing and unknowing, if a universal process of new knowing, new thinking and feeling, and a new language might then fall, transforming life on earth to a new stage, unknowable yet, until the influence of the discovery of the Gravity Star had touched first one, then another, then many areas of the earth most receptive at that moment to geological and spiritual explosions and earthquakes. What-ever happened in Puamahara, if it were an intimation of the future, built on the memory of the past, a memory treasured enough to be thought of as a precious flower, a fountain flower at the gate of the orchard of the Housekeepers of Ancient Springtime, or if it were merely a dream, the town would surely learn as other towns have done, to accept and profit from its new myth. Hamelin town in Brunswick, Lourdes, Jonestown in Guyana. No town could be immune to the planting of new myths and legends, for were not these the few ways in which human beings may live, without disaster, in both the known and unknown worlds? That is, until now, and the arrival of the knowledge of the Gravity Star. Or could the Gravity Star be simply a modern myth?

Mattina sat for two hours looking out at the back garden, the one or two cat-shapes appearing and disappearing in the grass; a heavily winged morepork flying slowly from the tall puriri at the end of the garden. She could still hear murmurs and cries from Kowhai Street; they were muted now like the sound of the wind, as if they had always been.

Then, at four o'clock, feeling too exhausted to know or think or feel or plan, Mattina returned to her bed. She did not ask again why the breathing presence had disappeared. She lay down, closed her eyes, and slept.

And woke. And it was morning.

She lay still, watching, listening for the night sounds. She heard the starting of car engines, the heavy traffic along the State Highways; dogs barking; distant voices of children on their way to school. She heard the street-sweeping machine, the trash-collecting truck, a train shunting just beyond the railroad station, towards Wellington; a freight train moving heavily, slowly, its wagons creaking; a chainsaw at work; hammering at the new house being built two streets away. The concert of sounds seemed to be so normal for Puamahara that Mattina began to think she had dreamed the midnight terror, and that, perhaps in layer on layer of dreams, she had known her entire visit to Kowhai Street; that she might waken suddenly in the apartment in New York.

Quickly she put on her robe and opened the front door. Morning had been up for hours. The sun had long ago arrived from its other world beyond the mountains where it always paused 'to get the day going', as if, having applied a firelighter to its 'other world' sun, it stayed to make sure the fire took hold. Now, in Puamahara, it was almost half way up the sky with the back garden in full sun, and, where Mattina looked on to the front garden and the street in shade, she could see her house-shadow, the tree-shadows, the postbox shadow staking their claim along Hercus Millow's front hedge. The street was clean. No trace of the midnight rain in the gutters, the hedges, the lawns and gardens opposite. Mattina could see no sign of the people of Kowhai Street.

Not wanting or daring to fetch her morning newspaper, she shut her front door and began to make breakfast. Later, sitting at the table by the window, she noticed the heap of letters and punctuation marks still lying on the tablecloth. They had not been a dream. The raging had not been a dream. She stared at the heap of letters. They looked faded, used, yet the morning sun, striking them, made them sparkle and shine, reflecting, perhaps, an old thought lying between the letters. Mattina wondered why she felt afraid to touch them, to brush them into a pan and drop them in the trash. After all, they were only a pile of old letters of old alphabets with a sprinkling of full stops and commas, seedlike with tiny sprouts not of life but of the final decay of the old languages that had lasted well, magnificently, but were now like the old gods and goddesses who no longer could change or accept new growth and must perish to feed the birth of the new.

And it had not been a dream. The midnight rain had fallen, its unique composition had been real, the events in Kowhai Street had been real. She and the people of Kowhai Street had entered the time of the coexistence of dream and reality, had absorbed and explored the principles of the Gravity Star. She felt now that when she saw her neighbours, she would think them unchanged; their clamour would have ceased, and what happened at midnight would never be publicly acknowledged or known but would remain in their and her memory as certainly as if they had lived through earthquakes, floods, tidal waves. The inner tempests of a street, a town, a country, a world may be sensed, perhaps measured and recorded by poets and other artists, and later by historians, but it is certain they are not announced at the time of their happening. They may even vanish from memory; yet Puamahara, the home of the Memory Flower, would hold each event through time in whatever new form time may develop. From the past the unique indescribable link had been forged with the dream future and the real future.

Then, for the first time since she had been at Number Twenty-four, Mattina burst into laughter.

'How serious I have been,' she thought. 'Yet it has been a serious time.' Although she was used to delving into abstractions she had seldom been so concerned for weeks at a time, or so intent in her obsession with her neighbours. Her visit to Puamahara, unlike her visits to other regions of the world, had become a crusade founded on love — for a person, a people, a cause. Like the Gravity Star she had achieved closeness through distance. Had she? If dreams are close, if reality is close, then, she thought, through the people of Kowhai Street I have come closer than at any other time of my life to Jake Brecon, my husband, my lover, the father of my child, John Henry.

Memories came to her. Scenes of her life passed one by one. It is nineteen sixty, the year of her marriage to Jake. She is twenty-three, slim, brown-haired, a rich young woman, Mattina Connors, visiting Europe with her sister Lucy under the terms of their grandmother's will. A small sum of money for Mattina and Lucy to exist frugally in Europe, then to return home with Nana's fortune to be divided between them. And of course Nana knew that both granddaughters would manage their budget successfully.

In Paris, on each excursion to the American Embassy or the American Express office to pick up their mail, they meet other Americans. It is early May, the time for 'discriminating' tourists to visit before the scorching June and the ragged burnt-out days of July and the shrivelled dusty August; and among these Americans are the young men with plenty of dollars who wine and dine the two sisters who then return to their tiny attic room of the Left Bank hotel. Then one day at the Embassy they attend a reception in honour of a young writer, Jake Brecon, lately out of the army, whose first novel, *The Battlefields of New York*, has already been signed for a film. Mattina meets Jake.

'And are you at work on your second novel?' she asks. 'A sequel, perhaps, to *Battlefields*?'

'*The Battlefields of New York*,' Jake repeats the full title.

'Oh. It's a great book. I'm glad it has had attention. So am I looking at the new Scott Fitzgerald? William Faulkner?'

Jake frowns. He is tall, heavily built with bushy brows and a moustache. He resembles Mattina's idea of a 'novelist'.

'I think my book has had too much attention,' he says sternly. 'And my title is too frivolous.'

Mattina smiles. 'I think it's wonderful. Being here is wonderful too. I'm rich and you're rich and we're young and. . . .'

'I'm thirty-three,' Jake says with another frown. His eyebrows move like antennae when he frowns. His blue eyes have the haunted expression that Mattina believes must be in the eyes of all *real* novelists. His skin is suntanned. In her twenty-three years of living as a rich young woman and lately meeting rich young men from Harvard or Yale, many of them clever, promising, and some also planning to write and publish novels, Mattina has met no-one like Jake Brecon, receiver of instant fame and fortune and entitled to call himself a novelist. Oh, the others have entitlements and privileges, many of which may send a young woman's heart into space, but Jake Brecon, novelist of now, the most promising young novelist, is a prize worthy of capture.

And so Mattina and Jake became friends. And lovers. And twelve months later they married in New York. They planned to live (on Nana Connor's fortune and Mattina's own wealth and on Jake's royalties, for *Battlefields* was still in demand), in Nana Connor's big old many-roomed apartment near Central Park where there was a small room upstairs from the sitting room where Jake could write his second novel. They planned to spend their summers at Lake George in the house given them by Mattina's mother, who had taken a permanent suite in a luxury liner, touring the world 'for ever'.

How simple it would be, young Mattina thought. She would have her own work at the publishers where she hoped to become a reader. They would wait up to ten years before starting a family, they decided, after traversing the old arguments for and against early parenthood. Mattina made the final decision by reminding Jake that the next important event in their lives was to be the writing, completion and publication of Jake's second novel for which Jake needed time, space, every consideration worthy of the newest most promising novelist.

They were very much in love. Before Jake settled to what he termed 'serious work', he and Mattina enjoyed a roving honeymoon throughout the United States with Jake reading from *Battlefields* and from the classic American writers. His audiences were enthusiastic; he was paid handsomely, invited to return whenever he wished, while he and Mattina enjoyed receptions and parties wherever they travelled.

'How marvellous it is,' Mattina thought. She could not quite believe that she was married to the famous young novelist, that it was she who posed beside him for the newspaper and the television cameras, who moved from famous person to famous person at their parties, then returned to Jake, *her* Jake; that it was she who shared his bed. Mrs Jake Brecon, wife of the promising young novelist, author of the bestseller, *The Battlefields of New York*.

At that time of their lives they moved in 'artists' circles'. An older novelist, hardworking, unspectacular, with impeccable prose, invited Jake and Mattina to an induction at the Academy (saying in an aside to Jake, 'You'll be up there one day soon'), where they met writers, painters, composers who had been mere dreams to Jake and Mattina but who now appeared and spoke to them and exchanged the current literary and artistic news ('who's in, who's out,' as Lear would say); and some, Mattina thought, were so old, she thought they had died years ago, but there they were, old artists, unseemly in a way, like old sheep that escaped the slaughter-house; but there they were, lively, witty, surrounded by their admirers and their fellow-artists; enthusiastic, fervent, reciting, not their own works, but the works of those they most admired who were often indeed long in their graves. The room was full of words of praise, a second, third helping of praise, praise to the nth power for all the artists; such praise, someone said, would have to sustain them over many years of hard work, little recognition, unfair and fair criticism and poverty; the praise and love of one artist to another.

There, Mattina had grasped Jake's arm. Poverty indeed! Nothing would prevent Jake from fulfilling his ambition and the expectations of the literary world!

In the early days of their marriage Jake accepted an assignment as a foreign correspondent for a London newspaper. It wouldn't take much time, he explained to Mattina, but would get him used to writing again. 'A note for the London paper. A couple of hours a day. Then I'll work on the new novel.'

And so for the next six years Jake wrote articles for the London newspaper. There were often visits to London, sometimes with Mattina, where they enjoyed meeting old friends. There were receptions, parties. There were visits to Paris, with Jake and Mattina seeking out the attic room in the small Left Bank hotel. They walked the familiar avenues, joking about how they had been lost in the 'Louvre'. Paris, they said, was their first love. It was after one of these visits to Paris that Mattina became pregnant: she and Jake were delighted.

John Henry was born eight years after they had been married, and after the publication of *Battlefields*. When Mattina became ill both during and after the pregnancy, they accepted the obstetrician's advice that further children might endanger her life, and so John Henry became their only child.

'He looks like a small dark comma,' Jake said tenderly. 'Or a big fullstop on a small exclamation mark.'

Mattina, exhausted after the birth, said impatiently, 'He is a small human being, and not to be likened to a mere comma, a punctuation mark!'

'A comma may be human,' Jake said seriously. 'All the marks and letters and signposts used in languages are created by human beings. And you and I have made John Henry.'

Mattina did not argue. She knew Jake's love for language. Her and Jake's love in their eight years of marriage had developed, changed, but had never died. They had watched it as parents watch a growing child, or a gardener tends his plants; and they often talked of it. 'Our love,' they said. 'Do you notice these days how our love. . . ?' Our love does this, does that, is this, is that. Day by day they read it as if it were a book they were writing together. They spoke it, in duet. They danced it with their separate rhythms. While making their love more complex, the arrival of John Henry also helped to change its course. Jake had not yet begun to write his second novel. When the film option on *Battlefields* had lapsed four years earlier (fashions were changing, the film company said; there was no longer the interest in Jake Brecon), Jake and a friend began an historical film script which was now put aside as being 'not the good idea they had thought'. Then followed eight months in London as a theatre critic. Now, with John Henry born, and everyone home, so to speak, Jake assured Mattina and his publisher that at last his novel was ready for writing. He might appear to be idle, he told them, but they could be sure he was working, inside himself; no-one could see, but it was a fact. Damn hard work. Then, even when John Henry was still an infant, Jake would read to him from the great American and English classics, a chapter an evening, sitting in the nursery telling of *David Copperfield*, 'I am Born', *Moby Dick*, 'Call me Ishmael', *Treasure Island*, while John Henry slept the sleep of infants, deeper than seas and farther away than ancient constellations. Sometimes, coming into the nursery, Mattina stood watching the way Jake's lips closed tenderly upon each word before in his beautifully clear diction he fed it to John Henry, the way a bird tastes a treasured morsel before transferring it to his fledgling.

As time passed, although Mattina and Jake no longer mentioned the second novel, she could see news of it in his troubled face, his anxious eyes that often stared far away as if his thoughts ranged along a distant horizon, grazing like a herd of beasts that, having found their freedom, were reluctant to return home. Gradually, also, friends or acquaintances who had surrounded Jake to share the fame of *Battlefields*, drifted towards other more profitable fires, leaving only those now qualified to be called 'old friends' who wrote or sent cards at Christmas, Hanuka, Easter, Passover, Memorial Day, Thanksgiving, and so on.

The rooms above the sitting room where Jake had privacy for writing were now occupied by John Henry and the Scottish nanny, Mrs Parker, hired temporarily during Mattina's convalescence and permanently when Mattina, recovering, found that John Henry flourished in Mrs Parker's care. Mattina began to feel like a spectator when she visited the nursery. She would stare at the child, needing to have him translated by someone who knew his language, trying to read him as if indeed he were a small comma or question mark.

And now, with there being no place for Jake to write, Mattina made plans; one evening she surprised Jake by giving him a ninety-nine year lease she had signed and paid for.

'Your new office on Third Avenue,' she said. 'Get that novel written.' And that evening she and Jake had their first bitter argument. Although Jake accepted the lease of a studio apartment he had not seen, he warned rather than promised Mattina that in future he would pay his own expenses, despite his dwindling royalties from what his agent and publisher now looked on as 'an old book, a dead book'. At least his small inheritance from his father would keep him in pipes, pipe tobacco, whiskey, and cognac.

'I don't want money thrown away on me,' he said. 'And you do throw money away, Mattina, as if it were in neverending supply.'

Her response, which he knew to be correct but could not accept, was that her supply of money *was* neverending, that she had so much that even its existence guaranteed more and more, far more than she could ever spend even on John Henry's education, Mrs Parker's salary and the rent of her small apartment downtown where she could spend her free days; Mattina's, Jake's, John Henry's needs and wants; utilities, the upkeep of their apartment, food — why, they could have had room service every day and still have money. The solicitor had advised that perhaps Mattina should invest in real estate in Canada or overseas countries to add variety to her portfolio and give the family the pleasure of travel, should they feel inclined, and while accepting the solicitor's advice, Mattina reminded her that her interest was people and that in spite of her and Jake's objections, she would continue, as Jake expressed it, to 'throw money after every down-and-out who could daub a canvas, compose a nursery rhyme or string two sentences together.'

Jake knew he was being unfair. Mattina's work gave her the chance to judge the quality of writing and artwork and prompted her to send cheques of support to promising artists and writers. And why should not Jake share in the support? Mattina argued. If he could forget his jealousy and guilt he would manage very well writing his new novel with his wife's support. His publishers had given up enquiring about 'the new work for the Spring or Fall list'. He had published a few good articles on current affairs in the better glossies. He had given readings and talks at universities. He was famous now for his stories at parties and his after-dinner speeches.

He was often approached by strangers who, complimenting him, asked, 'Have you ever thought of writing a novel? Or stories? You'd be a first-class writer.'

Sometimes when Mattina was walking home from her work in Fifth Avenue, she'd see Jake leisurely wandering up the Avenue, miles from his office; smoking his pipe and gazing skyward in a complete dream, but his step, the still-joyous step that Mattina knew and recognised, revealed him as a schoolboy playing hookey for the day: he hadn't even gone to his studio. And when he came home and was pouring his first drink of the evening, and Mattina said lightly, carefully, deliberately vague, 'How was your day?', knowing that he knew that she knew, she did not expect a detailed reply, and he'd say just as lightly, carefully, 'Fair, fair,' his tone trying to mask the guilt and helplessness he often felt, and Mattina knew he felt. Her deep sadness came from his reluctance, his refusal to talk about his 'day' which became his 'week', his 'month', his year after year.

And as the years passed and John Henry grew and Mattina became publisher's reader, and Jake left the apartment each day to work in his studio, their life, while keeping its framework, began to disintegrate from within. As if to insulate herself from the lack of details about Jake's existence, Mattina became more obsessed with her desire to *know* about the lives of people of other lands, distant people whose presence could not provide tears, immediate responses, longings; people whose lives, set in clear detail, were yet muffled by distance. Then when both Jake and John Henry caught mumps, and John Henry recovered and Jake was stricken with lassitude, his recovery delayed over many months, increasing his humiliation over what he and others thought of as his professional failure, of him as 'one whose work has come to nothing', the shame of impotence completed the near-destruction of their life together. Brought up in a Boston family of stern English extraction, educated in a private New England school that, between cold showers, cold baths, cross-country running in the dark and snow of wintry mornings, dealt lessons in manliness, playing the game concealing emotion while a wolf gnawed within, Spartan Jake was so determined not to admit his disability that he and Mattina found themselves rarely speaking to each other. Jake slept then in the small study beside the sitting room. During his convalescence he continued to sleep there. His reason, he said, was to 'get a good start' on his writing for the next day. The novel was taking shape, he said. He was jettisoning the dead wood. He was pleased, now, that the historical film script had fallen through for he was now into real stuff of the imagination.

He knew that Mattina knew he was deceiving himself and her. Day by day they lived a scripted lie that soon included all aspects of their life together, even to deciding what John Henry should and should not learn, how many drinks they should have before dinner, how they should pay the bills. Jake's prolonged convalescence now became the reason given when people asked insensitively, 'Has Jake written his new novel yet? Is he working on anything these days?'

Unable to bear Jake's suffering and feeling unable to help him, Mattina made her first journey alone beyond the United States. That was the six months spent in Nova Scotia, buying land and living, as she afterwards described it, 'in a small fishing village where I got to know the people, really *know* them.'

When she returned from Nova Scotia and there were Jake and John Henry walking towards her at the airport, the likeness of their gaits, the poise of each head, the way they both clasped their hands behind their backs, like British Royal Princes, and the contrast between big Jake, tall, broadshouldered Jake and smaller-than-average John Henry, yet patterned in the image of Jake, brought a surge of love within Mattina, and tears to her eyes. They hugged and kissed. They talked excitedly like children.

'Mom,' John Henry said. 'When I'm in bed tonight will you come and *chitter* with me?'

'Sure, John Henry,' Mattina said. 'We'll chitter and chatter. And I'll tell you about the people of Nova Scotia.'

That night Mattina and Jake made love, and the next morning, full of optimism ('things are coming right at last'), Jake set out for his studio. And Mattina, thinking seriously about her time in Nova Scotia, realised that the people she had come to know there had linked her and Jake in a new kind of loving. She hoped now that Jake's tortured anxiety over his work would be eased. Their new love was like a blessing given by the people of Nova Scotia. And was not part of the nature of love to include the world, although most of the world would never know how its influence made prosper the fragile, failing areas of loving?

23

When Mattina and Jake had their next serious rift, Mattina bought an island in the Bahamas, Cloud Cay, about five miles long and two miles wide with a jetty, three boats, a main house and three guest houses, much sand, many coconut trees and Australian firs, salt shrubs and a small village of a handful of Bahamians who for three generations had cooked, cleaned and waited on the household of the owner of the island. It was they who fished and filled the crawl, maintained the electric generator which provided light only, and the kerosene refrigerator and stove in the main house. Water was piped from the sea for cold showers, washing, and the flush lavatory, and drinking water and all food except coconuts and seafood were bought at the supermarket in Nassau, Taste Palace. The supermarket also had a small library (the Daily Read) to supplement its supply of new magazines, newspapers, and books.

At once Mattina made herself at home. Instead of sleeping in a bed in the house, she chose a hammock on the verandah. Each day she and her four servants (housemaid, kitchenmaid, waitress, cook) had breakfast on the terrace overlooking the West Beach, towards Florida, while the banana birds hopped about on the table, the hermit crabs crept laboriously up and down the sandy paths, and the local radio played West Indian music and the popular songs — 'Kingston Town', 'Yellow Bird (you sit all alone like me)', 'Oh what a scandal in the family'. Mattina and the servants and the lean old boatman who steered the boat with his feet, and the young man who chopped the wood and nailed nails on the walls when nails were needed, all became friends, with Mattina asking numerous questions and at first receiving suspicious guarded answers until the others realised that the strange American woman was not meaning to patronise them, make fun of them, show them how rich she was and what she could buy, she was simply being friendly in the way she knew best, and because it was not their way, and the leaks in her boat of friendship were stopped with dollars, and perhaps she herself had never been shipwrecked, they tolerated her, answered her questions, told her about their lives, and, shrugging, appeared indifferent to her horror when she learned of their meagre daily wage, what she herself was paying them, and to her shock when the young waitress, lifting the hem of her long dress, showed Mattina a coral wound oozing pus, that refused to heal. Doctors and hospitals were for the rich only, the young woman explained.

Whatever the servants thought of Mattina, she looked on herself as giving and receiving a friendship she treasured, and when she returned to Manhattan (with a promise to visit Cloud Cay at Christmas with her family), she felt she had again acquired knowledge of life in a foreign land. She had met and talked to and lived among the people. She had written cheques for thousands of dollars for the needy and the sick brought to her by the women of Cloud Cay, although the ease of her giving had quickened the old unease of knowing she lived within a palace of entitlement and privilege while the rest of the world spent its time aching for what it had never had and so had never lost — other lands, things, hopes, the marvels pictured on the television screens and in the cinemas. Mattina thought, What else but dollars could she have given the island people? They gave her much knowledge of themselves, their stories, their myths and legends. They showed her the shark reef and the octopus nest and where to look for scorpions. They pointed to the ocean where the American sailor, swimming to Paradise Island, had inhaled a Portuguese Man o' War. They taught her about the hermit crabs, the iguanas, the coral, the brain coral, the sand dollars; they showed her how to tame the Hawksbill turtle swimming in the crawl, how to read the clouds in the sky and how to use a silver knife to cut an advancing hurricane. They taught her about themselves, their families, their hopes. And as the plane left Nassau, looking down over Cloud Cay, Mattina thought, with a furious sense of possession, I *know* them, I *know* them. They are my friends. She refused to admit that perhaps dollars rather than the usual sacrifice and mutual confidence had bought her information and friendship. She rejoiced, however, knowing that Jake and John Henry would be waiting at the airport and again as after her visit to Nova Scotia, the ingredient she had gathered from the people of Cloud Cay would help to cement the love between herself and Jake and John Henry. Cloud Cay now belonged to them. They would spend Christmas there, Jake would set up a studio in one of the guest houses where he'd have no sound but the slightly metallic clatter of the coconut palms and the sigh of the sea on South Beach. They could hire a yacht, go fishing, swimming.

Later, standing in the Customs queue, Mattina frowned suddenly, remembering that she had used dishwashing liquid to shampoo her hair while she swam in the lagoon, and then she had noticed a shoal of dead fish floating by the shore. 'They've been poisoned,' Sam the boatman said. 'Probably some tourist with detergent.' And Mattina looked innocently at him as she thought, 'I *always* wash my hair with detergent. It's completely *harmless*. These people will make a song and dance about everything.'

She knew she had been unfair, that perhaps she had poisoned the fish, but she refused to acknowledge it. It's *my* island, she thought. I bought it, paid for it. The fish were most likely ill to begin with. She also remembered that a drop of her nail polish had killed a scurrying insect. Well, she thought, it might have been a scorpion and then I'd be thanking the nail polish!

Her unease like a mild indigestion passed quickly, and there were Jake and John Henry waiting, so near and loving that Mattina burst into tears. 'I'm not flying away again,' she said. 'Not ever.'

And within the next few days, enjoying the renewed love that surrounded, inexplicably, Mattina's feeding of information about Cloud Cay, Jake talked of his novel, saying it had definitely fallen into place.

'It had to be ripe,' he said. 'And who will ever know how much time is taken by the ripening process?'

Not daring to comment but full of love for him and sympathy for his unadmitted anguish, Mattina nodded.

Then when Jake returned from the studio that evening she sensed that the novel had not yet fallen into place.

'By the way,' Jake said. 'If we own Cloud Cay and those people you talk of are our servants, I think we should keep our distance. I don't think we should fraternise with the servants.'

Mattina said angrily, 'Oh you Bostonians, you English and your class system. I can't see, Jake, how you can be so impossibly old-fashioned and bigoted. It's because they're black, I suppose, that you don't want me to "fraternise", as you put it.'

Jake worked his lips, biting them and pursing them as if he were tasting an old theory that had lost its flavour.

'I'm not bigoted,' he said. 'It was grandfather who helped the slaves escaping from the South. But you have to show some dignity. You're terribly short on dignity. Look at the way you talk to the doorman and the mailman! You're too *familiar* with people.'

Mattina, subduing her anger, said, 'Let's go to Cloud Cay for Christmas. You'll see what it's like. And if you want to work you can use one of the guest houses. And maybe we can hire a yacht and go deep-sea fishing, or fish offshore with one of the island boats. There's a sloop — Sam navigates that — and a rowboat you can use on the lagoon. John Henry will love it. And we'll have guests, close friends. . . .'

Jake agreed it was a good idea. They planned three weeks at Christmas. Jake invited Corban and Shelly Croft and their two children, David (known as Dodge) and Louisa. Corban had recently published a bestselling novel, after painstaking years dedicated to the art of writing; and because he was originally from the South, he promised to bring a genuine Virginia ham. Mattina invited a friend, Myra Rose, and her cameraman friend Artie Kastermans and their small daugher Eugenia. David, Louisa and Eugenia and John Henry were pupils at the same private New York school known in a précis of privilege, entitlement, assurance, as Manhattan Academy.

It was now eighteen years since Jake published *Battlefields* although as it was now unfamiliar it was known by its complete title, *The Battlefields of New York*. The Brecons' routine for each year was well planned: summer at Lake George where Jake built a cabin overlooking the lake, to write in; winter in New York with John Henry at the Manhattan Academy and, later, at the prep school out of Boston. Mrs Parker's work was almost over. Her daughter and son-in-law who had emigrated from Scotland to the Midwest began to claim her attention, and on one or two vacations she took John Henry to stay with her family, and John Henry returned full of news about the farm and Nanny Parker's three grandchildren. At home, John Henry asked repeatedly, did Nanny Parker love him more than she loved her grandchildren? He wished there had been no grandchildren, he said. He wanted Nanny Parker to himself, she belonged to him, she was his nanny. And although he was now ten, his anxiety at having to share Nanny Parker and soon to say goodbye to her for ever persisted, and when he learned of the Christmas holiday at Cloud Cay he demanded, will there be other children and will Nanny Parker come with us and be my own Nanny? A keen observer could see John Henry's inward calculations as he tried to determine how much time Nanny Parker would be able to spend with each child and whether he, as Nanny's *real* child, would have more time than Dodge, Louisa and Eugenia. Eugenia was younger than he, but Dodge and Louisa were twelve and eleven.

That Christmas at Cloud Cay was to be Mrs Parker's last Christmas with the Brecons. She agreed to give up her Midwestern Christmas with her family to supervise the children for three weeks at Cloud Cay and accustom John Henry to the idea that Nanny Parker was to be shared with others and would soon return to her own family.

'But she's our family,' John Henry protested. 'Aren't you, Nana? You're *mine.*'

So Christmas that year became the event that would solve, soothe, enlighten; and banish the anxieties of the past year. 'When we get to Cloud Cay,' Mattina or Jake or John Henry would say, each relating the event to their own problems and ponderings. At Cloud Cay they would relax, play, write, without a care in the world.

'Is it really our island, Mom?' John Henry asked, and was satisfied when Mattina replied, 'Yes, it's our very own island.'

'We'll take books,' Jake promised. 'We must have books like *Treasure Island, Moby Dick, A Christmas Carol, Charlotte's Web. . . .*'

'*Charlotte's Web*!' John Henry gave a long sigh of anticipation.

And to celebrate what all now hoped would be a 'turning-point' in their lives, a reunion each with the other, Jake began and finished a short story called simply 'The Cloud', a tale of reconciliation between a man and his wife, that was to end on a note of happiness but became, instead, a moving story of a man's devotion to his dying wife and his grief at her death. Images of cloud and sky, of plants and the stars, gave an ethereal quality to the story which was later published and chosen as one of the Best American Stories of the Year. Jake was paid handsomely and given six copies of the paperback and for nine years he kept the copies stacked, spine inward, on the bookshelf of his study, and each time he determined yet again to begin his second novel, he would reach for a copy of 'The Cloud' and reread it and wonder why he had written it and why as a writer he had no choice, no choice at all. How could it have been that the work lay before him and around him, subject after subject, yet when he struck the first key on the typewriter and the word appeared on the white page, he always knew he had no choice. Ten years later with John Henry at college and Mattina on one of her visits to 'get to know the people', the pages of the anthology were discoloured, apparently streaked with water, although the apartment had no leaks in the roof or walls; and small silver insects with tails like fish had begun to devour the story and its pages. Jake would reread, remembering his feelings as he began to write the story — his happy anticipation, hope, joy. He did not ask himself why the grief and despair and love that filled the story had sprung from his then joyous state. He knew that among the great works of art, music of the dance had sprung from the grief of the composer. He thought of the painter dying in Antibes whose work captured then the essence of the wonder and light within the sea-bathed town.

A few days before Christmas, the Brecons set out for Cloud Cay. One of Mattina's suitcases was packed with fresh loaves of New York bread. Jake's suitcase had two dozen rolls of toilet paper, dishwashing detergent named Yellow Bird, and two dozen books. There were also boxes of typing paper, a typewriter, numerous Christmas presents: these were all the essentials. The remaining supplies could be bought at Taste Palace.

That was all ten, eleven years ago.

Sitting at the window overlooking the garden in Puamahara, Mattina remembered vividly the Christmas at Cloud Cay.

A tropical island. Coconut palms, silver-sanded beaches. Shells that had lain for years untouched, uninspected, unnamed — conches, the nautilus, pink and white coral, sand-dollars, smooth discs of shell earned or won in the trade between wave and shore. And always lying among the shells, the empty plastic containers, planks of wood, sheets of plastic foam — the flotsam of the ocean-going liners, the oil tankers, the freighters, and the smart high-stepping yachts from the Miami coast and the islands of the Bahamas, the Californian coast and the Mexican resorts.

An island with its calm lagoon and a natural rocky exit, the narrows to the open sea. Bays, jetties, bathing houses with rooftop observation and sunning platforms; a lookout tower at the entrance to the narrows; and at one end a deserted cottage where, they said, an old washerwoman lived with her mate, a giant iguana. An island that might be the fulfilment of many dreams for both children and adults. Mattina realised that after her first lone visit to Cloud Cay she had invested dreams for her, Jake's and John Henry's future in what she had seen and learned at Cloud Cay. The strength of her prior *knowing* created a reality out of every dream; it must be so, surely it must be so. She could not question why it must be so, simply because she had seen the scorpions and the hermit crabs, had learned the life-stories of the servants, and learned how a silver knife could cut a hurricane in shreds; she simply *knew* that her knowledge had the power to make reality from dreams.

And now, in Puamahara, she remembered Cloud Cay as the island where she and Jake first paid attention to New Zealand. That Christmas at Cloud Cay was one of the worst she had known, in the most idyllic surroundings. Their guests arrived all suffering the after-effects of the virulent 'flu that had struck New York. The children were raucous and dissatisfied, the adults morose, sarcastic and critical. Quarrels began as if they were a normal feature of Christmas celebrations, which indeed they often are, and continued until the guests returned home. On a strange island that in the children's opinion should have remained between the pages of a book or on a television screen for them to read about it and observe it in comfort, they spent their time following their parents everywhere, unwilling to let them out of their sight for fear they vanished, leaving the children orphaned and alone; and when the parents explained that Cloud Cay was a *real* tropical island with coconuts and palm trees and sharks and scorpions, where they could play at being shipwrecked and captured by pirates and live in caves with wild animals for pets, young Eugenia began to howl so much with fright and homesickness that the parents assured the children that Cloud Cay was just like home, not at all like one of those islands in books or on television. Pacified, the children spent their time on the sand by the lagoon, playing House and Home, home being Manhattan. When Jake suggested they explore, like real explorers, again Eugenia began to cry while the others looked afraid. They didn't want to die of thirst, they said, or be swallowed by lions and tigers or cannibals. They wanted adventures to stay where they belonged — in books and television. And so the Manhattan games resumed and were not given up until the party boarded the sloop for Nassau and the flight home.

Meanwhile, the adults argued and criticised among themselves. Corban Croft, depressed following his 'flu, became more depressed when someone unwisely broached the subject of his new novel.

'The fuss over the last one hasn't settled down,' he said. 'I'm sick to death of it. I feel like a dirt road with traffic passing over it night and day, sending dust everywhere that won't settle, and I can't see a thing.'

The others joked about it, reminding him that it was his bestselling novel that gave him the privilege of travelling in Air Force One. There was a persistence about the unpleasantness of one guest to another. Jokes were made each time Corban went to the kerosene refrigerator to check his Virginia ham. Then, later, at dinner of spare ribs and black-eyed peas and caramel coconut pudding, Corban made nasty remarks about the dessert. It tasted like sweat, he said.

When they were not lounging in the sun bickering or swimming, they played poker, bickering, with real money while Jake, always slightly withdrawn from the Christmas party, sat on the pleasantly open porch, smoking his pipe and gazing out to sea while he listened to his portable record-player, playing his only four records — Handel's *Messiah*, West Indian songs, Beethoven's *Emperor* concerto and *Bird-song of New Zealand*. Whenever Jake sensed that a record roused most antagonism, he replayed it, again and again, turning up the volume. The apparent peace of Cloud Cay was broken day after day by 'I Know That My Redeemer Liveth', the 'Hallelulia' chorus; 'Yellow Bird (I sit all alone like you)'; and, for some reason, the most disliked bird-song of New Zealand where all the party learned again and again through an excessively correct English accent that 'the male blackbird of New Zealand is a most unsatisfactory provider.'

'New Zealand, eh?' everyone said.

It was a drunken, difficult Christmas holiday that yet in the memories of both Mattina and Jake, as the next ten years passed, slowly reassumed, as unpleasant events are apt to do, the characteristics of an ideal holiday on a tropical island, and when reading of Puamahara and the Memory Flower and wanting to give Jake what both knew must be his last chance to start and finish his second novel after thirty years — thirty years — Mattina suggested she travel to Puamahara in New Zealand, 'to get to know the people, to look at some real estate, to research the story of the Memory Flower', both she and Jake laughed fondly, quoting 'the male blackbird of New Zealand is a most unsatisfactory provider,' and remembering their ideal Christmas holiday as perfect.

24

Remembering and thinking about her life gave Mattina courage to try to discover the effects of the midnight rain in Kowhai Street — her memory having given her temporarily a secure, fearless place to be. Again she opened the front door and walked down the path to the mailbox and, reliving again the events of the night, she scanned the empty street. Where were the children on their way to school? She was sure she had heard them, earlier. She looked at her watch. Eleven o'clock. Then where were the cars, the coming and going of neighbours, the distributors of leaflets, free samples and giant offers; and where was the genuine mailman on his bicycle, his knees in his summer shorts frost-burned with the mountain air? Where were the plumbers repairing roofs and spoutings and gutterings, the builders sawing and hammering to finish someone's dream home before the Labour Day weekend? Where were the cladders with their load of Temuka stone that was not genuine stone but layers of imitation wood painted the colour of stone? Where were the people coming from beyond the neighbourhood, the genuine people to the street of imposters?

Mattina then saw a fleet of dark vans arriving from Gillespie Street, and from each van two figures, men or women dressed in white, came bearing a stretcher, and with each of the four vans dealing with one Kowhai Street house at a time, their task was over quickly, with two, sometimes three covered stretchers being carried from each house and fitted in tiers, like sleeping bunks in a rail coach, in the back of each van. As they neared Number Twenty-four, Mattina, believing herself to be in danger, hurried from the path and hid behind the mauve-blossoming virgilia tree. She watched the stretcher-bearers walk to her front door, select a key from their supply (showing surprise to discover the door was on the latch), and enter; and she heard their voices as they moved from room to room, searching for her. She was thankful she had packed her bags the day before and had them checked in at the airport out of town, far enough away, she hoped, to be safe from whatever had afflicted Kowhai Street and Puamahara.

'No-one home,' she heard one of the men say to his companion, a woman.

'Are you sure?' the woman said. 'We should search the garden.'

'It's morning tea time,' the man said, quelling further argument.

They did not search further. Obviously their task was to remove all the inhabitants of Kowhai Street, and they may have thought that the real owner of Number Twenty-four was out of town and that the breakfast dishes may have belonged to a plumber sent to remove the traces of the rain.

Soon the vans with their load were driven beyond Kowhai Street. Mattina stole through the shelter of the trees to her front door. It was locked. Of course. Her heart thumped against her ribs, her legs and arms trembled. She sat on the wooden seat by the back door and tried to calm herself. She longed to be able to say, 'It's a dream,' then to close her eyes and enter a deeper safer sleep; or waking, say, 'It was a dream, only a dream.' She felt sick with fear. Perhaps they had sprayed some deadly chemical in the house? And who were they? And why did they appear to be so untroubled, so methodical in their actions?

Recovering a little, and slipping the spare key from its hiding-place behind the trellis, she went into the house. It was as she had left it. Nothing appeared to be changed. Evidently the stretcher-bearers had not felt it was their duty to speculate or investigate or indeed to feel fear or curiosity or compassion — and why had they not rebelled against the orders given them?

Mattina supposed then that the people of Kowhai Street had died, from the effects of the midnight rain — then would not she be dead also? Or perhaps the stretcher-bearers had quietly put them to death to advance a process of change: a people without a language was a lost people, a burden on the state.

During the remainder of that day several fleets of vans arrived in Kowhai Street. Cleaners, household removers. Watching from the safety of her garden Mattina saw the Shannons' computer, unshrouded, carried into the furniture van. Poor Renée, she thought. Her dreams of Auckland, the great elsewhere. She wondered about the James's daughter as she watched their piano wheeled on its carrier up the ramp into the van, and heard the few uncontrolled notes and resonances coming from the heart of the piano. Computer, piano, the instruments of the people. She wondered if the Hanueres had been out of town and escaped; and what of the Townsends and their mother in her new unit in Gillespie Street? Connie Grant would surely have escaped. And Hercus Millow? Dinny Wheatstone? She had seemed unharmed during the night. Mattina supposed that her own escape had been the result of confusion among the authorities about the tenancy of Number Twenty-four. The missing residents of Kowhai Street had been acknowledged residents, with Inland Revenue numbers, electricity account numbers, street numbers, bank numbers, even personal identity numbers. They had paid their rates to the Puamahara Council. Mail was delivered to them daily. They had not been unwanted aliens with no papers to prove their existence. They had relatives throughout New Zealand. They had been *known*. Or had they? But wasn't there always a strong link in a chain of people, with the urge to take action to discover missing links? Mattina was not so sure now. She knew that in many countries scores of people vanished each day without trace and were never heard of again: relatives and friends searched and inquired until they gave up hope, until perhaps they too vanished or died. The fate of many of the vanished was never known, and no action was taken. The force of the event gave it a qualification of rightness that defied protest. Who cared? It was believed that some died, others were questioned, tortured, or transferred to other lands, to newly built cities where they lived and worked until they died of sickness or age or accidents, three of the acceptable ways of dying.

Later in the day yet another van arrived in Kowhai Street, and outside each house except George Coker's, a sign was nailed to the fence or letterbox. For Sale. Apply Albion Cook, Real Estate Agent.

Kowhai Street was for sale.

Then when Mattina looked out she saw the children coming home from school, walking along Kowhai Street, playing their usual teasing games. There were no children from Kowhai Street. Mattina felt that her suspicions had been confirmed: everyone in Kowhai Street had died or been killed and removed. Except Mattina.

Cars passed as if the day were any day. People from other streets walked by staring curiously at the For Sale notices, and Mattina heard one woman say to another, 'That's unusual, a whole street for sale. There must be subsidence or the tone of the area has gone down and everyone's moved, in a body.'

Mattina, greatly daring but inwardly fearful, walked to the corner dairy. It was closed, with a group of people waiting outside for their evening newspaper.

'Isn't it usually open now?' Mattina asked.

A woman shrugged. 'It looks as if they've sold out and gone. I don't think they were doing too well. I think Hene and Hare have shifted up the river, further north.'

Others waiting and hearing the possible explanation agreed without further questions.

'That's it. The corner dairy has sold out. They've moved up the river.

Kowhai Street is selling out too. Everyone's gone. Up north. Down south. Funny things people do. Away in a flash.'

Mattina, venturing further into Gillespie Street, found it incredible to see the life of Puamahara continuing as if nothing had happened, or if, even supposing more than the selected officials or Council Members knew, no-one apparently worried or cared. The meekness of the population was uncanny. But, after all, they had their own affairs and the affairs of the town to see to, and people moved house every day, taking off without a word to anyone, and then just when others began wondering, they'd turn up in Auckland or Wellington or Invercargill. And that was life. Wasn't it?

Then, not willing to face the activity of Tyne Street but observing that everything seemed to be as usual there, with the trucks of sheep still thundering along the State Highway, Mattina turned back into Gillespie Street towards Kowhai Street. She used the phone box at the corner to telephone the airport. Her luggage had been checked in, she said, but she would not be flying for three days. She booked a through flight from Palmerston North to Auckland to Los Angeles and New York, cancelling her planned three days in Auckland. What a waste of words, she thought suddenly, realising that she had given the clerk twice the number of words necessary to understand her request. And if the supply of words was already dwindling, had her extravagant use of them been prudent? And should she not leave the country immediately before the midnight rain fell on every street in every town? Her thoughts confused her. How could she spend two more nights alone in Kowhai Street? The sooner I'm home in Manhattan, the safer I shall feel, she thought.

Then she remembered Jake's telegram. *Have completed novel. Love. John Henry and Jake.* The fact that Jake had completed his novel after thirty years of determined struggling was almost too much for her to bear. In the midst of the unreal, fearful events in Kowhai Street, she cherished the thought of that telegram and Jake's painful pleasure of achievement.

She walked home past the now tenantless houses of Kowhai Street. Even the house of Dinny Wheatstone, imposter novelist, had been emptied of her piano, her musical instruments, her books, her paintings, all possessions. And old Hercus Millow and his goods had gone; and the Shannons — the too-willing Peter (Mum may I mow the lawn?), Renée collecting atmosphere and events and needing a special mood like a paint-brush to remove them; Edmund the simulated pilot flying at last in Reality Mode; Dorothy Townsend with her reject carnations in the crystal vases; the Hanueres, lost between generations but still shy, tongue-tied in their mother and father tongue, yet the family proud again, having discarded their Charles and Jenny January for Hare, Hene Hanuere; and Joseph and Gloria James and Decima who would perhaps now stay a lifetime at the Manuka Home and never know about the midnight rain. And George Coker, and the penultimate Madge, both well vanished. Who would tend the cherished gardens? Who would paint, rebuild, build on, varnish, upgrade? Although it had seemed at first impossible that the residents of a street could disappear and few questions be asked, and the matter accepted and soon forgotten, Mattina sensed that even after a few questions were asked and vaguely answered, the inquiring relatives and friends would be satisfied, finding their own explanation, 'They never kept in touch with us anyway. There's no time these days for keeping in touch.'

Mattina again wondered why she had escaped. She had witnessed the falling of the midnight rain, the word-change overtaking the people in Kowhai Street. She had been aware of the consequences of the discovery of the Gravity Star and its possible effect on a place that held the legendary seed of memory, the Memory Flower. She was a stranger, however, something that all in Kowhai Street had claimed to be and perhaps were: trespassers. Yet her home was New York City, U.S.A.; and perhaps her city and country were not yet 'ripe' for such events.

Then recalling the experience of the midnight rain, she thought of the small crusted heap of letters and words lying on her table and how, discovering them in the night, she had given her thoughts almost entirely to memories of her past life and of Jake's almost unbelievable struggle to meet the expectations of himself and others by writing his second novel. Perhaps, Mattina decided, when the other residents of Kowhai Street were being destroyed by the experience of the night, she had removed herself, her real being, to New York City, that is, to Memory, and while races and worlds may die, if they are to change, to resurrect as new, they must remain within the Memory Flower. Mattina felt that her escape might have been assured simply by her clinging like an insect at the point of destruction to the Memory Flower which had been a consuming reason for her visit to Puamahara. Her sight of the heap of alphabet letters and punctuation marks had reminded her of Jake sitting in a wealth of millions of words and unable for so long to grasp more than a handful.

Mattina found few answers to her questions. She felt that in future someone who knew and remembered the people of Kowhai Street, a relative perhaps or a friend, coming to Kowhai Street or to any other street on earth, would use persistence of memory to uncover the story, and perhaps rebuild, in fiction, the individual residents of the street; not to say, deifying the novelist, that the street vanished to reappear only in fiction, but to hope that future artists with whatever materials at their command would forever ensure new versions of Puamahara with the Gravity Star, the light of unreasonable reason, shining on the petals of the Memory Flower.

25

Before Mattina left Puamahara she had one further task to perform. Having come to New Zealand to study Puamahara and to invest in real estate, she decided to buy the properties for sale in Kowhai Street and therefore she telephoned Albion Cook, the real estate agent, suggesting she inspect the properties that afternoon.

He arrived at two thirty-five outside Number Twenty-four Kowhai Street, and Mattina, waiting, came out to meet him.

'I suggest we walk along both sides of the street and return here,' she said, as if they were embarking on a journey through unknown territory of uncertain direction.

'Fair enough,' Albion Cook said. He was a tall, well-built man with a large pale face and light blue eyes beneath ginger brows. His receding hair was ginger. Every now and then he jerked his neck to turn his head while slightly lifting his left shoulder. Mattina tried not to notice the embarrassing tic and its repetitive suddenness that made him seem about to attack. His voice was pleasant, slightly hesitant at times but in the full flow of ideas he spoke to convince, to hush, to override, to assure the listener that in all matters of real estate he knew best. And when Mattina asked, 'Why are the houses being sold? What has happened to the people of Kowhai Street?', he replied easily, 'You know, people up and leave for no reason these days: that's the way things are.'

'But where do you send my cheque for the sale?'

Albion Cook frowned. 'It's going to a fund,' he said. 'A corporate fund. One of the new Government Corporations. I've been told the State really owned the houses.'

'But what about the relatives of those who lived here? You must know something of them?'

'Not necessarily. The lawyer is out of town just now. He would know. It's not often we have such a swift bulk sale, unconditional,' he said. 'But you Americans.'

'You Puamaharians,' Mattina said grimly.

They reached Dinny Wheatstone's. Albion Cook gave no sign that their inspection was unusual. He did say, 'There's no accounting for what people will do,' and when Mattina asked, 'In what way? What exactly do you mean?' he replied, jerking his neck and turning his head, that throughout history strange things had happened.

'For instance,' he began. 'For a whole street to take off and vanish is unusual — for Puamahara. It hasn't happened before, not here. But there's always a first time. You hear about it on TV, and, you know, they do keep telling us not to believe, as we used to do, that what happens elsewhere can't happen here. I tell you, we're out in the cold now. It's happened.'

Although he showed no sign of fear, he shivered slightly, and then, embarrassed as he read Mattina's keen glance, he converted the shiver into an out-of-rhythm jerk of his neck.

'Yes,' he repeated. 'We're out in the cold now.'

He was silent and then said suddenly, 'God help us, God help us.'

He then began to talk the language of real estate. He described each house, its age, the fifties and sixties, post-war solid building with some of the designs of the early State houses — three-bedroomed, bathroom, separate w.c., laundry near the back door, circular clothes-line at the end of a short concrete path from the back door.

'This house hasn't been updated,' he explained as they inspected Dinny Wheatstone's. 'Here's the old concrete tub in the laundry. You can see where the copper used to be, for boiling the clothes. There's an old-style wringer washing machine — good now for making wine and brewing beer — and in the sitting room that space-heater fitted into the fireplace with a wetback to heat the bathwater. You see the roof's tiled with the old tiles. Something new, though, from the corrugated iron. You'll need a stove in the kitchen. The chimney needs repairs. And out the back, those old citrus trees, the fruit thick-skinned and full of pips — they want taking out.' He pointed to other trees, diagnosing them and, like a dentist, urging their removal.

In each house his description was as detailed, with advice now and then as if Mattina planned to live in the house. 'You'll need this, you'll need that,' while Mattina, almost convinced of her future tenancy, murmured, 'I see, I see.'

Once, pausing to inspect a bare room in the James's house, he said, 'Not a trace. You'd think there'd be some trace of them. And the whole street!'

'Do you think perhaps there has been foul play?' Mattina asked, observing him closely.

Albion Cook laughed aloud. 'Foul play? In Puamahara!'

Each time they came out of a house into the street Mattina was aware of the grave-like silence of the afternoon. The pupils were not yet out of school. Cars, while not avoiding Kowhai Street, now seemed to have an extra quietness, driven slowly as if the street were a graveyard.

There was no breeze. The glossy summer leaves hung poised, immobile. No birds sang; no insects flew.

'It's uncanny,' Mattina said. 'Such quiet.'

'It's mid-afternoon in Puamahara,' Albion Cook explained, and Mattina believed his explanation as she remembered her first afternoon in Puamahara and the silence as of absence and loss.

As soon as they entered each house Mattina found herself remembering those vanished. She saw them, talking, planning; all had so many plans for the future of themselves, their land, their house, as if land and house and garden were members of their family. She recalled someone pointing to a corner of the 'section' describing what she hoped to plant there, as if the corner were an individual to be dressed; even the fence posts, the patio, the barbecue were spoken of as living things. 'See, there's the barbecue,' they said as if they named a new grandchild, their son's best friend, their daughter. 'That's our barbecue.'

Yet by the time Mattina had inspected the homes, the thought of the former inhabitants was beginning to fade as if, having been through a form of brainwashing with a head full of estate terms, descriptions, roofing requirements, coatings, claddings, paints, wallpapers, particle boards, floorboards, patio furniture, gradually Mattina found the houses and their structure had replaced those who had lived there. Once only, when they were inspecting the James's house and Mattina found a minute pile of alphabet letters and words crusted on the wooden windowsill of the sitting room, thoughts of the child who had no words filled her mind. Of what use was the small heap of old dead language to Decima James who had never known words?

As Albion Cook was leaving he said apologetically, 'Of course as you're leaving us in charge I should tell you we can't advertise for tenants until after a decent interval.'

Was he referring to the deaths in Kowhai Street?

The next morning Mattina cleaned Number Twenty-four and set the house in order for the return of the owner. The past few nights she had scarcely slept; she had wondered, awake in the dark, about the relatives of the dead who might try to visit them; again and again she told herself that the disappearance would be accepted finally unless at least one person, acting beneath the pressure of memory, inspired others to listen and also remember. 'Aunt and Uncle used to . . . I remember when I was a child and stayed in Kowhai Street . . . and where Gillespie Street is now . . . where the water-race used to be . . . I remember them so clearly.'

155

Although she had packed the small suitcase of belongings left when she checked her luggage, she still had her notebooks with her notes on the people of Kowhai Street. She sat at the table and smoothed open the pages and as she read the names and the notes an awful feeling of grief that she could barely understand came over her. 'I was beginning to know them' she told herself. 'But they were not related to me. I did not really live among them. Yet I grew fond of them, and of my visits to them. They were only people. The time has been like a war. People, like countries, move in to try to change, explain, describe what they see, to take control and credit. People are born interferers, intruders, changers. People infect people like a disease. And people love. The people of Puamahara could have been living at the end of the earth; and they were.'

As she closed the folder she repeated solemnly the familiar words spoken at ceremonies, memorials to the dead in battle, to the brave for their self-sacrifice. 'I will remember them.' She knew she would carry each life the near distance to New York, and like the witches and story-tellers of old tales, pour her memories, like a potion, in Jake's ear.

The taxi arrived at last.

'The airport out of town,' Mattina said. 'I don't want to miss my plane.'

'Don't worry, you won't,' the driver drawled. 'What do you think I run a taxi for?'

He spoke again only once during the thirty-mile journey.

'Funny things happening in Puamahara,' he said.

Mattina did not question him.

'Yes,' she said. 'I've heard.'

Later, from the plane, she looked down at the fresh dark green world of New Zealand; the milky grey winding rivers, the volcanoes and mountains, the misty interior where the foliage showed dark and more ghostly. From time to time on an otherwise bare plain or hillside she saw a red-roofed house like a dwelling capped with blood surrounded by sheep in white dollops of snow. Then, waiting at Auckland Airport, she ventured only once to look out from the entrance upon the blue-and-white air that seemed to be drunk with light, giddy with light, with the earth concealed with wire and an amulet or anklet of concrete, a green tree, sometimes with crimson or gold blossoms: the allowed bloom.

It was dark, with a violet-coloured sky, when the plane took off for Los Angeles and New York.

Part Four

Housekeepers
of Ancient Springtime

26

Home. Jake waiting at the Grand Central Station heliport on an early November morning. The day clouded, cool with an aftertaste of fall that Mattina received gratefully, welcoming the subdued colours of the impersonally noisy New York in contrast to the brilliance, the mechanical uproar, the clatter, incoherence and madness of a land of bright flowers, bright eyes, European, Celtic, Maori, South Pacific, all New Zealanders, pacifically peculiar people whose reason was upside down, who meekly accepted whatever happened, who behaved like cowhands, angels, snails, toads, who spoke loudly, their words returned to them, from mountain to mountain, as if they spoke for the world, from the Carpathians and the Southern Alps; who gesticulated vehemently, prayed with arrogance, sang divinely, cursed and mumbled; and dressed, the men like eighteenth century Southerners and the women like bumble-bees and flower gardens. The air of Puamahara had been attentively warm during the day, present at one's shoulder as if ready to help on with a wrap or, the next moment, snatch it away; cool at night; always accompanied by sharp edges of temperature, of colour, sound, and of pain. Seeing Jake in his winter overcoat, his bulky figure like a dark brown wheat sack, his face tanned with the moustache awry, like a false moustache, his New Zealand blue-sky eyes and his glance still full of love and anguish, Mattina felt the joyful sense of being home, of hope for no more pain, confusion, vanishings, questioning; now in a governed world of warmth and money and reason, foreignness forgotten — who cared, anyway, about the people of other lands, about small streets in small towns of flowers and sheep trucks and satin grass; and people unable to look beyond their Waitara stone cladding — now, in a world where others· attended to mundane daily services — meals, shopping, complaints to the electricity and phone companies — who cared now about the ordinary lives and chit-chat of an ordinary street; who cared about the Gravity Star, the Memory Flower?

Seized with a sudden pain of longing, of homesickness for Kowhai Street and its people, Mattina groaned; then she smiled.

'Good to have you home, Mattie,' Jake said as they hugged and kissed.

Mattina tensed.

'Sorry, Mattina,' Jake said, acknowledging her dislike of pet names for her.

Also, she had forgotten about Jake's English-style reticence, his laconic speech. Then, remembering the glorious telegram that cancelled a lifetime of suffering — *Have completed novel. Love. John Henry and Jake* — she hugged him closer, and they kissed again. Yet even now she was trying to convince herself that Jake's thirty-year torture, like the Thirty Years' War, had ended.

'It's wonderful,' she whispered.

'It sure is great,' Jake said, both as banal as new astronauts observing the beautiful earth.

Then Jake sighed.

'Something not OK?'

He sighed again. 'Nothing. Just the old story as we both know it.'

They taxied home to the apartment and as they rode up in the elevator to the familiar heavy carved wooden door with its carved lion door-knocker, and as Jake unlocked the door and swung it open, Mattina felt panic. Lately, not knowing what to expect, she had walked in many rooms of houses of the dead, and for a moment she was back in Puamahara, in Kowhai Street.

'The place seems empty,' she said. And laughed uneasily.

'Of course. Without Nanny Parker, and with John Henry in Boston, we do have empty rooms.'

She remembered her discovery that the telegram had come, after all, not from New York but from Boston, no doubt when Jake was visiting John Henry.

'I'm tired after the flight,' she said, aware that Jake's glance was puzzled.

'I'm exhausted. Jet-lag. I'm going straight to bed.'

'You'll eat? I'll have downstairs send up a salad.'

'No. I feel sick to my stomach. I'll sleep.'

'It's great to have you home,' Jake said again, sitting on the sofa by the window and reaching to the coffee table for his pipe. His movements were abrupt, uncertain. He stared, frowning, at Mattina, who wondered, 'Why is he staring so? I've been away from him before, and come home and slept the day away without his being so distressed and concerned. For himself? For me?'

She sat in the chair opposite him.

'I really don't feel like food or drink. And it's great to be home, away from your little old New Zealand and its male blackbird!'

Jake continued to stare seriously at her. Their separate poses reminded Mattina that she and Jake had never been a greatly smiling couple: they both laughed aloud, or their faces were serious, stranger to stranger; at breakfast they would sit opposite like two travellers in a train, a comparison made more credible by Mattina's habit of carrying her pocketbook everywhere, as if she were visiting in her own home.

'You received the cable from Western Union?' Jake said suddenly.

At last Mattina understood Jake's concern. She spoke excitedly, 'Oh yes, oh yes, it's wonderful news. Wonderful. I didn't know what to say in reply except that — wonderful news. I was so happy. Oh darling Jake. Even now I can't believe it. Tell me.'

Jake smiled bleakly with a subdued happiness.

'It was a surprise to me, too,' he said. 'After all my years of trying to convince myself I could write another novel!'

'Oh yes, oh yes.'

'John Henry told me he'd sent you a cable.'

'Oh. I assumed you sent it. It was wonderful, anyway.'

'I had no idea John Henry was writing a novel,' Jake said, biting the stem of his pipe.

Mattina felt a swarm of confusion as if all the bees in the orchards of Puamahara had entered her head, with honey and stings. She waited for Jake to speak.

'No. I had no idea. A firm in Boston is publishing it and they've pre-sold the first edition and are already reprinting. And he didn't say a word until it was written and accepted. And that was months ago, long before you left for — Pua-mahara.'

'Puamahara.'

'Puamahara. He sent the cable the very day he told me about the novel.'

'Oh Jake,' was all Mattina could say. 'Oh Jake.'

Jake rested his pipe in the ashtray and wiped his hand over his mouth, and Mattina thought wildly he was trying to prevent his words from escaping, trying to save, to store the words he had not been able to find over many years.

'I'm freelancing now, as always,' he said. 'And guest editing. I'm having a book of my literary essays published. And next year I'm assigned to the Presidential Campaign. I never was a fiction writer . . . oh, I have written a few more short stories . . . but I've confused being a lover, a student of fiction with having the talent for being a fiction writer. I always felt myself to be a kind of imposter. Do you see what I mean? *An imposter.*'

'You never were an imposter,' Mattina said angrily and fearfully, remembering Kowhai Street and the crusted heap of midnight rain. 'Oh Jake . . . the Presidential Campaign should be interesting.'

Jake smiled.

'I realised it was other people wanted me to be a novelist. And my enormous interest in literature, and my freaky first bestseller somehow convinced me and everyone else that here I was, the new Faulkner, Twain, Fitzgerald, Jake Brecon.'

'I feel dizzy,' Mattina said. 'I must sleep. But it is marvellous news, both for you and for John Henry.'

'He'll be home as soon as he can get away. The weekend, maybe. He'll tell you about it, I'm sure. Are you ill?'

He helped Mattina to their bedroom. The bed was made, the covers turned down. Not even waiting to shower, Mattina undressed and feeling dizzy and sick, she lay on the bed. Ten minutes later she was deeply asleep.

Not wanting to disturb her, Jake slept in Nanny Parker's narrow bed in the old nursery apartment along the corridor; he slept beside shelves of books, beside a Noah's Ark of wooden animals and others, beheaded, limbs, amputated, fur rubbed and fondled away; and by John Henry's toy typewriter with its narrow plate and minimum number of keys that could yet tap out the right words in the right place and help with the calm deliberate search for the lost words.

27

Two weeks later when the results of tests were known, the specialist diagnosed a malignant tumour so deep-seated that excision would sever an artery in Mattina's chest. Five months to a year, perhaps longer, 'they' said, the singular inevitably becoming the plural in such an important division of responsibility. There'd be increasing doses of medication to help in the last stages. Mattina's choice was respected — to be nursed and to die at home, to die also without being dressed in masks and tubes as if she were a deep-sea diver or a walker on the moon.

In the sitting room on the well-worn comfortable cream-coloured sofa, Jake sat while the specialist, Myrna Petrie, explained the diagnosis.

'I know Mattina,' she said. 'We were at school together, both in New England and in Switzerland. I respect her wishes to stay at home and die at home.'

Jake's shoulders in their abrupt heaving gave the only sign of his sobbing. As he wasn't used to crying, he had not the art of breathing as he sobbed, and therefore the breathing made a sound like an engineering fault that made him and Myrna smile. Then he sobbed again.

'She's only home from Noo Zealand a few weeks,' he said. 'With all her notebooks and records of her trip. And now this. And John Henry — it will break his heart.'

He paused.

'Could we have done something about this before?'

'It's hard to tell,' Myrna Petrie said. 'She had a variety of apparently unrelated symptoms; knowing Mattina, I guess she delayed consulting a doctor.'

Just then Mattina appeared in the doorway. Her face was paler than usual, her eyes tired. She smiled bleakly.

'What the hell,' she said. 'Am I not even allowed a drink?'

'It might be better not,' Myrna said. 'On the other hand — ?'

Mattina finished the sentence. 'On the other hand, what difference does it make, eh? Eat, drink and be merry. Except there's not much I can eat now.'

'You like yoghurt and ice-cream,' Jake said. 'Boysenberry yoghurt.'

Mattina smiled. 'OK, then. I'll think of something to eat to keep up my strength. After all, I have to relate my adventures Down Under in the land of the unsatisfactory provider, the male blackbird. I have to tell you of the people I met, the real estate I bought . . . years ago before I was robbed of my point of view.'

She looked accusingly at Jake and at Myrna who frowned, not understanding the reference.

'You see,' Mattina said to her still-puzzled audience, 'I had to fight for my life, my very days, and my point of view, with Dinny Wheatstone; and then to come home and find I must surrender both my life and the point of view that holds my life together. . . .'

Then she looked pleadingly at Jake. 'Let's not have a strange nurse for me. Let's get Nanny Parker again. You know she's a qualified nurse. And she knows us.'

'If we can,' Jake said. 'She may not want to leave her family now. She did give us many years of her life.'

Mattina, maintaining her relish of privilege and entitlement, urged, 'We can pay her any salary she wants; enough to make it worth her while; and employ an assistant for the messy jobs.'

She thought, I'm dying, but I can still buy some comforts. And Nanny Parker wouldn't turn down a huge sum to ease her own retirement and the disabilities of her approaching old age.

Then with a sly smile and another reference, whispered, to 'getting back my point of view', she murmured, 'I'm going back to my bed.'

Jake helped her to the bedroom, and into bed. He plumped her pillows, pulled the covers over her and kissed her; embracing and kissing, they both wept, thinking of their life together, of John Henry, of the one time each had been unfaithful, of the novel that once separating them so sharply now united them with its thirty years of phantom existence, having a life in its unwrittenness, in their years of focusing on it. Both knew of Jake's deep store of sadness. He had been mocked, his inability to produce his second novel had been remarked upon in literary columns, with explanations that bore no relation to the truth as Jake perceived it. Once, at the publisher's, Mattina had heard a visiting literary agent ask one of the editors, 'Have you heard anything of Jake Brecon's new novel, the one he's been writing for thirty years?' She'd heard the laughter.

'It's a brutal world indeed,' Mattina said, thinking of Jake's past years while Jake, supposing that she referred to her illness, murmured, 'We're together again. We'll spend all this time together. Nanny Parker will be here too. And John Henry as often as he is free.'

'And I'll tell you about Puamahara and Maharawhenua, I'll tell you stories of the southern land, spinning out each day and night with the

164

memory of Puamahara.'

'And John Henry's novel will be out and everyone will be reading it,' Jake said, blinking his eyes and biting his lower lip in the way he'd always shown strong emotion. There was a 'used' part of his lip, like the kissed stone of the pilgrims or the trodden paths of centuries gone.

'Well, I'm around sixty now,' Jake said. Then he smiled, trying to look modest. 'Meakin — my publisher — thinks my book of literary essays is . . . well . . . he thinks highly of it. And I'm no longer — what was it I used to say? — "biding my time". Such a phrase is dead, as far as I'm concerned.'

'Dead. Let's forget it for now,' Mattina said.

When Jake had gone from the room, Mattina felt a terrible depression creeping over her, a grief for all she would lose and leave, all that 'belonged' to her, her human and financial possessions, her real estate in Nova Scotia, the Bahamas, New Zealand, and all that was open to possession by everyone — morning, noon, night, the seasons, the weather, landscapes, seascapes, mountains; and the inward possessions like memory, love, time, the yesterday and Now, the awful tomorrow; and her own being, her self, her point of view which, she noticed, was shifting almost imperceptibly to Jake, and in the weeks to come might be taken over by others as her self, like a character in fiction, became less important and vanished. She could not believe in her coming death, and when she tried to think about it, a feeling like a dull coverlet spread over her mind, concealing and soothing. She thought, 'One thing I must do before . . . in the days or weeks to come . . . is tell Jake of Puamahara, preserve the memory of Kowhai Street and its people — who knows? — in future years he may visit there . . . or John Henry . . . soon . . . about the Gravity Star . . . and the Memory Flower.'

She fell asleep. This was to be her routine for the next few months of winter. She would wake, wash herself or bath, (until Nanny Parker took over these duties), dress, and spend the day lying drowsily on the sofa in the sitting room. Jake would come home from the uptown apartment where he still needed to work, though he spent less time there as the weeks passed, and together they'd have lunch and talk and Mattina would doze, and waking she would talk of Kowhai Street, the Gravity Star, the Memory Flower; of her house and the neighbouring houses. Jake learned of the penultimate Madge and her murder, of old George Coker and his rose bushes and his silver cups 'for egglaying'; of Dinny Wheatstone, the imposter novelist, the thief of roving points of view, and her novel shown to Mattina.

'What became of it?' Jake asked. 'Was it good?'

'I returned it to her,' Mattina said. 'I found it interesting, also alarming.'

She could not try to tell Jake about her own presence in the novel, about her existence within parentheses, nor about the breathing creature, nor the cardboard world, the reduced dimension, the people of Kowhai Street existing briefly as cut-outs between the pages of a book. She described the Shannons and Ed, the simulated pilot flying in Reality Mode, the Jameses with their piano tuning and their daughter in the Manuka Home out of town; the Hanueres, trying to rescue their language and their name; she described Hercus Millow the ex-sergeant-major in the German prison camp; the Townsends and their bereaved mother; Dorothy in the carnation fields, Rex in the dyers. She told how one afternoon, hearing a noise outside, she had surprised Rex Townsend wheeling away a barrow of earth from her place to his, with the explanation, 'This is really *our* earth. When the fence was built, earth was mistakenly transferred to your property, and it's lain there, but it doesn't belong to you, it's ours.' She told how she'd let Rex Townsend remove his ten barrows of lost earth that had been 'in the wrong place'. 'A godlike action, don't you think?'

They laughed.

'Risky too. In a country of earthquakes where most of the earth ends up in the wrong place — your earth or mine, eh?'

Then Mattina told Jake of the Gravity Star. He'd heard of it, vaguely, he said — wasn't it a star that was at once close and distant? How could that be?

'Yes,' Mattina said in a slightly singing tone, 'Near is far, heavy is light, here is there. It adds up to nothing until. . . .'

She supposed, she told him, that the Gravity Star and its meaning had homed in like a honey-sucking insect upon the Memory Flower, upon Kowhai Street and Puamahara, as a beginning. . . .

Jake frowned. 'I don't quite understand,' he said. 'A beginning? A beginning of what?'

Mattina sighed. 'It's so hard to explain. I've written it somewhere in my notebooks. You know, there are times as in a chemical reaction when all the ingredients are present in the required amount; they combine; and it happens.'

'It?'

'Something strange. Or terrible. Or marvellous. Or merely just a volcanic eruption with molten lava flowing down a hillside burying towns and people and trees and animals. . . . But if it happens, and it's *invisible* —'

'I understand that well enough,' Jake said. 'What really happened in Kowhai Street?'

166

Mattina could not describe what really happened. The thought of the midnight rain made her shiver. She lay back on the sofa and closed her eyes and when she reopened them she said, 'Some time soon perhaps you or John Henry will visit Kowhai Street to check on what will be your and his real estate. You must meet Albion Cook, the agent. I don't know how much of the story he will tell you. I think you should see Puamahara. And don't forget to walk to the orchards out of town where the Memory Flower is said to bloom. And visit the James's daughter in the Manuka Home; she is quite alone now. And don't forget what I have told you of the people of Puamahara. Please remember it and remember your own experience when you travel there, and tell it to John Henry. That's important. When all the other threads are broken, either through necessity or carelessness or ignorance of use, your remembering will renew the thread. In Puamahara I watched a saddler strengthen and proof his sewing thread by drawing it through bees-wax — keep drawing your memory through your experiences; and know — as you must know — that our John Henry has written a novel because he is our child, and he remembered your reading to him and your remembering the great works of literature; and so he wrote a novel, trying to continue the memory, replanting the orchard . . . oh I talk of saddlers and sewing and trees and blossom. I never talked like this before, did I?'

They were both silent then until Mattina sat suddenly upright.

'Do get the roulette wheel and let's play roulette. Nanny Parker has bought me a child's toy shovel and rake to rake up my earnings. Come on, Jake. *Faites vos jeux. Les jeux sont faits.*'

Sometimes instead of roulette they played poker and blackjack and Strip Jack Naked; and when John Henry came to visit, they played Happy Families and Donald Duck. And sometimes Jake in his wonderful clear voice read prose or poetry or talked, thankfully and with melancholy, of how his life from its beginning had been accompanied by the works of Chaucer, Shakespeare, Spenser, Milton, the New England writers — Emerson, Thoreau, Hawthorne; the modern Americans — Fitzgerald, Faulkner, Hemingway, Steinbeck, Hart Crane. And the women writers too, he conceded — Dickinson, Willa Cather, Welty, O'Connor, McCullers. . . . And because their Christmas at Cloud Cay was now cancelled, Jake read again the Christmas books, Melville, Poe; and as had been his habit when he read to John Henry, he pointed out the special choice of words, the apt phrases almost as if he were the teacher, Mattina his pupil; just as she, her diminishing life enlarging the view of others, became teacher to Jake.

Often Mattina listened to his readings. Other times she dozed. And often she could think of nothing but Puamahara; and then she talked on and on of the residents of Kowhai Street, the midnight rain, the words and letters of the world's alphabets falling everywhere, as rain but never rain for they would fertilise and feed nothing, although some showed a spark of light, a diamond spark among the dead languages.

Her talk became rambling. When Jake tried to question her closely, she was not able to explain.

'Poor soul,' Nanny Parker said. 'She's delirious.'

And because Mattina pleaded with Jake to listen, to listen and remember, he could not leave the room, to let his tears flow freely. He stayed to listen, to try to remember, until Mattina exhausted, fell asleep again.

And when John Henry came down from Boston, Mattina thought as she watched him and listened to his excited talk of the new novel he was writing, 'The young Jake.' Tall, young, too young, blooming with confidence.

'I'll bring you and Dad a copy of *The Diviner* as soon as I can,' he said. Then he turned, wonderingly, shyly to Jake, 'Dad, I didn't know you were one of the editors of *Wordwork*. It's printed in *Paris*! And I didn't know it was you who wrote all those essays for *The Times* and the *Coast Monthly* — we had to *study* them at school; you, the great American critic! And I've only just realised how much your reading to me has enriched my life and my attempts at writing. I never dreamed. My father, the editor of *Wordwork*. Why, *everyone* reads *Wordwork*, everyone quotes it, it's the highest thought of.'

Jake laughed and shrugged.

'All through those days of *Charlotte's Web* and *Treasure Island* and *Tanglewood Tales* and *Dracula* — remember when you were reading *Dracula*?'

'*The Diviner* is being advertised in the *Monthly Review*,' John Henry said. 'With quotes.'

Both Mattina and Jake smiled indulgently, proudly.

In spite of having come from a family with grandparents, sisters, Mattina felt now as she had always felt, that her real allies, enemies, rivals and accomplices were aspects of New York City. These and her immediate family — Jake, John Henry, Nanny Parker — were her world now, with the dark wintry New York City itself looming beyond the storm-windows, watching over her as she lay on the sofa in her nightgown and robe, snugly tucked under a New England patchwork quilt. And although she had never worn visible make-up except for the eyeliner, shadow and mascara for her eyes, and nail-polish, she always had various creams and potions for her skin and hair. Now, for the first time, she hid her pallor with rouge, and, reclining like a woman conducting a salon, about to receive the wigged and powdered aristocracy and their young protégés, the artists, musicians, composers, writers, she received Jake, John Henry and Nanny Parker. And Dr Myrna Petrie. Often Mattina was bored with her family; she tired too easily. She hoped once, slyly, that Big John Henry, the lover from the past, might visit her, and she daringly asked Jake to get in touch with him. Their bitterness over her affair with Big John Henry had laugh at it now, but Mattina still felt nostalgia for the one time when she played the role of domesticated wife, preparing and cooking meals for Big John Henry in his apartment uptown. And when she cooked Big John Henry's meals she had always been nervous waiting for approval of herself as a *real* housewife as well as a man-wife, and not the spoilt rich hussy Jake sometimes called her. He had been a slighter version of Jake. His voice, too, was musical. He read poetry to Mattina, although she did not care greatly for poetry. Yet he was separate from the literary world known to Jake; he had never wanted to write novels or follow an artistic career.

Mattina had no last visit from Big John Henry. He was out of the country, Jake said, with his wife and daughter.

'No matter,' Mattina said, accepting the pangs of regret, jealousy, and melancholy.

Sometimes Jake played records remembered from the early years of their marriage, their Paris days, and the few wonderful summers they spent at Lake George; but even then Jake had not been able to forget the world of the novelist. 'Theodore Dreiser was here first,' he said wistfully. They played the Beatle songs, too, that were part of little John Henry's birth and infancy. Mattina requested again and again, *Hey Jude, don't make it bad*. And together they listened to the reconstituted Bach, the fresh youngsters from Liverpool allying themselves to the grand old cathedral master with his talented wife and their seventeen children, and now speaking for Mattina and Jake in their New York sitting room, pleading for them.

'Hey Jude. . . .

'Here a minute, Jude. Wait. Hang on a second, Jude.

'Jude, don't make it bad.'

28

Mattina died in February, surrendering at last her point of view. It was a day of blizzards when the streets of New York City were almost empty of people while those who ventured out sheltered in store and apartment doorways. For two days the blizzards unleashed their blind fury. February, Mattina used to say, was the worst month, and why did the groundhogs choose then to waken from their winter sleep?

For months after the funeral, Jake sank out of sight 'like a swimmer whose strength is going'.

There was the publication of *The Diviner* with John Henry appearing on television, the interview with the promising young author; and Jake, as he watched, thinking, how thin his face has grown; he looks older than his twenty years; he's a Brecon, but he has Mattina's eyes. John Henry had fought long against growing up, and in the last days of Mattina's illness he had reminded her and Jake again and again, 'Remember when you used to come to the nursery to *chitter* with me? I'd say, Mummy, let's chitter; as if the whole world depended on it.'

For those months when Jake retreated with his grief, Nanny Parker stayed on, cooking his meals, washing his clothes, doing all the household chores; and helping Jake and John Henry who came home in the weekends, to decide what to do with Mattina's clothes and personal possessions. Her small high-heeled shoes were so hollowed out with wear they looked like shaped wooden clogs. Why hadn't she bought more, Nanny Parker wondered. More shoes, more clothes, gowns. The few clothes in Mattina's closet were sweaters, jeans, one evening gown, short, black. There was little to reveal her wealth unless it was the diamond bracelet and necklace. Nanny Parker felt she would never understand Mattina and her chosen way of spending her money — having everything done for her, her clothes picked up from the floor, her shoes reunited one with the other after one lay under the bed, the other by the bath; entertaining promising young artists with a banquet at the Russian Tea Room while she herself ate a simple bowl of wonton; travelling in a private plane between New York and Lake George. . . . Obstinate, self-willed, Mattina paid for and took what she wanted but what she wanted was seldom what others want: Mattina Brecon was different.

Nanny Parker, a member of the Brecon family for twenty years, was now able to admit to herself if not to many others that her personal life had been bought (paid for handsomely) by the Brecons; but in spite of her sacrifices she had been paid security and love as well as money. She had enjoyed her work and as a young grandmother bringing up John Henry she had loved him and was loved by him and amused by him as if he were a creature not part of the human race. His grave questions, his solemn thoughtful face — even as an infant he was precocious. From the time he could talk he had his own record player, recorder, television, typewriter; and books, of course, with his father reading aloud to him at every opportunity, talking literature to him, transmitting to him his love of prose and poetry, while his mother and he, each night, pursued their fantastic 'chittering' about everything under the sun. Nanny Parker realised that the few times she had overheard Mattina and John Henry laughing was during the 'chittering'. And now Mattina was dead, Nanny Parker felt ashamed of the many times she had resented the Brecons, as she waited on them, said Certainly Mr Brecon, At once Mrs Brecon, I don't mind at all, Mrs Brecon, looking after little John Henry during the holidays, I can easily delay my vacation, work extra hours, fetch those goods from uptown. . . .

That had been her role; a servant; mixed with being a mother-substitute to the wee fellow while his parents lived and loved and separated and were reconciled, and finally worked out their differences. Too late, perhaps, was Nanny Parker's thought.

It had not been too late, however, for both Mattina and Jake to understand that their obstinate love over many years had become devotion; the love that was at first a deep narrow stream, confining, turbulent, had widened, deepened, to flow through every area of their lives, steadily, its mood changing with the seasons but without the brutal assaults of unusual weather; with passion in its darkness and light, but without mutilating abyss and fire.

In the weeks that followed Mattina's death, Jake tried to be patient with those who kept affirming, 'You always have memories. Whatever happens, you have memories of Mattina.'

And that, Jake felt, was false. You grow old and your memory fails, often completely. You don't know who you are, your name, you fail to recognise friends you once loved, relatives, places; what price memory then? Yet why, particularly in the weeks before her death, had Mattina talked so often of memory and of that place in the Southern Hemisphere — Puamahara? She had talked of memory not as a comfortable parcel of episodes to carry in one's mind, and taste now and then, but as a naked link, a point, diamond-size, seed-size, coded in a code of the world, of the

171

human race; a passionately retained deliberate focus on all creatures and their worlds to ensure their survival.

I will do as she wished, Jake told himself. I will visit Puamahara in the deep south of the world: a place we've never really accepted or learned to think about as it is, with different seasons in different months of the year, different time; we've ballooned our northern existence into all four corners of the world; even in the farthest places without roads, schools, without food, barefooted children with swollen bellies play Rambo and the heavens are filled with Star Wars and not the Gravity Star. Yes, I'll travel to New Zealand to Maharawhenua, to Puamahara and Kowhai Street. I'll inspect the real estate, the people. I'll visit Decima James in the Manuka Home out of town, and, at Mattina's last request, the orchards, the place of the Memory Flower.

29

Six months after Mattina's death, Jake sold the apartment and moved to his uptown studio which had one guest room, the study, the sitting room and Jake's large bedroom. He then wrote to Albion Cook, the land agent in Puamahara, with news of Mattina's death and the transfer to him and his son of the real estate in Kowhai Street. He would be arriving in Puamahara, Jake said, in September, and would Albion Cook reserve him a room on a daily basis at a local hotel?

Although John Henry, completing his second novel, was tempted by Jake's invitation to travel with him first to Nova Scotia, then to Cloud Cay, then to Puamahara, he preferred to stay in Boston. During a weekend visit to Jake, John Henry was shocked to find how much weight his father had lost, how his back appeared hunched as if he still carried weight. Jake now used a walking stick, although he had no limp, and when John Henry remarked on this, Jake laughed, embarrassed. 'It feels right,' he said, 'walking with the aid of a stick. And it's useful — to lean on, to prod with, and maybe in some circumstances to strike with. The old man and his walking stick!'

'Dad!'

'It's true. I feel old.'

'Dad, you've years and years ahead of you,' John Henry said, lavishing an unsuspected gift of time in the generous way of those who have an abundance.

John Henry felt that Jake should travel alone on his pilgrimage to Puamahara; and, as a more unusual version of the newly bereaved widower 'travelling the world', it would give Jake stories to tell when he returned. And later, John Henry thought mournfully, aware that he as an instrument must receive, like notes of music, the continuity of generations and other lives, he too, when Jake died, would make a similar pilgrimage to the places where his parents gathered their knowledge and memories and where the event happened which his mother could not describe or explain. She had seen the blossoming of the Memory Flower — oh not as a real flower on a stem nor as a flower sculptured out of stone, but one sprouting from the crevices of centuries, tended by 'the Housekeepers of Ancient Springtime'. She had murmured of such things before she died; and John Henry had been certain that her murmuring was not entirely delirium.

Both he and his father, numbed by Mattina's death, dwelt in it in their thoughts as each day they lived in a desert where nothing grew now, with each day acres and acres wide and long and the night like a distant land to be travelled through; yet when daylight approached it at once receded almost out of their lives and the long journey began again. And there were times when both Jake and John Henry yearned for the human mind to be released from the bonds of time and space, to be able to accept and know the Gravity Star that Mattina, even in her last confusion, talked of lucidly with excitement.

'See Puamahara, visit Puamahara,' she had cried out one night.

Then, with Jake and John Henry at her side she woke and together they played card games, Happy Families, with Jake playing Mattina's hand against John Henry, stacking and shuffling and dealing and winning and losing a share of John Henry, of his talents, his new career as a writer.

'It's true,' Jake acknowledged. 'I was never a writer of fiction. I write essays and read. And it's writers who must thank providence for readers.'

The day before Mattina died, Jake read to her from the poems of Stephen Spender, one of the 'golden' poets of Jake's younger days at the end of the age of the gold cocoon, and at the beginning of looking at, feeling, describing events as they were; poetry written in a warm bed, a warm room with 'honey for tea'; as well as poetry written while fire-watching during an air-raid; or after, at home, in a half-ruined street of the dead. Spender had known the anguish of both worlds.

Jake read, finally:

> Yet those we lose, we learn
> With singleness to love:
> Regret stronger than passion holds
> Her the times remove:
> All those past doubts of life, her death
> One happiness does prove.

174

30

Jake's visits to Nova Scotia and Cloud Cay were unremarkable. It was the hurricane season in the Caribbean with a storm attacking Cloud Cay, and watching through binoculars from Nassau wharf, Jake could see the coconut palms leaning with their heads in the sand; some were violently uprooted. The main house had half of its roof dislodged. There was no prospect of a visit to Cloud Cay and standing in the boisterous but harmless winds of the main island, Jake was shocked by the fury of the hurricane as it passed rapidly like a whip across the back of the many small islands, then travelled away to the Miami coast and the north. Jake remembered Mattina's story of cutting a hurricane with a silver knife. How unlike the sceptical Mattina of her younger days, to put faith in a tale told by an ill-educated person living on a backward island, Jake thought. Mattina had changed following each visit she made in what Jake thought of as her 'peculiar exercise' to 'get to know the people'; yet returning, she had been full of new love and delight and in the midst of their loving, their most private world, she seemed to bring her new knowledge of the people of Nova Scotia and Cloud Cay, and her new experience of the land and the sky and the sea, the foreign daylight and dark, to share, as she shared herself with Jake, as if the people of *Our Beautiful World*, the other lands, themselves were invited guests at their loving; how mystifying yet satisfying it had been! More satisfying than the former 'chat' or 'chitter' that used to develop into an argument. There had been times when, overcome with crippling shame at his inability to write his second novel, Jake had the wild suspicion that Mattina, realising his anguish, may have been deliberately 'feeding him' characters and stories that might inspire his writing, as if in their overpopulated bed they were engaged in mutual insemination.

Jake was not an enthusiastic traveller. While he waited in the long queue in the Customs Hall of the Auckland airport, he consoled himself with the thought that the visit to Puamahara was a necessity, different from Nova Scotia where he had been unable to find the people or the atmosphere described by Mattina; even different from Cloud Cay, the memory of which was gradually settling in his mind as a nightmare with its mixture of Mattina's impressions of her first visit, the Christmas party of escapees from the New York plague, the *Messiah* with its constant reference to 'dwellers in Zion', the recording of the blackbird, the unsatisfactory provider, and his recent visit where he witnessed the destruction of the main house. The wait in the Customs queue, the wait to transfer to the flight to Palmerston North, were tedious, dream-like, and finally his boarding of the plane referred to as a 'jet-prop' was not without apprehension as the plane seemed reluctant to leave the earth and during the flight it stayed well in view of the plains and mountains and rivers, and only during the path through the central North Island enveloped in mist and swirls of cloud, it flew as if blindly into nothingness. 'It's always like this,' Jake's neighbour explained. 'Don't worry. The centre of the North Island is always shrouded with mist whether you travel by car or plane; it's a strange, secretive part of our land, full of legend.'

Mattina had talked of the Maoris. Glancing at the rows of passengers behind and in front, Jake saw no Maoris; there were several rows of Japanese tourists slung with cameras; the rest were what Jake would have called 'ordinary' people, just like Jake, from the top half of the world. And this was Down Under. Jake had also noticed that when he spoke to the passenger beside him, heads turned, faces stared, the expression in the eyes said, 'He's American.' There was little joy in the faces; quite different from the days after the Second World War when Jake and others even younger than his nineteen years helped to 'clean up' Europe, and the faces and eyes that said, 'He's American,' had been full of joy. There'd been Vietnam and Korea since then; and others since. At first the Americans had bought love with their deeds; then, with food and bombs — everyone found that easier, and easier to strike than to talk. Talking, you needed a hard-working brain, ideas, a language; words just didn't fall from the sky when you needed them.

A hostess in a crisp patterned overall held a dish of sweets in front of Jake who smiled at her, 'Thanks.'

Unfolding the paper he drew the sticky red sweet from its niche and sucked at it while the strongly chemical-raspberry flavour swirled through his mouth. Crumbling the wrapper, and poking it into his ashtray, Jake read: 'Puamahara. Reasons Sweets. R. T. Reason & Co.' Then turning to his neighbour, a young man wearing a yellow tie and a grey suit, he said, 'Excuse me. . . .' The young man had an open, pleasant face with room for feelings to come and go as on a large screen. His hands too were large.

'Excuse me,' Jake repeated. 'Do you know Puamahara?'

The man's glance was questioning. Then he said, 'Oh. Puamahara?'

'Yes, Puamahara.'

'It's up the coast from Wellington. Has some good restaurants in the main street. A horticultural centre. Fruit, flowers and so on. You going there?'

'Yes. Do you know it?'

'Not personally.'

Both were silent, then as a buffeting wind struck the descending plane, sending it riding up and down like a ship on seawaves, the young man said, 'You get crosswinds here.'

Jake was the only passenger to disembark at Palmerston North. The others were flying to Wellington.

As he walked across the concrete strip to the terminal he felt the breeze fresh and cold in his face. There was a touch of ice in the air. Everywhere appeared clean and green and deserted, and as he waited for his one travel bag to appear in a corner marked Selfclaim Area, he noticed a cab driver standing by the kerb outside, apparently waiting for his fare. Picking up his bag from among the suddenly arrived heap of boxes, Jake approached the driver who said, 'You Brecon? City Hotel, Puamahara?'

'Sure. Albion Cook arranged a cab for me.'

'Right,' the driver said. 'Settle in for a fifty-kilometre drive to the Maharawhenua. Roses, carnations, kiwifruit, berryfruit, apples, car bodies, carpets, plastics, the lot. And sweets.'

'And people?' Jake inquired gently.

'Sure. People.'

For half an hour they followed a long straight road close to the sea and wild surf with the cab buffeted by the wind and showered with seaspray, while on the eastern side a plain extended to distant cornflower-blue-topped mountains with slopes streaked with grey and white rock and the hollows shadowed with dark green forest. Soon, on a winding road, they crossed the mountains, and then passed a succession of villages each containing a group of old wooden houses, all faded, some blackened by fire and weather. A row of concrete buildings, garages, factories, and a large old hospital, Manuka Home, with groups of faded wooden buildings set in its carefully landscaped grounds, heralded the approach of a large town. Then the sign, Welcome to Puamahara, the Home of the Memory Flower; then the main street, Tyne Street, with the outlying motels vying for trade: Best Mountain View in Puamahara. Waterbed. Electric Blankets. Adult Video. Spa Pool. Microwave. All the latest enticements of lust and pleasure. . . . Then into a stream of cars, trucks, cattle trucks, noise, sidewalks with pedestrians walking alone or pushing small-wheeled shopping trolleys or baby carriages with babies dressed Alaska-fashion against the chill September wind from the eastern or northern mountains or (as the cab driver explained), the 'raw southerly' from the South Island.

The cab then turned a corner and eased into a parking space. 'There.

City Hotel. Brasserie and all. Bang in the middle of Puamahara. That's eighty dollars, eighty-eight including tax. But it's only forty American, remember, so it's cheap to you.'

Bemused by his thirty hours travelling and the fact that his 'real' time was now nearly midnight, while in New Zealand it was early afternoon the next day, Jake thrust a handful of Kiwi notes into the driver's hand, then picked up his bag.

'We don't get many Americans in Puamahara,' the driver said. 'Except for the horticultural experts; and an American woman who stayed a while last year.'

Jake checked into the hotel. He carried his suitcase up two flights of stairs to the top floor into a large room with two single beds, and windows overlooking the traffic lights in Tyne Street. The smell of animal manure came in the opened window; Jake shut the old-fashioned sash window, drew the heavy brown drapes and prepared to sleep. His room (the only one with 'private facilities', the receptionist had said) had a small bathroom with w.c., shower, a bath-towel, hand-towel and bath-mat; and a wafer of khaki-coloured soap, the same colour as the old houses they'd passed on their drive to Puamahara. There was no washcloth, no writing paper and envelopes, but two postcards of Puamahara showing fields of carnations and distant mountains, silver-topped and forested. A folder gave details of food at the Brasserie, a list of recreational benefits to be enjoyed in season by visitors to Puamahara, the Agricultural and Pastoral Show; art shows in an old house converted to an arts centre; dog obedience club meetings; rugby football; soccer; tennis; horse racing; a rose garden display; shopping malls; the sweet factory; and the cinema or movies. There was no art gallery or museum or concert hall. There were churches of many denominations. Sleepily, lying in bed after a quick shower and shave, Jake, out of habit, read the form of literature offered by the hotel, together with the tourist brochures — Fishing; Hunting; Shooting; Golf, Circuits for Jogging. At the end of the brochure there was mention of a town library, and a brief note on Puamahara as the source of the legend of the Memory Flower, a legend that clearly was valued although the writers of the brochure had not known how to define the value in their breezy account of the hang-gliding, flying, swimming, running and ball handling that appeared to be the chief preoccupation of the Puamaharians. Had Jake not learned from Mattina about the residents of Puamahara, he might have believed the brochure's portrayal of a hunting-shooting-fishing-rugby-playing population. As it was, when he slept he dreamed of his visit to the orchards out of town, and to the Manuka Home where Decima James lived.

178

Waking at seven that evening, Jake phoned for room service and a recorded voice said, 'I'm sorry. No further meals are available until seven-thirty a.m. We wish you a pleasant goodnight.'

He drew aside the drapes and looked out at Tyne Street where there were fewer cars than earlier in the day, but as many heavy eight-wheeled trucks with tarpaulined loads charging along the street and belching black smoke; and a truck, stopped at the traffic lights, gave Jake a glimpse of marble-eyed dusty sheep jostling one another for a view from the red-painted slatted three-tiered enclosure. Jake could hear the sheep's hooves scraping sharply on the wooden platforms, as if they wore boots with toe- and heel-caps, and in their restless shifting to and fro they seemed like tap-dancers trying to get space to stage their 'routine', while their heads pushed in panic and their mouths opened in shrill bleating.

The lights changed and the truck was on its way north. Jake closed the drapes and recalling that he'd seen an electric jug or kettle in a small corner cabinet, filled the jug from the bathroom tap and plugged the cord in the wall outlet. In the cupboard above the cabinet he found a plastic dish of tea bags, coffee bags, sugar sachets, and three-inch-wide containers labelled Milk; and on a side plate, three small plastic-wrapped parcels each enclosing twins of cookies — coconut, chocolate and plain, the plain labelled in large letters PLAIN PLAIN PLAIN. Jake drank a cup of instant coffee, ate two plain biscuits, and deciding against exploring Puamahara's streets that evening and feeling too tired to care, chose the phone book rather than the Gideon Bible for his bedtime reading, and fell asleep embracing the phone book.

He woke in the night. There was dead silence except for an occasional truck, and a freight train shunting on the railway tracks near the hotel. Its light beamed through Jake's window. Thank God, he said to himself, I'm here for only two or three days. Why on earth did I come here? I can't hope to relive Mattina's experience. He thought of her intense pleas for him to visit Puamahara and Kowhai Street; the orchards, the Manuka Home where she herself had not visited. For him to remember, only remember. Remember what, he wondered, looking around his hotel room with its standard linen and its slabs of food and its assumption that first thing next morning he would be away to fish, hunt, jog or play football. Remember what? Where? As far as he could judge, Puamahara was an ordinary town, much smaller than was cunningly suggested by the name City Hotel; about the size of Saratoga Springs or Schenectady. In his dozing state he tried to assure himself that his visit was significant, that the Memory Flower and Mattina's request warranted flying thousands of miles to the

179

end of nowhere.

What he had seen of Puamahara gave him little encouragement to remember; in the night with the glare of the passing trucks like roving animals searching the corners of his room, he was sure he would forget Puamahara. He reminded himself, however, that although not a writer of fiction, but having practised for the past thirty years the art of writing, that a writer's forgetting is not ordinary forgetting, nor is a writer's remembering: a writer's remembering is never quite merged with usual life, as part of the day and night, but is set as on a stage with curtains drawn, prepared to be floodlit instantly to reveal every detail of sight, sound, colour, and once these are noted the lights are changed to bathe the scene in the remembered feelings and thoughts; the memory is then set in its own drama with the writer the sole audience until that memory is chosen to be described in words. Perhaps, Jake thought, I must not be impatient with Puamahara. My stage of its memory has this night only a huge sheep-truck full of sheep performing their song-and-dance routine in a rage of fear upon slatted wooden panels painted the colour of dried blood.

Early next morning Jake phoned Albion Cook to arrange to be shown the Kowhai Street real estate.

'I'm just along the road from the City Hotel,' Albion Cook said, speaking with a deference that Jake felt was out of proportion to the occasion, Perhaps Puamahara was a genuine small town where small events like the arrival of someone from America loomed large?

'Imagine my being just along the road,' Albion Cook repeated.

'You did reserve my room at the City Hotel,' Jake reminded him impatiently.

'I certainly did. There's no denying that,' Albion said.

Jake felt that Albion Cook had a large supply of useless, sparkless words that he was determined to use. Where he might have used a crisp yes or no, he enlarged them into sentences that merely parcelled the yes and no for delivery by his easygoing voice; but after the unwrapping of the delivered words, only yes or no remained. Words deserve more care, Jake said to himself. Even the sparkless words can be made to sparkle, not picked off the assembly line prepolished and prearranged.

'We can walk along Kowhai Street together,' Albion Cook suggested. 'And I'll show you your real estate.'

At half past ten Jake met Albion Cook outside the Post Office opposite the hotel and on Jake's insistence they walked and did not drive down

Gillespie Street towards Kowhai Street. Albion Cook talked constantly about Puamahara with the words spilling out of his mouth, while Jake, tense, his tanned face worried, looked uneasily at Albion's word-working face that seemed to be moving without inner substance, like a glove puppet with no hand inside it. Albion Cook had an explanation, a reason for everything. He expressed sympathy at Mattina's death.

'She was rare,' he said.

'Oh. Did you know her?' Jake asked, surprised, whereupon Albion made a jerking movement with his neck and looked over his shoulder.

'I sold her the Kowhai Street real estate,' he said, implying that the intimacy of a real estate transaction could be equated with knowing.

'She was a friend of the people of Kowhai Street,' Jake said. 'She was really interested in each one.'

'I believe she was a writer?' Cook said.

Jake smiled a tired smile.

'In a way,' he said.

They had walked past the veterinary hospital, the two Funeral Homes (one a branch of the local furniture store), the Nonconformist Church, the Medical Centre, and the Hospital and Home for the Aged from which already the daily aroma of stew was wafting into the street. They were about to walk into Kowhai Street when Albion Cook said suddenly, 'There are no tenants yet for the Kowhai Street properties. There's only the young couple who keep the wool shop in the Mall and they bought well before the . . . events.'

Jake was surprised. 'No tenants? I understood Mattina to say that she came to know each resident of Kowhai Street.'

'There were various upheavals,' Albion Cook said, moving his hands upward and outward like a fountain, but as an illustration of 'upheaval'. 'Just around the time your wife left Puamahara.'

'Upheavals? Earthquakes? Eruptions?' Mattina had said that New Zealand was prone to earthquakes.

'Not exactly. Just . . . upheavals. . . . Your wife was here when . . . this happened . . . you know how neighbourhoods can become . . . say . . . restless . . . someone moves away . . . the rest move . . . and quick as a flash they're all gone. You see?'

'Yes, I do know that happens. I've seen it happen. In wartime. But — in Puamahara? Did it happen in Kowhai Street? Mattina said nothing about it.'

'I believe it did happen here. Neighbourhoods are quite secretive, you know, about this sort of thing; and the towns keep the secret. I bet each town in this country has its deadly secret!'

'But Mattina said nothing about it.'

'Everyone moved away quite suddenly — up north, down south, over to Australia, you'd hardly believe it. I think your wife was amazed and bewildered by it. I think she bought the homes in Kowhai Street as a memorial to friends who had gone to other parts of the country. There were strange rumours around, but the Council put a stop to them. I saw nothing untoward about being given the properties to sell for the Corporation. Also, you can't have rumours in a tourist town like Puamahara. And our tourism is growing, because of the Memory Flower.'

In Kowhai Street almost the only sign of life was the flowering trees.

'Kowhais,' Albion Cook said. 'You pronounce it "korfy", or some such.'

He repeated the pronunciation, making a sound like an angry cat. 'Though why we should have to be so exact beats me. All this language business.'

'Oh?' Jake was interested. In her last days, Mattina had talked or rambled persistently about language and Puamahara; words; the Memory Flower; the Gravity Star.

'I should think all words deserve the dignity of correct pronunciation,' Jake said sternly. Albion Cook had spoken so angrily about the pronunciation of 'kowhai', calling it a 'mere word'. A mere word. Dear Mattina, always trying to warm Jake with a coverlet of words. Wanting words to rain down on him, thirty years of downpour to help him complete his second novel! Words, Jake felt, should be treated with no less or more dignity than if they were human beings; the two supported each other with an intimacy and ease; they were as close as senses, skin, bodily function.

Jake saw Kowhai Street as an ordinary shabby, deserted street. He felt distaste at the thought of entering each empty house, playing the landlord to the vanished or dead. He tried to recall the list of people Mattina had known, the details she had given about their lives, their feelings, their plans for themselves and the future of their house, their garden. If anyone had known Kowhai Street it was Mattina in her two months' stay. John Henry had her notebooks now, to study them in detail. What a strange two months, Jake thought. And now she was gone, and the residents of Kowhai Street had vanished as if they had never been. Albion Cook had spoken of them as if they too had died. He decided to test Albion Cook's memory.

'Who lived in the house opposite Number Twenty-four?'

Albion frowned.

'I used to know the bloke quite well. I'm afraid I've clean forgotten him.'

Jake persisted, 'And what of his neighbours? Who were they?'

Again Albion Cook frowned, then shrugged.

'I don't recollect who lived there. Or there. Or there. The fact is that this shouldn't concern you. We're inspecting your real estate. It can't matter to you, who lived here. Things change. People come and go.'

'But new people haven't come to live here,' Jake said irritably.

'Of course not. But they will, they will. Give it time.'

'Give what time?'

'You know.'

'I sure don't know.'

'I mean give us time to forget. I shouldn't be expected to remember everything about those who used to live in Kowhai Street. Life goes on, you know. And you're sure you don't want to inspect the houses? The valuer has everything in writing for you to study and he's in touch regularly with your New York solicitor. You needn't worry about Kowhai Street, just accept the cheques when they start coming in.'

As they returned towards Gillespie Street, Jake asked again, 'Are you sure that the people of Kowhai Street all decided to leave at once, overnight? It seems incredible.'

Albion Cook, his face and eyes showing little feeling, said solemnly, 'That's the story.'

Just then, near the corner of Gillespie Street, Jake noticed an elderly woman standing as if unsure which direction to take, glancing cautiously around her as if she were fearful of being observed. She was thin, wearing a threadbare coat and carrying a shopping bag.

Jake called out to her, 'Say, Ma'am?'

She was clearly afraid, deciding whether to reply. He walked quickly towards her.

'You live here near Kowhai Street?'

The woman's face paled. Her eyes were tired and her grey hair had straggled loose from its once-waved setting.

'I live in the brick unit two doors up,' she said. 'but my son and his wife and family lived in Kowhai Street. Rex was a Full Gospel businessman, went to meetings regularly. He was highly thought of. And now they're all gone, the children too. They found me this nice brick unit to live in after I came out from England.'

'Where did they move to?' Jake asked.

The woman's voice increased in pitch as she became more distressed.

'They didn't move. They had no plans to move. They just disappeared.

183

The whole street disappeared.'

Albion Cook grasped the woman by the arm.

'Now Connie, be careful what you say. You know you're only dreaming. You're not well.'

Connie shook herself free.

'I know what I'm talking about,' she said. 'The whole street disappeared. They were taken away. They died. It was horrible.'

Albion Cook, his feelings carefully concealed, turned to Jake.

'It's better for us to go now,' he said. 'Poor old Connie Grant. They let her stay here in town, but believe me, she raves day and night about her so-called family in Kowhai Street. She couldn't believe they would shift house without telling her and then not get in touch with her. You'd be surprised what loving relatives do. Connie Grant will have to be put away, I fear.'

'Did you know her family?' Jake asked, hoping to prise a memory from him.

'No. Haven't a clue. Don't remember them.'

Connie Grant turned fiercely on Albion Cook, plucking his sleeve and shrieking at him, 'You don't remember them, you don't *remember* them? You're a criminal not to remember them when I know you knew them, and you sold them the brick unit!'

Then she turned to Jake and whispered, 'He doesn't *remember* them. I'm the only one now who remembers, the only one left. And it's a real memory. And I'm keeping it, I'm keeping it. And there was a woman here, an American like you, who escaped, she'll have the memory too, she took it with her; in her notebooks, in her bag, in her head, she won't lose it. She wrote it down on paper to be made into a book. Her husband was a famous writer, she said, and she was working for him. They'll *remember*.'

Albion Cook pulled roughly at Jake's arm as if to try to prevent further conversation with Connie Grant.

'She's crazy,' Albion Cook said, as they walked towards the town. 'She's quite crazy. And now there's really nothing further to keep you in Puamahara, is there, now that the arrangements are made about Kowhai Street.'

Jake smiled slyly. Connie Grant's outburst had gripped him with a feeling of unease that he was tempted to disregard, thinking that after all it was none of his business, an apparently inexplicable event in a small town thousands of miles away from New York City; except that Mattina had linked her life with Kowhai Street and Puamahara, and therefore Jake felt that his own life and memory had also become part of the property of Puamahara, while Puamahara became his life-property and memory-property; apart from his *real* estate.

'I have the impression,' Jake said to Albion Cook, 'that you're trying to be rid of me.'

'Not at all. Certainly not. You're a long way from home, though, and maybe it's best for your sake and the sake of your poor dead wife to return to New York, now you've inspected Kowhai Street. You could fall ill with the strain, you know.'

Jake looked sharply at Albion Cook's expressionless face. Funny, he thought. Mattina had said Cook's face was full of expressions, changing from one to the other.

'I don't plan to stay more than a day or two,' Jake said. He did not confide his plan to visit Decima James in the Manuka Home, and the Memory Flower at the gateway to the orchards out of town. He remembered Mattina's description of Decima as the child with no spoken words. Jake felt that he and the child might share a vein of understanding, they were or had been kin, one in a desert where she apparently knew no thirst, the other thirsty in the same desert surrounded by borders of overflowing streams. People such as Decima, Jake felt, spent their lives in institutions because the opposing frailties of themselves and of those who loved them induced a collapse of the will and strength to care for them, yet they would always be like special touchstones, gauges set with diamonds, to measure human possibilities and impossibilities, fountain-sources where the supposed strong could replenish their strength of being; and in the instance of Decima, to measure the usual need and dependence on spoken words against an infinite silence where the buffeting, battling, hurting world is met with no castle and keep of spoken language.

And as Jake thought of Decima James, and of Mattina's description of Joseph and Gloria James, the conversations, the tuning of the piano (another adventure in wordlessness), he felt joyful, thinking, 'I'm remembering them. They are not dead entirely. I shall visit the Manuka Home and see the residents, many of whom will never be *spoken for*, that is, wanted within a close family, and I shall go to the orchards out of town to see the legendary source of the Memory Flower.'

31

That night at the hotel Jake thought again of Connie Grant and her claim about her son, her daughter-in-law and their children. Mattina had described them. And although he had been able to read only intermittently from Mattina's notebooks, he remembered now the strange descriptions she had given him as she lay on the sofa in the sitting room: he had thought she was delirious. He knew now that the disappearance of the people of Kowhai Street had been a fact, not a dream. Surely, though, her descriptions had been exaggerated — a town emergency, a disaster, an event of terror for her and everyone else in Kowhai Street? When she talked of it, he had supposed her death was seconds away, he could only rock her in his arms to try to ease her terror at facing death or the thought of death; he had not witnessed a 'domestic' death in peacetime. He had known the inevitable 'distant' deaths within his family (his mother and father, a cousin, an uncle) as news only, as printed words of a letter or a newspaper item, or spoken words, whispered, within the family; over his lifetime he had known and lived through, suffered and survived, more fictional deaths; and in his inevitable rehearsing of Mattina's death, he would choose from the descriptions within his complete Library of World Literature; in the end he had simply an image of the woman he loved looking suddenly startled and interested, as if struck by a new idea but not afraid. Then her death quickly put into words by Jake: 'She lay abruptly back on her pillows. She was dead.'

It had not been that way. After a night of vomiting, Mattina fell into an exhausted sleep from which she did not waken. And after all the words that might have been used, the event itself had its own speech, and because it was death it had the power to destroy any waiting words, to break them into small pieces and bury them. Was that so? Jake was now beginning to feel more kindly towards those well-meaning friends who had said, 'You'll always have her memory.' The word 'always', he supposed, would have to do in the meantime, as would the phrase 'in the meantime'. Trusting eternity to the vault of Albion Cook's 'mere words' made Jake feel sympathy for Cook's sentiments. Should words be given such complete trust, Jake asked himself. But ah! they were not 'mere words'; their intimacy gave them all power.

That evening Jake slept more peacefully, unawakened by the freight trains shunting or the sheep trucks changing gear at the traffic lights or the drunken shouts outside the Public Bar downstairs; or the motor-cyclists using the streets as a late-night raceway.

He was awakened by bird-song, the dawn chorus from the plane trees in Tyne Street. Drowsily he listened, identifying only the thrush, the blackbird (ah, the unsatisfactory provider), and . . . was that the grey warbler . . . the riroriro? The Christmas present of New Zealand bird-song was useful at last. The blackbird again, having most to say and sing and singing very well. Then suddenly the chorus stopped, taken over by the street sounds of Puamahara.

As Mattina had been, Jake was surprised at the assumptions about his daily life in America, his pursuits, his feelings, and about his country. The common phrase, 'As you're from the States you would know,' or 'You wouldn't understand, you're from the States,' showed the wide range of his deemed areas of ignorance and knowledge. At the same time he realised that he had a fund of unspoken thoughts beginning, 'These New Zealanders wouldn't know . . .' and 'These New Zealanders don't understand. . . .' He was surprised to find that *his* thoughts always contained the negative.

'How do you like being in Puamahara, away from the United States?' the waitress asked as she served his 'full English breakfast'.

'OK,' he said. As expected. He enjoyed the waitress's respectful glance. He had always imagined, and many of his friends had told him, that he resembled Douglas Fairbanks Senior from the Golden Age of Hollywood, and now when the Hollywood classics were screened on tele-vision, Jake's likeness was remarked upon. For the past twenty years his appearance had been that of a man of sixty. Sometimes, looking at his image in the bathroom mirror and seeing the handsome face, summer-tanned, the cornflower-blue eyes, he used to feel like someone in disguise, an imposter, with the only genuine part of him reflected in the worry lines on his forehead and the desperate expression in his eyes. Am I para-lysed? he'd wonder. What is preventing me? Why am I constantly hovering over my theme, my characters, unable to land, to settle, to swoop with accuracy and mastery upon my quarry?

Then, over many years, Jake's before-dinner drink shifted slowly to become his before-noon drink, then his after-breakfast drink. He gained weight, his persistent worry not even offering him a cosmetic advantage. He took to wearing around his enlarging waist a cylinder of sand sewn in a cloth bag which, the salesman explained, would force his muscles to work and his body to shed weight, 'As if you carried around each day enough stones to build a memorial.' The weight of the sand had caused

Jake to adopt the stance of someone hauling stones or coal or sacks of wheat: he was harnessed, like a packhorse, to the weight. He looked on his two years spent wearing the sandbelt as time in prison. It had never caused him to lose weight. Yet now, after Mattina's illness and death, Jake's excess weight had vanished.

He smiled as the waitress brought his coffee.

'It's instant coffee,' she said, 'the way Americans like it. Not the real stuff.'

'That's good,' Jake said, amused. The coffee tasted like lukewarm water flavoured with cigarette butts. No wonder the blackbird is an unsatisfactory provider, he said to himself.

At mid-morning Jake took a cab to the Manuka Home, after first phoning to make sure Decima James could receive a visitor, a stranger. He felt apprehensive. Visiting a home for the intellectually handicapped was not his custom; had Mattina not made the request, he would not have dreamed of going there. His encounters with 'such people', young or old, had been like his encounters with death in the midst of life: through fiction only, the spoken and written word; and film images. His war experience of death in the midst of death bore little conscious weight; it had been like a heavy burden that melted, vanished when the war ended and the world convinced itself it had returned to 'normal' times.

Approaching the grounds of Manuka Home Jake felt his fear increasing. He had left the cab driver at the gate, to return within the hour, and as he opened the gate he was surprised to find it unlocked. He read the notice: Manuka Home and Training Centre for the Intellectually Handicapped. He walked along a gravel path beside a wire-fenced enclosure where children played on swings, bounced on trampolines, and climbed over an old red-painted steam-engine with driver's cab, all on a bright green lawn separated from a field by a wire fence where a group of black-and-white cattle, mightily interested, stood watching the children play. A closer glance told Jake that only a few playing were actually children: the others were older, perhaps in their late teens or early twenties. On the left of the playground was a fenced concrete yard where two or three who were clearly more seriously afflicted played with apparent aimlessness. One boy wearing a helmet sat rocking and banging his head against the concrete wall of an adjoining building. Another boy, older, and helmeted, rolled upon the concrete, likewise banging his head. A girl in her teens leapt up and down tirelessly, without stopping for breath or rest, and then raced like an engine from fence to fence letting out a series of wild cries and screams.

A woman in a white overall came from the building.

'May I help you?' she asked like a storekeeper protective of the goods that may be shoplifted. Her smile, though, was friendly. Jake was surprised that she was perhaps no more than twenty.

'I called to see Decima James,' he said. 'I don't know her. My wife met her and her parents in Kowhai Street, Puamahara.'

The young woman looked startled. 'Oh,' she said quickly. Then she calmed. 'You say you didn't meet the parents?'

Jake, not a patient man, said sharply, 'I said I had never met them.'

'You're American?'

The woman looked embarrassed by her question and quickly followed it with, 'But your wife met them?'

'Yes. She was in Puamahara last year. Living in Kowhai Street. From New York.'

'Oh. You're Mr Brecon? You phoned?'

'Yes.'

'I'm sorry, but Decima's parents have disappeared completely, I'm told. No word to us about Decima. I'm told they took off to another part of the country, perhaps to Australia, and can't be traced. Some parents do this, you know; can't face it. You can see why, I suppose. There's Decima, over in the play area.'

She pointed to the young fair girl who had been leaping and running and who was now standing inscribing circles with her arms. She was looking at Jake and the woman and smiling and laughing in bursts.

'She has never spoken. She has a world of her own and no-one knows what it is and no-one can find out. No-one will ever know her. And now her parents have gone and she'll be in an institution for the rest of her life.'

Jake felt the pressure, the guilt.

'I — my wife and I didn't know the Jameses as friends. My wife was only a visitor, as I am. She lived a while in Kowhai Street.'

'In Kowhai Street?' The woman spoke grimly. 'And is your wife at home now?'

'Yes, in New York.'

An unwillingness to deal with sympathy and explanation came over Jake.

'Yes she is,' he repeated comfortably, feeling the advantage of the distance. What could he and Mattina do to help Decima James? Nothing at all.

The woman received his words with an air of triumph. 'The rumours that have been circulating about Kowhai Street! Some said the entire population of the street had vanished. But there's your wife back in the U.S.A. It's as I and most people supposed — those living in Kowhai Street were visitors who went home or others who happened to be up to their ears in debt or wanting to escape personal problems or from people — as in the case of Decima's parents, who couldn't face having such a daughter and caring for her. I'm told the people disappeared because all were at odds with their daily life. Even that woman who called herself an imposter. She went too, they said. The whole street. And I'd move out myself if there were a murder in my street. I'm told some rich American bought most of the properties. But it's all blown over now. How quickly everything settles, is forgotten! Who thinks of the *Wahine* these days? I bet that even a few years after Noah's Ark when someone mentioned the Flood, most would say, "Which flood? I don't remember a flood." And they're even naming a street after a General who killed our boys in the Second World War, or so Granny tells me, but what do I care. I don't remember the War because I wasn't even born then!'

'Those things are not forgotten,' Jake said harshly. 'Forgiven, maybe, but not forgotten.'

'How do you mean?' the woman asked.

Jake did not reply. He pointed to Decima.

'It's a shame her parents are gone.'

'She won't remember them,' the woman said.

'How can you be sure?'

'We can't. But she has no speech. She has no words even to tell us about herself. She has gestures, cries, movements of her body — an incredible range of communication — but no words. She'll never say, "I remember."'

Jake struggled to argue, thinking of Mattina and her insistence on remembering, but an awful depression came over him suddenly as he realised that some day he would lose his personal image of Mattina just as he had lost her presence; he could do nothing to stop the movements of 'Time you thief'; and even now the alarm bells were ringing as the thief approached.

'I think maybe my visit is of little use,' Jake said. 'I'll just wait here for my taxi.'

'As you wish,' the woman said. 'All the same we do like to have visitors, even if they're not relatives. We see so few visitors.'

And as she turned to walk towards the administration building, she said, 'Sad, isn't it?'

'Indeed,' Jake said as he walked towards the wooden seat just inside

190

the gate. He brushed away the night-dew from the seat and sat facing the playground. He closed his eyes and was almost falling asleep when he was awakened by the sensation of being pulled, clung to, crawled over, and for a second he felt as if he were an illustration in *Gulliver's Travels*, Gulliver waking in Lilliput. Then he realised that only five persons had hold of him, those who had been playing on the swings and the trampoline, and two others who had been watching. They had hauled along the driveway an old wooden trailer with wooden sides and shafts like an old horse-drawn cart, which perhaps it had been. One called, 'Pull us, pull us, give us a ride,' while the others screamed their delight, piling into the cart so that Jake felt bound to respond. His taxi was not yet in sight.

There was room only for three at a time in the old cart. Jake did not know he had such strength. Standing between the shafts, he grasped one with each hand and began to haul the wheeled cart which once in motion moved easily with the three travellers shrieking their delight. When Jake had gone about twenty yards he scooped the three out, enticing them with a wave of his hand, while the others piled in, surprisingly showing no anger or argument about possession and 'rights', while Jake turned the cart and hauled it and its passengers back towards the seat where, tired now, gently dropping the shafts, he surrendered the cart.

'Out,' he said, like a sergeant-major. 'Or you might unbalance yourselves.'

The children climbed from the cart and the group at once held tight to Jake as he returned to his seat. His impulse was to brush away the clinging hands from his sleeve, his coat, his hands. His shoulders ached with the unaccustomed exercise. He remembered his days of wearing the heavy sandbag around his waist and the hunching of his shoulders as he walked in what seemed to him now, in contrast to his recent living burden, as a dead walk, a nothing walk. He thought again of the waking Gulliver and he felt less panic in being in a hospital playground with young people wanting his attention. Slowly he removed the reality of the Manuka Home. He gently uncurled the clinging fingers.

'My taxi,' he said. 'It's waiting.'

He opened the gate and hurried to the taxi and as they drove away from the Manuka Home Jake looked guiltily back at the group that still danced and clamoured for giant-sized attention and love.

A fleeting visit only. Enough, he thought. This afternoon, the orchard. And then home.

32

That afternoon Jake walked slowly down Gillespie Street towards Kowhai Street and beyond to the orchards. He was not a practised, eager walker, yet he declined offers of a lift.

'It's a breeze,' the driver said. 'The orchards. Straight down, straight back. You from America?'

Jake could not stop thinking of Kowhai Street and the disappearances. He could not understand why so few of the people he talked to showed signs of having been shocked by the loss of an entire street. He had expected to see in each person's face, the fear, anxiety, wondering, that each must have felt. Had they all been brainwashed, drugged? He didn't think so. They appeared to be normal everyday citizens of an ordinary town. The powerful erosion or obliteration of their conscience or memory or compassion or sense of outrage had been accomplished by the natural workings of the human mind and heart, with perhaps a little help from the spirit of evil?

The day was crisp and blue and Jake found himself walking almost directly beneath the afternoon sun that even in early springtime directed its scorching rays upon Gillespie Street, the sidewalks, the houses and the gardens and those few out walking. Jake took off his sportscoat, mopped his hand over his sweating brow, and paused outside the store signposted temptingly Dairy Ice Cream Sold Here. Cone or Block. He was about to go inside when an elderly woman appeared from one of the brick flats nearby.

'You remember me?' she called to him. 'I'm Connie Grant. I saw you yesterday in Kowhai Street. You *do* remember me?'

'Yes, I remember you,' Jake said irritably. 'Of course I do.'

'You look hot. Would you like to come inside for a cup of tea?'

Jake hesitated.

'It won't take long. You'll be refreshed.'

He followed her into the flat, to a room where he sat on a rose-patterned sofa that stood along one wall facing two rose-patterned easy-chairs. There was a gas fire and at the other end of the room a dining table and chairs and a china cabinet. The mantelpiece above the fire held two vases of dead flowers. The vases were china, shaped like hens, and obviously once containers for Easter eggs.

'Excuse the dead flowers,' Connie Grant said. 'They're carnations. I haven't had the heart to throw them out. My daughter-in-law, Dorothy

Townsend, gave them to me before she disappeared. First, I lost my husband, then my house and furniture and china, in England; and my new towels and sheets, brand new; and now I come out here to my son in New Zealand, the Full Gospel businessman, and I lose my son and his wife, such a sweet woman, pretty too, but she didn't care to have me in the house, there was no room for me; and young Hugh and Sylvia, they're gone; they had no time for a grandmother, and they kept these birds that deliberately threw their birdseed on the carpet, just stood in their cage and kicked the seed everywhere, just to spite me. I've lost everything. Don't go. I'll make your tea.'

Jake drank his cup of tea. He felt refreshed, and was glad to sit out of the sun. He kept thinking of the children who were not children, who had clamoured for his attention, and how he had hauled them in the old horse-cart. Play with us, amuse us, be with us, love us.

'I'm walking to the orchards,' he told Connie Grant as he gave her his empty cup.

'I say take care,' she said. 'The people of Kowhai Street disappeared overnight. My son and his wife and children were killed, murdered, I tell you. They were all murdered.'

'But who would murder them?' Jake asked.

'I don't say it was a person or people. Something must have happened. No-one else knew or wanted to know or wanted to remember. It's all slipped away as if it had never been. But there's nothing wrong with my memory.'

Jake had the image of a cliff, the size of populated Kowhai Street, falling into the sea or over the edge of the world into nowhere, and the wound in the earth healing overnight; and no-one remembering. But the kowhai trees remained in the street!

'Or could it have been a satellite or something else modern?' Connie said.

'Or an idea,' Jake murmured.

And as he thanked her for her tea and said goodbye, she called after him, 'Take care. I warn you, take care.'

To Jake she had the manner of one of the old women who, with the old men of myth and legend, wait by the side of the road, by the river bank, the edge of the forest, to warn, advise and assist.

He stopped briefly at the corner of Kowhai Street and glanced along the street. Already the kowhai blooms had faded, the area beneath the trees sprinkled with old gold mingled with the dark red petals of other blooms from the front gardens. The sun, angled now towards the mountains, shone full on the east side of Kowhai Street, leaving the houses on the west in shade with their giant shadows blotting the light from the street and their front windows dark, mirrorless, while the windows in the houses opposite glinted as if on fire. It reminded Jake of an old street in a New England town with everyone indoors lunching or away at the ocean; no sign of habitation. And as Albion Cook employed a maintenance firm to garden and mow, there was no air of neglect; except perhaps in the profusion of unpicked flowers, new buds pushed side by side with flowers dead on their stems. Jake remembered Mattina's description of the Shannons, how Renée carefully trimmed the dead flowers from each plant, or picked them for vase displays. Flowers in populated Kowhai Street, Mattina had said, were never allowed just to *be*.

Perhaps I may never return to Puamahara, Jake thought, as he continued his walk beyond Kowhai Street. Unlike Mattina, he had never been interested in accumulating real estate. Words were his only valued property and he had enough money to live on: he was now wealthy. He disliked the idea of receiving real estate income, accounts and statements from properties in Kowhai Street. After all, the only news he needed from Kowhai Street and Puamahara had already reached him — the story of the Memory Flower; and Mattina's news of the Gravity Star, with Kowhai Street the first place to experience the overturning of the old ways when distance is near and the eastern mountains of Puamahara could be the Carpathians; and weight become lightness; and the trees, as in Rilke's poem, have their roots in the sky. Jake decided, musing as he walked, that the next visit would be John Henry's.

He walked past another store to the open country where houses alternated with fields of black-and-white cattle with glossy flanks, full udders and swishing tails, congregated by the gates to the milking sheds. He passed a retirement village. A man stood in front of the gate of the village, by the cattle-stop. He carried a stick and he wore a hat ringed with fishing-flies; his face was tanned. Jake supposed he might be a retired farmer. He stood staring at the traffic passing on its way to the orchards and the nurseries in the fertile land near the foothills.

Jake walked on. He was surprised to see that the next field was occupied solely by a bull, also gazing over the fence at the traffic; a very old bull with its leather coat marked and patched and its eyes red-rimmed and watery. Perhaps, Jake thought, the bull also had retired to live in an allotted acreage to stare at the traffic roaring by.

At the turn of the road, Jake came to the orchard, its entrance concealed by great trees, firs, macrocarpas, Australian firs, poplars and one native tree that Jake recognised by the now-familiar dark evergreen leaves. These dark green trees of New Zealand, Jake felt, had a tenacity not shown by deciduous trees; also a tirelessness in their tiring. They reminded Jake of people who grow up and grow old and then ancient and refuse to part with their life, refuse to give up part of each year to decay and sleep and rest, maintaining their watchfulness over their world; certainly losing leaves from time to time, but strong in their year-long force of being. To be surrounded by such trees, Jake thought, must produce, surely, a similar tenacity in the population.

He paused by the orchard gate near a dusty driveway lined with scores of fruit trees already in blossom — some, like the plum and cherry, already shed; others, like the apple, just beginning to bloom.

Then Jake saw the sculpture, the Memory Flower. Mattina was right; it wasn't a thing of beauty, why there must be hundreds of sculptures of white flowers symbolising everything from purity, virginity, serenity, mourning . . . but wasn't that the story, Jake told himself, feeling that his response to the Memory Flower was inadequate after the way Mattina had stressed its importance, 'more important than life' she had said in what Jake then felt was a moment of unreason . . . but wasn't that the story, the ordinariness of memory? No-one need be special to be able to remember; everyone was rich in memory.

Jake felt at ease then, gazing on the sculpture, remembering the legend. The orchard was quiet with subdued afternoon bird-song, with even the blackbird abstaining. And in the orchard, in spite of the modern methods of chemical spraying, of constant pollution that diminished the necessary swarms of bees and gave to those who survived a sickly convalescent appearance, and in spite of the drifting air from Puamahara's factories and motorways, the blossoms had survived one more year. The acres of rows of glorious white and pink were no more nor less than a plan of time and space recorded by memory, the Housekeeper of Ancient Springtime, and reinforced by human memory using words, spoken and written language.

Jake thought then of John Henry. Yes, John Henry would surely visit Puamahara and the source of the Memory Flower. I shall tell him the full story, Jake thought, of Kowhai Street and Mattina's knowledge of the residents, their ordinary, extraordinary, daily lives. I shall tell him of the Gravity Star and the determination to understand and not understand its consequences. He will have my telling, and Mattina's telling in her notebooks. Some day, perhaps, New York City may suffer the fate of Kowhai Street; there may be a new world, a new language for all; new people turned out of their old minds and hearts. And perhaps John Henry will then write a novel of Puamahara, the novel I never could have written.

*

Yes, he told me. And I travelled to Puamahara. And what I have just written is the novel he spoke of; or perhaps it is merely notes for a novel? And perhaps the town of Puamahara, which I in my turn visited, never existed? Nor did my mother and father in the way they are portrayed, for they died when I was seven years old, and so I did not know them. What exists, though, is the memory of events known and imagined, and the use of words to continue the memory through centuries, despite or with the Gravity Star, to a future when today, our Now, will be known as our past has been known as Ancient Springtime, while we, who treasure the Memory Flower, are the Housekeepers of Ancient Springtime.

John Henry Brecon
Lake George, New York, 1987